Portrait of Ignatius Jones

A NOVEL

PETER DAVID SHAPIRO

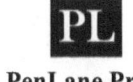

PenLane Press
11 Wachusett Drive
Lexington, MA, USA 02421

Grateful acknowledgement is given to the Wittgenstein Archive in Cambridge, UK, for permission to use a photograph from its collection as source material for cover art.

This book is a work of fiction. References to real establishments, organizations, or locales are intended only to provide an air of authenticity, and are used fictitiously. All characters, and all procedures, processes, incidents and dialogue, are products of the author's imagination and are not construed to be real.

For information please write: PenLane Press, 11 Wachusett Drive, Lexington, Massachusetts USA 02421

www.peterdshapiro.com

ISBN 978-0-9839244-4-9 (pbk)
ISBN 978-0-9839244-5-6 (ebk)

FIRST EDITION 2014

To my parents, Helen and Herb, with thanks

"I am the Light that shines forth, that gives joy to the souls."
From a Manichaean prayer, <u>gnosis.org/library/kins.htm</u>

"Rage, rage against the dying of the light."
Dylan Thomas, 1951

One

1896

*Testimony of Mrs. Eugenia Stephenson Concerning a Meeting
at the Boston Spiritualist Lyceum*

I WAS SEATED AMONGST THIRTY others in the audience in a meeting hall of the Boston Spiritualist Lyceum on Tremont Street when Ignatius Jones entered, accompanied by his close friend and tour manager Mr. William Price following several steps behind.

Ignatius Jones seated himself behind a table at the front of the room.

To be sure, I'd heard the whispers emanating from certain quarters in Boston, that he takes liberties with women without regard to their marital circumstances, and that his appetites in that quarter cannot be sated.

They say that unaccompanied women enter and depart his house on Pinckney Street at all hours in plain view of his Beacon Hill neighbors, that they flaunt their identities without shame, even some who are well-known in polite society.

Such calumnies failed to dissuade me. I resolved to see for myself the most renowned spiritualist in Boston and to hear his words directly.

Now that I was in his presence, I had to acknowledge that he was as striking a man as I had imagined, exhibiting no indicia of the horns and tail that might be inferred from the malicious stories about him. Tall, strong featured, and elegantly dressed in a fine wool suit and purple silk cravat, he made a wonderful impression. In particular, his eyes, as dark as coal, which at first glance appeared harsh in their intensity, in truer fact expressed a most powerful empathy once they were met with an open accepting mind.

In short, I cannot deny that my heart beat faster on seeing him in person for the first time.

Mr. Price also offered an attractive appearance, being about the same age and height as Ignatius Jones, and very light complexioned with long blond hair and blond eyebrows. He grasped in his arms a painting that he carried in such a way that we could not see its subject. He carefully leaned the painting against Ignatius Jones' table so that it continued to face away from us, and then strode to the back of our meeting room where he stood to watch the proceedings.

We remained completely quiet, except for a gentleman behind me who could not control his infernal cough, while Ignatius Jones surveyed each of us, saying nothing. When his eyes met mine, I felt with the greatest certainty that they were penetrating into my very soul.

Finally, he spoke to us in a voice so deep that it rumbled like thunder even while his tone remained conversational as if he were addressing just one other person.

"This evening I will conduct five readings," he said.

He reached into a straw basket on the table. It contained note cards on which I and other audience members had written our names. An assistant had dropped the cards in the basket after we paid a fee, ten dollars each, to attend the session.

"Mrs. Eugenia Stephenson."

"That's me!" I ejaculated, incredulous that Ignatius Jones would ever have occasion to utter my name, let alone in public before an audience.

"Please come forward, Mrs. Stephenson, to join me at my table."

I did so, not daring to look at the others in the room. I dreaded to see the envy they must have felt that I was selected for his first reading.

His firm, warm hand enveloped mine as he held it on the table.

"You have lost someone," he said.

That was true. I was recently widowed.

"Yes," I said. "My husband."

"He is with us now," Ignatius Jones said. "He is telling me that he died unexpectedly. Is that correct?"

"Yes," I replied.

"He suffered a mishap of some kind. Am I making sense to you, Mrs. Stephenson?"

"Yes," I said. "An accident."

"He is telling me that he lost his balance and he fell. Is that what happened?"

I was struck speechless. Indeed my poor husband had fallen while hiking in New Hampshire.

"Is that what happened?" he repeated.

3

I nodded, still unable to speak.

"I regret having to recount this history," he said, looking at me with the kindest sympathy imaginable, "but it is important that you know that my communications are truly with your husband."

"I understand," I said, finally locating my voice.

"He is telling me that he was present with you in spirit when you learned about his accident. He says that that you should not worry about him, that he passed into spirit so quickly that he didn't suffer."

On hearing this, I felt tears welling in my eyes. Ignatius Jones pressed my hand, and said, "He is telling me that he remains near to you always."

Then, to my growing wonderment, Ignatius Jones recited to me facts, one after another, that he could only have learned from my dear departed husband or from me, except that the great man and I had never conversed before this evening. He noted that I had been ill but had now mostly recovered; that the brooch I was wearing was a gift from my husband that he gave to me just after we were married; and that I was introduced to my husband by a close relative, my dear older sister, now also passed.

After I returned to my seat, my mind was too occupied with all that I had just experienced to pay close attention to his next four readings, although I did join in the audience's exclamations as undeniable proofs were delivered that he was in contact with his subjects' loved ones.

Then, having completed the readings, Ignatius Jones addressed all of us in the room.

"I will now show you a truly wondrous object."

4

PORTRAIT OF IGNATIUS JONES

He turned the painting that was leaning against the table so that it faced us directly.

It was his portrait, a perfect likeness, in which he wore the same suit and cravat as he did this evening. But it was more than his image captured by skillful application of oil paint on canvas. The portrait that Ignatius Jones held in his arms was alive. It glowed, positively radiant from an internal source as if charged with Edison's electricity. His eyes, as represented in the portrait, exerted a magnetism that was almost beyond description; they touched my soul as profoundly as those of the living and breathing man who stood before us.

"As you can plainly see, this is my portrait."

Some members of the audience chuckled. Yes, that was plain to see.

"It was painted by Desmond Wilkins."

All around me I heard murmurs of recognition. Of course we knew well of Desmond Wilkins, the most sought-after painter of members of Boston's leading families.

"However what I hold here is more than an oil painting," Ignatius Jones continued. "For a full day and night after it was completed, I clutched it in my hands, staring into the image of my own face and of my own eyes. By sheer force of will, I invested in this object a portion of my aura, of my very self, so that it will forever remain part of me, and I of it."

A quiet settled onto the room as we contemplated the portrait that we understood now to represent so much more than it first appeared.

"Someday I will pass into spirit."

"No!" cried out a large young man in the front row.

"Yes, I will pass into spirit, like all men, indeed like all creatures," Ignatius Jones replied. "Even so, I will continue to communicate with you from the Other Side."

We tried to comprehend. Were we beholding a man who was in truth an immortal being who would speak to us from his grave?

Upright men of the church held spiritualism in low regard as I well knew having suffered their lectures on that topic, and in particular they looked askance on wonderful personalities such as Ignatius Jones. How would they react to what he was telling us now? How should *we* react? Were we like the Israelites in the time of Jesus when they heard prophecies of His resurrection?

"You are wondering how I will speak to you," Ignatius Jones said. "My answer is that those who possess the gift of sensitivity will feel my presence in this very portrait, and they will hear my voice."

"But how will we know the truth of what we hear?" persisted the large young man, clearly still in distress.

"You will know," Ignatius Jones said. "Believe in me, and through this portrait you will witness proof of life eternal."

Two

2009

Tudorsville, Vermont

SETTING UP for the rummage sale commenced well before daybreak.

Doreen Marrone, Ladies Auxiliary President in Bethel Congregational Church, marshalled her troops to lay out the items donated by church members on eleven tables, one each for toys, kitchen utensils, electronic devices, books, tools, household products, collectibles, and clothes piled separately for babies, children, men, and women.

Doreen also organized a food table offering delectable home-made baked goods, and the cashier's table to collect payments for purchases.

She designated an area off to the side for additional items that were too large for tables, kids' bicycles, a manual lawn mower, plastic lawn chairs, suitcases, and a rocking chair.

By the time the early morning sun had warmed sufficiently to consume the mist rising from the damp grass and from nearby Loon Lake, all the tables were ready, each in its appointed spot on the lawn in front of the white wood-frame church just across the road from charming old Loon Lake Inn.

The women of the Ladies Auxiliary took their places behind their assigned tables.

Weather was predicted to be sunny for the Saturday of the rummage sale, so Doreen opted not to erect a canopy over the tables. A good decision, as it turned out. The dappled morning sunlight made everything look fresher and nicer, and it brightened the mood of the early-bird customers who were sauntering up from their cars in search of bargains.

Suzie Prestowicz presided over the collectibles table. Which made sense, since she'd donated almost everything on it, plates, old photos, silverware, porcelain dolls, vinyl records, and other well-worn treasures. Sturdy, energetic, and known in town for her readiness to take on new tasks that needed to be done, Suzie waited behind her table eager to chat while also watching that her smaller items didn't end up sliding into people's pockets.

Suzie had affixed little red stickers on each of her collectibles with prices ranging from fifty cents for the old photos, to two dollars for a plate depicting the Eiffel Tower, up to fifteen dollars for her late husband's silver-plated shaving brush and razor that he inherited from his father, who brought it back from Europe after the war.

A man stopped in front of Suzie's table. He appeared to be about her age in his late forties, or early fifties. He had thinning brown hair, a round face, and soft smooth-shaved cheeks. His light-weight powder-blue cashmere sweater rested gently on his generous belly, the serene casual look favored by Hollywood agents, not that Suzie had met any, but she'd seen them on TV.

His trousers were well cut of fine wool, and sharply pressed, in Suzie's opinion a welcome change from the scruffy blue jeans favored by most men in Tudorsville.

He looked like a man who could afford what he wanted and denied himself nothing.

"Does anything here catch your fancy?" she asked, laying the groundwork for a friendly chat.

"It's all wonderful stuff," the man replied.

Normally, Suzie was good at connecting with people but this man was a challenge. He revealed nothing through his wide-set eyes and tight-lipped smile that reminded her of a turtle after swallowing a fly.

"Let me know if you have any questions," Suzie said, gamely smiling back. "My name is Suzie Prestowicz."

The man nodded and continued lifting and inspecting her items, and then putting them back down.

"What's your name?" she asked, after a moment passed.

"Charles."

"Where are you from, Charles, if you don't mind me asking?"

"Woodstock," he replied, without raising his eyes from her table, a hint maybe that he did mind.

A hint that she chose to ignore.

"Woodstock is such a pretty town."

"I like it," Charles said, to Suzie's ears sounding simultaneously dismissive and self-satisfied.

Tudorsville and Woodstock had little in common except for sharing the same regional high school.

Tudorsville's modest lakeside cottages, plain American family restaurants like BJ's with its all-you-can-eat buffet, the Aubuchon hardware store, and its Victorian-era Loon Lake Inn, all occupied far lower rungs on the social ladder than Woodstock's gracious houses, pretty shops, and the grand Woodstock Inn built by Laurance Rockefeller, one of *the* Rockefellers.

Residents of Tudorsville entered neighboring Woodstock mostly as house cleaners, shop clerks, and town employees.

For their part, residents of Woodstock tended to drive straight through Tudorsville on their way to somewhere else, such as the ski resorts at Killington or Okemo, or summer theater in Weston, down past Ludlow, or Rutland for business. Few found reasons to stop except to fill up on gas or to get hardware items at Aubuchon's.

Suzie entertained the notion, before banishing it as uncharitable, that the man standing at her table was indulging in a bit of slumming by dropping in on a church rummage sale in Tudorsville. He looked too urbane for such a humble community event, in fact too sleek even for wealthy Woodstock which was, after all, still only a small town in Vermont.

"I would have figured you were up from Boston or New York," Suzie said.

"Nope."

Charles picked up a bunch of her old photos.

"May I?" he asked.

"Of course," Suzie said.

He leafed through them. They were all in black and white, and were taken before people smiled while their images were captured for posterity. They were of men in rough work clothes and women in loose-fitting dresses who posed solemnly in front of farm equipment or wood fences, and also of men, women, and children in their Sunday best in studio portraits to commemorate important milestones in their lives.

"Who are these people?" he asked.

"They go way back. My husband called them 'ancestor' pictures."

"Fascinating," Charles said, although there was no hint of particular interest, let alone amazement in his surprisingly high-pitched voice. "What about this painting?" He gestured languidly towards an oil painting in a wood frame that was propped against Suzie's table.

Suzie lifted the painting up onto the table to catch the sunlight. It was a portrait of a man dressed like a late 1800s dandy with wavy brown hair and a purple cravat that shone like lustrous silk. A large gold ring with a red stone embedded in it adorned the baby finger on his hand that grasped at the lapel of his jacket as if he were about to make a speech. But the most remarkable feature of the man in the portrait were his dark eyes that glared out with such intensity that Suzie, for one, could only look at them directly for a moment or two before breaking off contact.

"We've had this for years," Suzie said. "We found it in my mother-in-law's attic after she died."

"Who is he, in the portrait?"

"I don't know. My husband never said, if he knew."

As Charles gazed at the portrait, Suzie added, "It's spooky." Immediately she wished that she'd kept that opinion to herself. It was hardly a recommendation to a prospective customer.

But the man was undeterred. "Why do you say that?"

11

"The way he stares at you, he's like the ancient mariner grabbing onto your shirt to tell you his tale of woe."

"See what you mean," Charles said. And then, in an offhand way after he'd returned his attention to Suzie's old photos, he asked, "Even so, how much are you asking for it?"

"For the painting?"

"Yes, just curious."

Suzie wasn't fooled by 'just curious.' Tourists who visited her Suzie's Wool Store on Main Street in Tudorsville, next to the Aubuchon Hardware, often pretended to be less taken by the products on display than they actually were. She could see that the man, Charles, was intrigued by the painting.

She wanted it sold. She dreaded taking it back home. She detested the damn thing, to be honest. But John, her late husband, latched onto it as a family heirloom the moment it was found wrapped in brown paper in his mother's attic. He was adamant that the painting would be displayed prominently in their house, and there was no more to be discussed on the topic. For too many years it had haunted her front hallway like a guard dog of Hades.

In its favor, Suzie figured that the painter must have been a serious artist given that his handiwork made such a strong impression.

Including on their daughter Lily when she first saw it as a two-year-old toddler.

~ ~ ~

She looked like an angel back then, with her curly blonde hair like her dad's, and her sweet pink cheeks.

During one of her tours of the house, testing her skills as a new walker, bowlegged, swinging her legs forward like

Frankenstein's monster, she lurched from the kitchen to join her parents who were talking in the hallway.

"Lily, look at our new painting," John said.

Suzie interrupted, "Don't, John, she's just a baby. The horrid painting will frighten her."

"She'll get used to it," John said.

Initially Lily didn't understand what her dad was telling her to look at. John turned her towards the painting.

She stared at the man in the portrait, as if mesmerized. She stepped towards the wall on which the painting was hung, and stretched her arm up towards it.

She couldn't reach it.

"Up!" she said, raising her arms to her father.

John lifted her so that she was at eye level with the man in the portrait.

Lily strained to get closer.

"Careful, Lily," John said.

"Closer!"

When her father failed to move close enough to the painting for Lily to touch it with her tiny outstretched fingers, she cried, "Closer! Closer! Want to touch!" Frustrated by her father's inexplicable non-compliance, she screamed, and when that didn't work, she screeched even louder.

"Lily, if you don't stop, we'll have to put you in your room," he said.

She squirmed and twisted in John's arms and her screeches reached ear-splitting, glass-bursting ferocity.

"For God's sake," Suzie said, "what's the harm? Let her touch it. See what happens."

The tips of Lily's fingers came into contact with the painting, and she went completely still, totally absorbed.

Even now as a teenager, Lily would touch the painting when she passed through their front hallway. The man in the painting spoke to her, she said. She could hear him calling her name.

She'd be upset that it was sold. But John was gone, Lily was away for the summer, and it was time to clean house.

Suzie had procrastinated on setting a price for the painting. Now, hoping she'd judged her prospective customer's interest correctly, she resolved to go for a high number.

"Sixty dollars," she said, and held her breath.

He responded without any hesitation. "Fine, I'll take it."

Damn, she thought, *I should have asked for more*. But the deal was struck and she pressed a red sticker showing the agreed amount to the frame of the painting.

"Thanks," Charles said, and carried the painting over to the cashier's table.

Three

CHARLES PHILIP TUCKER laid his newly-acquired painting on a table beside his flat screen monitor. Although he didn't know a lot about art, he did have an eye for money. The frame alone was worth more than he paid, and the painting... it was exceptional, and compelling, and he had trouble pulling his eyes away from it.

His best clue about the painting was the signature in the lower right corner, 'Desmond Wilkins 1896.'

Charles typed 'Desmond Wilkins 1896' in his Google search bar.

According to Wikipedia, the artist was renowned for his portraits of eminent Boston personalities, and many of his paintings were exhibited in major art museums, including in Boston's prestigious Museum of Fine Arts.

So far, so good, thought Charles, feeling increasingly pleased with himself.

A list of the artist's works showed that in 1896, Desmond Wilkins painted a Boston matriarch ('Mrs. Emeline Whipple'), and separately her two children ('Master George and Miss Susan Elizabeth'), and a Boston psychic named Ignatius Jones.

Charles entered 'Ignatius Jones' in his search bar.

15

Wikipedia reported that he was a founder of modern-era mediumistic readings in the late 1800s who inspired psychic mediums during his own time and was revered by them and their successors ever since.

He was murdered in 1903.

Charles clicked on a *Boston Evening Globe* article about that shocking event:

Spiritualist Murdered. Witnesses Identify Assailant. He Escapes. Police Request Assistance.

BOSTON. July 7 -- Ignatius Jones, the famous spiritualist, 37 years old, was shot dead today in the gentlemen's changing room of the University Club on Beacon Street. According to police, he was assassinated by bullets fired at close range into his head and chest.

Members of the Club who witnessed the shooting identified the assailant as Mr. William Price, brother of Miss Melissa Price, a young lady with whom Ignatius Jones was believed to have had a personal relationship.

It was Mr. Price, a longstanding member of the Club, who sponsored Mr. Jones for membership despite objections in some quarters. Mr. Price was associated with Mr. Jones as director of the Boston Spiritualist Lyceum on Tremont Street.

Witnesses state that a loud altercation ensued between the two gentlemen in the changing room. Mr. Price accused Mr. Jones of causing Miss Price to become with child. Mr. Jones objected to the tone of Mr. Price's accusation. At which moment Mr. Price revealed that he was carrying a pistol. He fired shots at Mr. Jones and then fled the Club.

PORTRAIT OF IGNATIUS JONES

The Reverend Artemis Hutchins, a spokesman for the Price family, told the Boston Evening Globe that the family would have no comment.

Police are searching for Mr. Price and request the assistance of the public in reporting his whereabouts.

Followed by another report the next day:

Theft in Spiritualist's Home. Portrait Missing. Police Confident.

BOSTON. July 8 -- A thief gained entry last night into the Pinckney Street home of spiritualist Ignatius Jones, who was murdered yesterday.

Mr. Jones housekeeper, Mrs. Shirley Kennedy, told police this morning that the only object missing, to her knowledge, is a portrait of the noted spiritualist that he had commissioned from Desmond Wilkins.

Police are questioning persons of interest with previous involvement in thefts of fine paintings. Although they have yet to announce any arrests, they are confident that this crime will be solved quickly. They declined to speculate whether the theft of the portrait of Ignatius Jones might be related to his untimely, violent death.

And then, the day after that:

Body of William Price Found in Charles River. No Sign of Wounds.

BOSTON. July 9 -- The body of William Price, 38 years old, was discovered by a Harvard University student yesterday evening in the Charles River, floating near the Weld Boathouse.

Police have been searching for Mr. Price in connection with the slaying of famed spiritualist Ignatius Jones.

According to police, there are no signs of wounds on the body apart from the effects of being in the river.

Mr. Price is survived by his sister, Miss Melissa Price, who resides in Boston, and by his three brothers, who reside in Cambridge and in Concord.

Mr. Price's family has submitted a claim to the police for his body. Services will be private.

Charles refined his Internet search to look specifically for the portrait, 'Ignatius Jones portrait Desmond Wilkins 1896.'

He found a grainy black and white photograph of a man standing next to a painting that he was holding on a table beside him. The photograph caption read, 'Ignatius Jones and his Portrait.'

Except that it was shown in black and white, the portrait in the photograph looked identical to Charles' painting. Even the gilded wood frame was the same.

He printed this image and others that he retrieved from his Internet search and arrayed them on the table. They all matched his painting.

In 1922, the *Boston Evening Globe* reported that the portrait had yet to be found:

PORTRAIT OF IGNATIUS JONES

No Leads on Spiritualist Portrait.

BOSTON. Oct 9 – Boston Police admitted today that they have no leads on the Desmond Wilkins portrait of spiritualist Ignatius Jones that disappeared shortly after his murder almost two decades ago.

Mrs. Richardson of the Boston Spiritualist Lyceum told this newspaper that the portrait embodies more than just a fine work of art by the noted portraitist, Desmond Wilkins. She said, "Ignatius Jones commissioned his portrait to serve as a portal for him to communicate with us after he passed to spirit. Spiritualists in Boston and around the world pray for its safe return so that we may once again hear his voice."

Commissioner Herbert A. Wilson of the Boston Police Force asserted that the investigation into the painting's disappearance will continue.

Charles didn't buy psychics' blather about communicating with spirits any more than he believed in ghost visitations, UFOs, alien abduction, extrasensory perception, reincarnation, fortune telling, mind reading, or time travel.

But he did appreciate the potential for him to make good money if *other* people believed that the painting had extraordinary powers.

He'd learned that all that was needed to make good money was a certain kind of flexibility.

Some might conclude from his soft skin and expensive clothes that Charles Philip Tucker was born to wealth. Not so. He was the only son of two middle-school English teachers who called him Pip, short for Philip, and did what they could for him given their modest circumstances.

Charles never gave them a second thought once he moved on to better things.

To Charles, what counted in the end was not whether people had good hearts, or meant well, only whether they were useful.

He put this insight about people to good use on Wall Street where he promoted Internet start-up stocks. He had a great run until the dot coms collapsed and the SEC filed charges of fraud, which were completely unfounded but he had to settle rather than attempting to fight the government.

Next he sold consumer electronics on eBay. His cost was close to zero for his inventory of cameras, watches, mini-TVs, MP-3 players, and GPS sat nav devices. Being damaged or defective goods, they'd been designated by their factories in China to be destroyed, until they were intercepted and saved on Charles' behalf by managers of the disposal facilities. Charles had his resurrected products cleaned and shrink-wrapped in clear plastic, and sold them as new. A very profitable business, before eBay overreacted to negative reviews and expelled him from its site.

Moving on, he wrote up a plan to sell sports memorabilia with promotional tie-ins to former sports heroes. His venture attracted early-stage investors like flies to sugar. They virtually begged that he accept their money. Unfortunately, the former sports heroes got greedy after they learned of their involvement. He had to fold the still-nascent business after his investors' capital was exhausted.

Thanks to such ventures, Charles could fund a very satisfactory life-style, indulging in exclusive restaurants, top-rated wine, bespoke fine wool suits, a Mercedes with all the latest features, and the company of stunning models at his elbow at high-profile public events.

His classic white-brick Federal style house on Elm Street was among the finest in Woodstock. It was large, and solid, and pleasing to the eye. Matching black shutters framed all of its windows and its front door. Lunettes capped its first floor front windows and front door like arched eyebrows. His grounds were landscaped meticulously with closely cut grass, manicured shrubs, and stands of white birch bark trees.

And now, he'd found another money-maker, possibly his best yet, in his newly-acquired portrait of Ignatius Jones. The question was, how to exploit it?

One idea: Sell the painting at auction. Art collectors would bid like crazy to buy a long-lost Desmond Wilkins.

Another idea: Display the painting in a gallery which might be called, say, the Gallery of Afterlife Art. Charge admission to see the painting, and then charge more for official reproductions sold exclusively in the Afterlife Gift Shop, and then still more for rides through a haunted tunnel and for personal readings from psychics in the Gallery's authentic Psychics Corner.

Lots of possibilities.

Four

BUT FIRST, he had to verify that his painting was the real thing.

To find an art expert who wouldn't ask too many questions, Charles called Richard (Dickie) Wainwright, his former Wall Street colleague and currently a financial advisor to the newly rich in Greenwich, Connecticut.

Dickie answered his phone, "Richard Wainwright."

"Hey Dickie, it's Pipster," Charles said, resurrecting his Wall Street nickname.

"Pipster, long time no hear! How're they hanging?"

"Can't complain."

"Heard you were up in Vermont."

"Yep. How are you doing, Dickie?"

"Doing great. So, to what do I owe this honor?"

"Just catching up, Dickie."

"Pipster, I know you. What do you want?"

"I recall you collected art, back in the day."

"Still do. Paintings, sculptures. Why?"

"You purchased some of it from sources that preferred to remain anonymous."

"Better deals that way. Nothing wrong with it."

"How did you protect against forgeries?"

"Sounds like you just bought some art."

"Not at your level, Dickie. Did you have an expert check the art for you?"

"Of course. A guy in Boston."

"Can he be trusted to keep quiet about what he sees?"

"Wouldn't last long otherwise."

"Can you give me his name?"

"I don't know, Pipster. He's kinda shy."

"I won't identify you as my source."

"How about we trade favors? I'm looking for a place in Vermont, lakefront, near ski resorts, not too rustic. I'll give you his name if you promise to buzz me when you see something I might like."

"Deal."

"I'm expecting to hear from you on this, Pipster. No bullshit."

"I promise."

"Denny Sullivan. I'll text you his phone number."

Charles called Denny Sullivan from a desk phone in the lobby of the Harvard Club in Boston where he was a non-resident member, so that Caller ID would show the Club as the caller.

"Mr. Sullivan?"

"Yes?"

"I was referred to you by a friend who told me you evaluate works of art."

"And you are?"

"Call me Mr. Smith. My friend said you would be comfortable with that."

"If I'm paid in advance."

"No problem. I have something to show you. Can I bring it to you now?"

Denny Sullivan's condo was a fifth floor walk-up in a brownstone on Beacon Street. Charles climbed the first two flights of stairs fairly quickly. He slowed to a more deliberate pace on the next two flights, and had to slow further on the last flight to the fifth floor, stopping to catch his breath every couple of steps.

"Christ, am I out of shape," he told himself. "Got to lose some weight."

When he made it to the fifth floor, he waited until his heartbeat subsided back to normal before whacking Denny Sullivan's door with its brass knocker, the head of an angry Leprechaun.

"So you're Mr. Smith," said Denny, when he opened the door. Denny had the pale haggard look of someone who spent most of his time indoors. One of his eyes was wandering off-center, and his brown hair and beard were laced with grey. "What've you got for me?"

Charles took the painting out of its flat cardboard box, and held it in the light from Denny's windows that overlooked the Boston Esplanade and Charles River.

"Aha," Denny said.

"So what do you think?"

"My fee," Denny said, "is one hundred dollars for a ten minute verbal opinion, or one thousand for a written technical evaluation with carbon dating of the canvas, x-ray analysis, database review on the painter's work, and digital image analysis. Either way, cash in advance."

"Let's start with your ten-minute opinion," Charles said. He pulled five twenties from his wallet.

Once his fee was pocketed, Denny propped the painting on an easel for closer examination.

"You see the Desmond Wilkins signature?" he asked.

"Yeah, I did notice that," said Charles, not overly impressed with the first ten seconds of Denny's ten-minute opinion.

"Even without his signature, I'd have recognized it as one of his," Denny said. "The mix of brushstrokes is typical of his portraits, fine brushstrokes for the face, especially around the eyes, nose, and lips, and more textured brushstrokes for the coat and background. The palette, especially for the skin color, and the extraordinary life in the eyes, are typical Wilkins."

"How about the age of the painting? Was it done in 1896 like it says in the signature?"

"For my ten-minute opinion, I can tell you whether it's old or not, but not the year," Denny said.

"Okay, whether it's old or not, what's the answer?"

Denny pulled thick curtains over the windows, shut the door leading into other rooms in his condo, and switched off the overhead light.

"Close your eyes to get used to the dark," Denny said.

A moment later, Charles heard a clicking sound, and Denny said, "Now, open your eyes and look towards the painting."

"Okay."

"I'm shining a black light on the painting, scanning it up and down. If the paint fluoresces, it's new. If the paint stays mostly dark with no irregularities, it's old."

"I don't see anything."

"That's your answer: It's old."

Denny opened the curtains, and turned the overhead light back on.

"One more thing," he said. "I know all of Desmond Wilkins' work and I recognize the man in this portrait based on photographs from that time. It's Wilkins' portrait of a famous psychic named Ignatius Jones."

"No kidding," Charles said.

Denny looked at him. He didn't like to be played.

"Did you already know that?"

"No, how could I?" asked Charles. "Is it a big deal, that it's a portrait of the psychic?"

"This painting went missing more than a century ago."

"Is that right?"

"It was stolen," Denny added.

"Should I be worried about that?"

"I wouldn't think so, not after all this time. Unless someone comes out of the woodwork to claim it, you should be in good shape, assuming you purchased it in a proper transaction, of course."

"Of course," Charles said.

Staring at the painting was starting to make him feel uneasy. Something wasn't right in the room. Denny seemed harmless, and he hadn't said anything threatening. But still, Charles wanted to leave. He had what he needed.

Charles said, "You won't tell anyone that you've seen this painting, right?"

"Lips are sealed," Denny replied, drawing his forefinger across his mouth.

"So, just so we're clear, the painting is old and you believe that it's the Desmond Wilkins portrait of the psychic, Ignatius Jones."

"That's my ten-minute verbal opinion," Denny said. "A more definitive written opinion that you could take to the bank, so to speak, would require the technical tests that I mentioned, which would take more time."

"Understood," Charles said.

"But based on what I've seen here, you've got yourself a very valuable painting. Congratulations."

"Thanks."

"You're most welcome. Goodbye, Mr. Smith."

Five

DENNY SULLIVAN'S LIPS stayed sealed until he heard Charles descending the stairs outside his door. Then he dialed Carter Haas, the Stanley R. Levison Curator of American Paintings at the Boston Museum of Fine Arts.

"I just saw the Desmond Wilkins portrait of Ignatius Jones."

"No way!"

"Yes way."

"Are you sure?"

"I had a good look at it here in my apartment. I'm pretty sure. It's in great condition. Minor age cracking in the paint but nothing more than you'd expect."

"I'd love to see it," Carter said. "Where is it now? Who brought it to you?"

"I can't say."

"Tell me, Denny. I'll make it worth your while."

"No, in this case, I mean it. The guy was very careful."

"What *can* you tell me?"

"The painting's as good as any Desmond Wilkins I've seen, maybe better. Technically superb. And his image of Ignatius Jones is real intense. It looks like he's about to step right out of the canvas, like he's more than real."

"I'd love to see it."

"Shouldn't be too big a deal for you to find, now that we know it still exists and as of today, is somewhere in Boston."

"What about the guy who showed it to you?"

"He goes by the name of Mr. Smith. He paid me in cash for my opinion. I think he obtained the painting only recently."

"Why do you think that?"

"Otherwise he would have said it's been in his family for a long time, something like that, and he didn't."

"That's it?"

"He wears expensive clothes. Well fed. Well groomed. Doesn't get a lot of exercise based on the fact that he was red-faced and sweaty from climbing the stairs in my building. He watched and listened but didn't say much. I think he knew more about the painting than he let on. Also, when he called before he turned up here, he was phoning from the Harvard Club on Commonwealth Ave. That's all I know."

"Well, that's a start, anyway."

"If you do track the guy down and get your hands on his painting, I'll expect a little something from you."

"Which you shall receive," Carter said.

Carter pondered how to find the Desmond Wilkins portrait of Ignatius Jones that Mr. Smith was carrying around Boston.

He checked on the Internet for reports of recent sightings. Nothing there.

No point in contacting fellow curators at other Boston-area museums: Those who'd gotten wind of the long-lost Desmond Wilkins wouldn't reveal what they knew. Those who hadn't would only join the hunt once he asked them about it.

Ditto for his contacts among private art collectors: They wouldn't hesitate to outbid the MFA for the famous painting.

He *could* call Dr. Frances Gourmelon.

As Boston's leading psychic medium, she would have heard any news relating to Ignatius Jones or his portrait. She'd be less likely than the others to compete with him to buy the painting.

He wondered how she would respond when he told her about it.

Not on the phone. He wanted to see her face. He'd tell her in person.

Six

DR. FRANCES E. GOURMELON lived alone in her downtown Boston condo on Essex Street, on the floor above her Institute for Psychical and Paranormal Research.

Being sociable by nature, she customarily ventured out for her full English breakfast to the Horse & Plow Café in the Millenium Hotel, only two blocks away from her condo.

Each morning, she entered the Horse & Plow as soon as it opened at seven o'clock. She claimed her favorite table near the door where she greeted her fellow patrons as they came in.

Usually they returned her greeting in kind. Frances was hard to miss and at first glance, easy to like. She had a warm, friendly demeanor, curly grey hair, pink cheeks, and grey-green eyes that shone kindly behind her gold-rimmed glasses. She always wore a brilliantly-colored muumuu, today's being deep purple garlanded by yellow and red slashes. Her large gemstone rings glittered like holiday lights on each of her fingers. Each was gorgeous to behold and also, Frances believed, had special powers, the Amazonite to dispel her negative energy, the Amethyst to calm her down, the Blue Topaz to help her think more clearly, the Rose Quartz to strengthen her personal relationships, the Sapphire to deepen her intuition, the Prehnite to clarify her dreams, the Turquoise to bring prosperity, and her precious orange Moonstone to enhance her psychic abilities.

Frances was amply proportioned.

But not *fat*.

She did not take kindly to the f-word. She might drop the f-bomb about herself in a joking way but anyone else who bandied it about in her presence received a scowl that would freeze a volcano. She did keep physically fit, thank you very much. Every day, regardless of weather, she huffed vigorously around Boston's Public Garden to work off her breakfasts and her home-baked chocolate chip cookies.

Call her full figured, plump, buxom, *zaftig*, sturdy, large, or stout.

Not fat.

Jeremy Stanger, an affable Brit who managed the Horse & Plow, made a show of bringing over a menu. He already knew what Frances wanted, the same as on every other day, but he would grant her the courtesy of awaiting her order. It would be presumptuous to do otherwise and Jeremy was not the sort to presume.

Also out of politeness, Frances made a show of reading the menu. She clucked appreciatively as she read what was on offer.

Jeremy asked, "May I bring you tea?"

"Yes, please, dear, black with milk on the side."

"Have you decided what you'd like?"

"This morning I'll have your Full English with my two eggs poached, bacon very crisp, your marvelous British sausages, fried tomatoes, and a toasted English muffin with butter and jam on the side."

"Very good, Dr. Gourmelon," Jeremy said. "I'll bring your tea shortly."

While she waited, Frances scanned the obits in her *Boston Globe* to prepare for the calls she'd soon receive from the bereaved, her future clients.

Her tea arrived, then her breakfast, and Frances set aside the paper to give her meal her full attention.

When she was done and Jeremy had removed her plates, except for her tea, which he refreshed, Frances returned to her *Boston Globe*.

Her cellphone buzzed, a text from Carter Haas at the MFA.

"Are you available later this morning? Need to see you urgently."

Thinking that perhaps he wanted another session to communicate with his beloved sister, Frances replied, "I have a client this morning. Can you drop by after eleven o'clock?"

Carter's return message: "See you then."

Back in her condo, Frances still had ninety minutes before her morning appointment, just enough time to make fresh batch of chocolate chip cookie dough and then to take her fitness hike around the Public Garden.

She followed a recipe that she'd received from her mother when she was twelve and took over making chocolate chip cookies for their family bakery, Masnaghetti's Italian Bakery on Hanover Street in Boston's North End.

After the usual mixing, beating, stirring, and tasting, she scooped her newly-made cookie dough into a plastic container.

Before covering the container, she dug out a teaspoonful for a final taste test, just to be sure. Delicious! She placed the container in her refrigerator to chill prior to baking.

Then she washed her bowls and utensils, wiped her kitchen counters, and marched out for her daily hike around the Public Garden.

Seven

CHRISSIE BALDWIN'S boy Jimmy was discovered hanging from a tree limb near their home in Belmont, a leafy western suburb, on the day that he was due to self-surrender at MCI-Concord to serve an eighteen months sentence for dealing cocaine.

A suicide, according to police.

Unable to comprehend the finality of her loss, Chrissie called Dr. Frances Gourmelon.

She told Frances that she couldn't manage her grief. She started crying.

"Take your time," Frances said.

When she could talk again, Chrissie said, "I can't go on like this. Can you help me?"

For Frances, being a psychic medium was not just about the money, although the money was important, no question. It took plenty to maintain her space in downtown Boston, and to pay for her annual pilgrimages to England where she'd lived her earlier lives, and where in her current incarnation she shopped at Harrods in Knightsbridge for her Sylvie Bertone designer muumuus.

But the real bottom line for Frances was to help people. By putting them in touch with their loved ones, she comforted them no less than priests, therapists, and others in the helping professions.

It was in Frances' nature to get involved. Even while growing up, she took sides in her neighbors' dramas. Their business was her business! She threw herself into campaigns of all kinds, solicited signatures on petitions, made phone calls, knocked on doors, and held signs on street corners. She stayed available for her ex-husband after their divorce when he struggled with alcohol, and reliably sent birthday greetings to his two children from his second marriage. She cared for her nephew Teddie Bulger after his dad passed to spirit and his mom, her sister Portia, was too frazzled to cope.

So when someone asked for her help, Frances was inclined to respond.

She jumped Chrissie ahead of a long waiting list to give her a special emergency appointment, which that morning brought Chrissie and her son Daniel, Jimmy's younger brother, to the front door of her Institute.

"Come in, come in," Frances said, grasping Chrissie's hand in both of hers. "I'm so glad to meet you."

She led them down the long hallway to her meeting room.

The room had black walls and ceiling and no windows. On the wall to the left of the door, framed certificates confirmed that Frances' Institute for Psychical and Paranormal Research was accredited by the National Spiritualist Association, and that she personally was certified by the Skybridge Center of Santa Fe, New Mexico, as a Level Seven Research Medium.

PORTRAIT OF IGNATIUS JONES

On the opposite wall, to the right, were photographs that showed Frances mingling with notable Bostonians. One had her standing next to Boston's beloved Mayor Tom Menino, both of them beaming towards the camera, and another placed her at a gala between Robert DeLuca, the Speaker of the Massachusetts House of Representatives, and his wife Amanda Menegakis, who had scrawled across the bottom of the photo, "Always your dearest friend, Amanda."

In the center of the room, there was a round wooden table surrounded by chairs, including Frances' own hand-crafted teakwood chair that was a gift from one of her clients.

She invited Chrissie and Daniel to sit in the chairs opposite hers.

Chrissie, a slim woman with light brown hair and glasses and deep circles under her eyes, looked apprehensive but also hopeful, whereas Daniel, a gangly teenager showing signs of facial hair on his upper lip, wore a scowl that conveyed more clearly than words that for him, every minute spent in Frances' meeting room was a minute totally wasted.

"This is our first time together," Frances said.

Chrissie nodded.

"So before we start, we must set our expectations. I do mediumistic readings, which means that I communicate with spirits who have crossed over to the Other Side. I hear them speaking to me and I sense their emotions. Sometimes what they tell me is very clear. Other times I hear fragments, or phrases, that are subject to different interpretations. Often I hear a lot of voices at once. So maybe I'll misunderstand a word or two and when that happens I'll need your help to clarify the messages that I'm receiving."

"We understand," Chrissie said.

"I believe that you do understand, Chrissie. And it's wonderful that you brought Daniel with you to share this experience."

Daniel didn't acknowledge Frances' mentioning his name. He was looking around the room, everywhere but at her.

Chrissie dabbed her eyes with a tissue from the box on the table. "I'll do my best," she said.

"I am feeling Jimmy's presence now," Frances said. "This is so hard, Chrissie, but I feel, it seems to me, that he is terrified."

"He was very scared," Chrissie said.

"What I sense is that he regrets causing you such trouble and such pain."

"He was a good boy."

"Duh, he was a drug dealer," Daniel interjected. "And yeah he was scared. He was going to jail."

Frances said, "The feeling I'm getting is that Jimmy concluded he had no choice but to do what he did. He wants very badly for you to understand that and to forgive him."

"I do," Chrissie said. "I do, I do."

"And he is aware when you are thinking of him, Chrissie. That means a lot to him."

"This is such total bullshit!" Daniel said.

"Daniel!" Chrissie said. "Please!"

"Mom, she's just telling you what you want to hear. She's making it up."

Frances said, "It's okay, Daniel, you're right to be skeptical before you see proof."

"Yeah, and I am."

"Still, you must try to stay open to whatever is coming through. Negative energy might stop Jimmy from communicating with us. You wouldn't want that, would you, after all that you and your mom have suffered?"

"Whatever," Daniel said. He leaned back in his chair, crossed his arms.

"Let's just you and I talk a bit," Frances said.

"Whatever," Daniel repeated.

"You were close to Jimmy, weren't you?"

"He was my older brother."

"He confided in you?"

"Yeah, well, he told me stuff. Just talk."

"I'm sensing from Jimmy that he trusted you. That although you were younger, he believed you had good judgment. Does this seem right to you, what I'm sensing?"

"Maybe. I don't know."

"I'm getting from him that he believed he could share his thoughts with you. And sometimes you talked about things that your mom didn't know about."

"I guess," Daniel said, glancing at Chrissie.

"I'm feeling that Jimmy let you know, maybe not in so many words, maybe just hinting, about what he was planning to do."

"He didn't..."

Chrissie looked sharply at Daniel. He turned pale. He stammered, "I... I... didn't know that he'd...."

"He told you?" Chrissie asked.

"Mom, he was just talking about not going to prison, about dying first. I told him to suck it up. I had no idea he'd go through with it."

"Why didn't you say something?"

Daniel's voice broke. "It was just talk. I had no idea."

"He was your older brother," Frances said. "It was his decision. I think he very much wants both of you to know that no one else is responsible."

"Alright," Chrissie said, glaring at her son. She and Daniel had more to discuss, but not here and not now.

"Was there a gift that he may have given to you, Daniel?"

"No."

"Like a memento of some kind? Something he owned, perhaps, that he wanted you to have."

"He gave me his high school graduation ring because he couldn't take it into prison. It wasn't a gift. I was going to return it to him when he got out."

"I'm feeling that he wants you to hold onto it, Daniel, to look at it from time to time, perhaps to think of him."

Daniel just looked at Frances.

"Will you do that?" she asked.

"Yes."

"Don't blame yourself, Daniel. Jimmy is always nearby. You can take comfort in that."

When their session ended, Frances said, "Chrissie and Daniel, I feel so sad for what happened, but at least you've been able to hear from Jimmy now.

"Yes," Chrissie said. "Thank you!"

"It's important for both of you to realize that he has found a kind of peace where he is, after such terrible distress."

"I do realize that," Chrissie said. "Thank you."

As they said their goodbyes, Frances pulled Chrissie in to her large bosom for a long hug, and then did the same for Daniel, who did not resist.

Frances wished that she *could* hear the voices of those who had passed.

She tried everything to get them to speak to her in words she could understand. She gripped their photos, relics, and clothes with her right hand, her left hand, and both hands. She experimented with different room environments, darkness, strobes, incense, candles, and music. She enhanced her sensitivity through fasting, chanting, incantations, and marijuana.

None of these special measures made any difference.

She could sense the spirits' presence, and she could feel their emotions, but in hard factual truth, she could seldom make out what they were saying.

For that, she needed help from her clients.

Frances: "He seems to be telling me that he felt ill, or perhaps disappointed, or anxious."

Client: "He did worry about his work."

Frances: "Yes, that's what I'm hearing, that he felt anxiety about his work. Am I getting that right?"

Client: "Yes, that's exactly how he felt."

When Frances was called out on mistakes – "no, my Dad had no hobbies" – she recovered seamlessly by stating larger truths. "What I think he's telling me is that for him, being a good family man was the only hobby that he ever wanted."

Her clients scarcely noticed.

And anyway, who could say that the messages that she delivered were not what the spirits intended?

Frances used the time between Chrissie's and Daniel's departure and Carter Haas's arrival to bake her chocolate chip cookies.

She scooped chunks of her cookie dough onto a baking tray lined with parchment paper.

She inserted the baking tray into her oven once it was preheated to 350 degrees Fahrenheit.

Twelve minutes later, she removed the tray from her oven and laid out the cookies onto a wire rack for cooling.

Carter Haas arrived at the Institute promptly at eleven.

"Come on in," Frances said.

"I'd love to but I can't stay," Carter said.

"Don't be silly," Frances said. "You can have one of my chocolate chip cookies while we talk."

Carter sniffed the air. "I was wondering what smelled so good."

Carter was finishing his second cookie, washing it down with tea, and wiping his fingers with a paper napkin, when Frances asked, "So why did you want to see me, Carter?"

Carter said, "I have incredible news."

He paused, watching Frances carefully.

"Yes?"

"The Desmond Wilkins portrait of Ignatius Jones has been discovered."

Frances looked at him, momentarily speechless. Then she asked, "*The* portrait of Ignatius Jones?"

"Yes."

Frances does seem surprised, Carter thought.

"Where is it?" she asked. "Have you seen it?"

"I don't know, and no, I haven't seen it. One of my contacts in the art world said that he examined the painting which was brought to him by a Mr. Smith. He believes that it's the real Desmond Wilkins portrait of Ignatius Jones."

"After more than one hundred years."

"Yes."

"And you're here to find out how much I know about the painting turning up now."

"I figured you might have heard something, being a leading member of our spiritualist community."

"This is the first I've heard of it," Frances said. "Honest."

Carter said, "In that case, I'm hoping you can check around, see what you can find out."

"I'll let you know," Frances said, patting Carter's hand.

Each month, Frances chaired a board meeting at the Boston Spiritualist Lyceum to discuss programs at the Lyceum and other developments of interest to the spiritualist community.

She didn't recall anyone at recent board meetings mentioning Ignatius Jones or his portrait.

At her next board meeting, a week after her visit from Carter, Frances brought up 'Ignatius Jones' as an example of something or other, and saw no reaction of note, although everyone there certainly knew who he was.

No one from the spiritualist community contacted her with news, or even rumors, about the portrait.

She checked Boston-area spiritualists' blogs and websites: No mentions there either.

Frances emailed Carter that she could find nothing to add to what his contact had told him about Mr. Smith and his painting.

Eight

CHARLES HUNG HIS POSSESSION on a wall in his office where he could look at it while he worked at his desk.

He had confirmation from a Boston art expert that his painting was valuable, but now he was in no hurry to let it go. He liked having this great work of art all to himself. Being a connoisseur of the finer things in life, he liked being able to gaze at it whenever he chose. He owned it. He was going to enjoy it.

The man in the portrait stared back at him.

The more that Charles looked at the painting, the more trouble he had focusing on anything else. *What was the man thinking while the artist captured his image on canvas? What did he see on the street when he left the artist's studio? Did he have a carriage waiting? Did he meet someone?*

He kept coming back to it, trying to grasp what the man in the portrait was attempting to communicate.

Days passed when he missed meals, failed to respond to emails, and neglected his money-making schemes.

The painting was too distracting. Charles resolved to limit his time with it. He banished it to a room in his basement where he left it on an easel in the dark.

There, it was out of sight but not out of mind. Charles couldn't stop wondering about it every time he looked at the blank space on his office wall, or walked past the door to his basement. The day after he removed it to his basement, he decided to check on it, just to take a quick look and leave.

He turned on the light in his basement room. The man in the portrait glared from the canvas with fierce black eyes. Charles sensed that he was not alone with the painting. It was just a sensation; the room was small and uncluttered, and it took but a second to verify there was no one else there. He listened intently for sounds out of the ordinary. He heard no creaking of floorboards, no doors opening or shutting, just a car passing by outside. He was positive that he'd locked his front and back doors and the glass slider to his patio. He shuddered, involuntarily. Why was his skin prickling?

The man in the portrait, Ignatius Jones, was *watching* him. Not possible. He'd had been dead for over a century. If Charles had learned one thing from growing up with a lapsed-Catholic father and a lapsed-Mormon mother, it was that life after death, and ghosts, and spirits, existed only as religious fables to distract the weak-minded.

It was just a painting.

He couldn't shake his unease, however. And he couldn't help but return the psychic's mad stare.

And then, in his mind, he heard a man's voice.

"Charles Philip Tucker."

Charles froze. He couldn't move. He could hardly breathe.

"Charles Philip Tucker," the voice repeated. It reverberated inside his head as if there were speakers implanted in his brain.

"Yes," Charles replied.

"You know who I am."

He did know.

"You are Ignatius Jones," Charles said.

Even as he decided, *I'm getting the fuck out of here!*

Charles shoved his chair back so abruptly that it tipped over. He switched off the light to the basement room, bolted two stairs at a time out of his basement, slammed the basement door behind him, then on the other side of the door, leaned over gasping, hands on knees, his chest thumping.

He felt foolish for having panicked. He was *Charles Philip Tucker*, cool, calm, always seeing the angles. No way would he allow a weird hallucination to chase him out of his own basement.

After several hours thinking about it, he resolved to find out whether he'd hear the voice again if he returned downstairs. If so, he'd stay in control this time, whatever happened.

He faced the painting again, looking into the black eyes of Ignatius Jones.

Once again, he heard the voice, "You know who I am."

Charles again replied, "You are Ignatius Jones."

"You will be my Messenger," the voice said.

Charles had no idea what that meant except that he was expected to do something for Ignatius Jones, and serving others was not his style.

He heard, "You will transcribe my words."

"Why me?"

"I have selected you."

"What *are* you?"

"I am spirit."

"Like a ghost?" Charles could scarcely believe that he'd ever ask such a question, but he couldn't deny hearing the voice, to which he was responding, and which was responding back to him.

The voice said, "You will hear my words and report them to my followers in the physical world."

Charles thought, *This spirit, or ghost, can't make me do anything against my will.*

"Not going to happen," he said.

He left the basement, resolutely this time, calmly, and without panic.

Next morning, he returned for another visit with the painting. Nothing happened. He looked at the man in the portrait and asked, "Are you there?"

No answer.

He missed hearing the voice.

He tried again that afternoon. Again the man in the portrait, Ignatius Jones, glared out at him from the canvas but stayed silent.

Back in his kitchen thinking about his interactions with the man in the portrait, it came to Charles that he was mistaken to reject the task for which Ignatius Jones had selected him.

It was like an epiphany. He realized now that he *wanted* to do what he was asked. He wasn't obeying an instruction. It was *his* choice.

He returned to the basement and stared into the black eyes of the man in the portrait.

"I *will* serve as your Messenger," he said.

At that moment, he knew again that he was not alone. Relief flooded through him, and he gave himself up to it as he heard the voice say, as it did before, "You know who I am."

Charles replied, also as he did before, "You are Ignatius Jones."

"You accept the role I have given you."

"I do."

"You will not exploit it for crass personal gain."

"I won't."

"You will now transcribe my first message."

Charles reached for a notebook on a table beside the easel. He opened it to its first page and waited, ready to write, with his gold-plated Cross ballpoint pen in hand.

The man in the portrait spoke again, and Charles took down his words.

After the voice fell silent, Charles moved to the side of the easel to reflect on what he'd just heard and done.

He couldn't just have imagined it. Otherwise, where had the words come from that he transcribed in his notebook?

I am Ignatius Jones.

I will communicate through my portrait with those who believe in me.

My Messenger Charles Philip Tucker will transcribe my words in a Book for my followers in the physical world.

Do not doubt my words.

Defend my Book against defamers and blasphemers.

Defend my portrait against all enemies.

Believe in me.

Charles understood now that to serve as Messenger for Ignatius Jones, he had to retain the painting, so auctioning it off was out.

Also, he now realized that it would be crass to display the painting in a tacky street-side gallery with a gift shop, haunted tunnel, and psychics' tables. So that idea was out, as well.

Charles pondered the words he'd just transcribed.

Ignatius Jones said that he would communicate with those who believed in him.

He must be referring to psychic mediums who revered him as a founder of modern spiritualism.

What if psychic mediums were invited to see Ignatius Jones' portrait so that they could hear his voice from the Other Side, just as Charles had heard it?

They'd be happy. Ignatius Jones would be pleased. Money would be made, non-crassly.

Charles stretched and yawned to gain control over his nerves. He felt good: A new scheme was taking shape.

Nine

CHARLES COLLABORATED with Murray Gattis and with Buddy Choate when each found it mutually advantageous.

Charles was the big-picture guy.

Murray scoped out their schemes, identifying means and methods. He found opportunities in the nooks and crannies of bureaucracies, laws, regulations, policies, and everyday common practices. With his deeply furrowed brow and neatly trimmed goatee, he could have been a college professor.

Buddy put their plans into action. He came across as a regular fellow, stocky, dressed by Sears, with a gap between his two front teeth. People thought, "He's like us," and were reassured.

Of the three, Buddy was the only convicted felon, having served two years for assault with intent to inflict serious injury, after he hit a neighbor with a baseball bat and almost killed him. Earlier, as a teenager, he was sentenced to a Juvenile Detention Center for beating a fellow student with a rock. The judge might have sent Buddy home on probation except that his foster parents at the time told the court that they couldn't manage his behavior. They were afraid of him, and didn't want him back.

All that was safely in the past, now that Buddy had learned how to control his impulses. He presented himself as an easy-going good guy, and others had no reason to perceive him differently.

Their current venture involved registering homeless men for a free mobile phone service.

Murray and Buddy were accosting prospective customers in a ragged part of Burlington, Vermont's largest city, while, back in Woodstock, Charles was processing the paperwork to collect subsidy payments from the federal government for each one they signed up.

The fact that their venture didn't actually provide mobile phone service was less consequential than one might expect because their cheap wireless phones were quickly lost or sold and the few homeless guys who kept them long enough to attempt to make calls soon gave up.

They planned to shut their venture down as soon as they made their revenue target, at any rate before the government's next audit.

"Pigs get slaughtered," Charles told his colleagues, recalling one of the many pithy Wall Street sayings, this one cautioning against excessive greed.

Buddy's cellphone chirped just as he was reassuring a bearded gentleman outside a liquor store that the free wireless service would not be exploited by the government to track the gentleman's whereabouts and curtail his freedoms.

"See," the man said, "they know where you are."

Answering his phone, Buddy said, "Hey, Charles. What's up?"

"You and Murray need to drop what you're doing. Come back to Woodstock."

"Why?" Buddy asked. "We're making great progress here. Lots of new customers for our excellent service." He winked at the bearded gentleman.

"Just get down here," Charles said. "You'll thank me."

"What's this... manifesto... that says you're the *Messenger* for Ignatius Jones?" asked Murray, holding up the sheet of paper that Charles had handed to him and Buddy.

"What about it?" Charles asked.

"I mean, where did you get these words, Charlie?"

"From Ignatius Jones, the man in the portrait."

"Seriously?"

"That's what I'm telling you," Charles said. "Direct from him to me."

"Is the painting for real?" Buddy asked, gesturing towards it with his thumb.

"Absolutely," Charles said. "An expert in Boston confirmed that it's old and that it matches other work by Desmond Wilkins."

"Who is?"

"A famous artist who was commissioned by Ignatius Jones to paint this portrait back in the 1890s."

"Charlie, just so we're clear," Murray said, "you're telling us that the dead guy in this portrait dictated the words on the sheet that you gave to us."

"That's exactly what I'm telling you."

Murray shook his head, and Charles asked, "Don't you trust me?"

Murray stifled his reply when he saw that Charles wasn't smiling.

"You know about psychic mediums, right?" Charles said.

"What they do is phony," Murray said. "Just tricks."

"Maybe," Charles said. "But they make big money, the ones who go about it the right way. There's one psychic, she calls herself Ms. Josephine, who gets twelve dollars a minute for her private phone sessions, which if you do the math adds up to three hundred sixty dollars for a half hour. Another one gets four hundred seventy five dollars for one hour in-person sessions, and even more for larger group sessions. She has a year-plus waiting list. There's also a guy, a psychic for celebrities, whose obit in the *New York Times* says he made millions promoting a psychic hot line on late-night TV."

"A lot of money," Buddy said.

"A shitload of money, and Ignatius Jones is our ticket to tap into it."

"How is he our ticket?" asked Murray. "All we've got is his portrait."

"Ignatius Jones is like a god to psychic mediums. Do your research, Murray. You'll see. They'll pay whatever we ask to see his portrait and to hear his voice. All we need is a place where they can come to communicate with his spirit."

"Like a church."

"You have a problem with that?"

"No. Good money in religion."

Murray glanced at the image of Ignatius Jones glaring at him from the easel and quickly turned back at Charles.

"Look, Charlie, tell us the truth, no bullshit, do you truly believe that you're communicating with the spirit of Ignatius Jones?"

"Of course I believe it," Charles said. "I'm his Messenger."

"Yeah, okay, sure."

Charles said, "Move your chair to the side of the portrait, facing me."

"If it makes you happy," Murray said, humoring Charles, seeing where it led.

Charles looked into the eyes of the man in the portrait.

He heard the voice of Ignatius Jones, in his head, like telepathy. "Listen to his father."

What Charles heard next were mutterings that he could barely make out over background noise that sounded like leaves rustling, radio static, and anguished groans.

"Murray," he said, "I'm feeling a connection through the portrait."

"Great."

"Ignatius Jones tells me that I'm now in contact with your father. I have to admit, it's hard for me to understand what your father is saying but I'm picking up a feeling of anger, and of regret."

"He could be a real SOB."

Charles thought he heard a word like "sorry" in the stream of noise.

"Well, he's sorry now."

"Too late for that."

"He regrets the arguments you had. Possibly he lost his temper."

"Yeah, well…"

"He's sorry that he attacked you when you were young and couldn't defend yourself."

"My father never hit me."

"I mean psychological attacks on you, questioning your motivation, your discipline. Am I getting that right?"

"Pretty much."

"Also I sense from him that there were arguments about money."

"True."

Several sounds that Charles heard may have been words like "care" and "son."

"He wants you to know that he cared for you as his son, and still does, even if he didn't tell you that often enough, or hardly ever in fact."

"More like 'hardly ever.'"

"He regrets that he didn't have a chance to tell you that before he died."

Charles continued to stare at the portrait. Heard garble. Perhaps a word. "Summer."

"What I'm receiving now is a memory that your father has about time you spent together when the weather was warm, doing something pleasurable for both of you, just the two of you."

"Doing what?"

"I'm not sure. But I'm sensing that it was warm, so it must have been during the summer."

56

"Well, in the summer we did go fishing sometimes."

"That's probably why I'm getting an impression of a lake or stream."

"We rented a cottage on a pond in New Hampshire."

Another muttered word. Charles heard it as "Sick."

"And one more thing," Charles said. "Maybe this happened when you were out fishing, or some other time, but you got sick or were injured, and he took care of you."

"Well, I almost drowned and he pulled me out, if that's what you mean."

"Yes, well, that must be it. Also, there was something he said to you when you were arguing, like he wanted to 'make a man out of you,' along those lines."

Murray replied, in a quiet voice, "When I messed up, he'd tell me, 'be a man.'"

Charles broke away from the portrait and turned to face Buddy, whose mouth was hanging open.

"You got all that by looking at the guy's portrait?" Buddy asked.

"I told you. I'm his Messenger."

"Wow," Buddy said.

Murray said, "Well, Charlie, you've got my attention. I'll do the research on Ignatius Jones and on psychics. If the money's there as you say, I'm in."

Buddy asked, "So this portrait of Ignatius Jones is like a portal to the spirit world?"

"You got it," Charles said.

"But, if we can reach these spirits through the portrait, what's to stop them from coming through the portrait to reach us first?"

"You mean, to haunt us?"

"Yeah. Like a two-way street, with spooks coming our way."

"That's not how it works, Buddy."

"Ignatius Jones told you that?"

"Yes," Charles said, stretching the truth a little. "That's what he told me."

Buddy stole a sidelong glance at the portrait to confirm that Ignatius Jones remained securely on the canvas.

Ten

ON THE DAY that Suzie Prestowicz was selling the portrait of Ignatius Jones to Charles Philip Tucker, her daughter Lily was setting tables for lunch on the veranda of the historic Atlantic Seaside Inn on Block Island, surrounded by ocean, twelve miles out from Point Judith, on the Rhode Island mainland coast.

It was Lily's first summer job outside of Vermont, and her first time at the ocean, and she loved it.

Tall, with long blonde hair, and sixteen, Lily loved the laidback vibe on the tiny island, the guests at the Inn who greeted her by name and asked where she was from, and her fellow workers with whom she bunked in the staff dormitory, especially Anna from Bulgaria, Dorina from Romania, and Oksana from Ukraine.

Still, at night after the lights in the dorm were turned off, and she was listening to the breathing of the other girls, she missed being home.

She missed her mom, despite how everything was a big argument, like when she came home with alcohol on her breath and her mom refused to acknowledge that she should be grateful that at least her daughter didn't smell of tobacco, and then when her mom had an even bigger fit because of the condom in her purse, where her mom had no business looking in the first place, although using a condom was better than not using one if you were going to have sex anyway, which Lily made quite clear she was, and soon after that her mom got her started on the pill.

She missed her dad, and would always miss him.

She missed the man in the portrait in their front hallway who told her, "I will always love you."

Once, when Lily was sniffling in her bunk bed after the lights were off, Oksana, who had dyed her hair raspberry red to celebrate her arrival in the US even if only for the summer and who wasn't fazed by anything, asked softly, "What's wrong, Leelee?"

"Nothing."

"Are you crying?"

"No. I'm fine," Lily said.

How could she explain to Oksana about the man in the portrait? Lily never lacked for company. Boys were drawn to her like moths to a candle, including several who worked at the Inn, and she reciprocated their interest. But the man in the portrait was different. She could tell, from the way that his dark eyes gazed into hers, that he knew her more completely than anyone else, more even than her mom, who never tried to hide that she hated the portrait.

Lily needed to hear his voice, and to touch his portrait, to remind her that she was not alone in the world.

Her summer on Block Island was a dry run for going off to college.

Her high school guidance counselor assured her and her mom that she'd be accepted, no problem, at her top choice,

Boston University's College of Fine Arts, as well as at other schools she might consider. She had a 3.9 grade point average and her extra-curricular accomplishments included, during her junior year alone, winning the southern Vermont high school speed skiing competition at Mount Okemo, leading the high school debate team to regional state victory in Rutland, playing Nellie to rave reviews in her high school's rendition of *South Pacific*, and volunteering for her third Thanksgiving in a row at the Rutland Food Pantry.

She knew now that she could tolerate being away from home.

All she needed was to return home occasionally to re-connect with her mom and with the man in the portrait.

The summer drew to an end, as summers inevitably do in the Northeast, and it was time for Lily to return to Vermont and to Woodstock/Tudorsville Regional High School for her senior year.

Early on an overcast Saturday morning in late August, she huddled with Oksana, Dorina, and Anna at the dock in Old Harbor below Water Street, waiting to board the ferry that would take her back to Point Judith on the mainland. Copious tears shed the night before by Lily and by her friends had left each of them with reddened cheeks and puffy eyelids. They hugged, their arms around each other, sharing their exquisite sorrow. Two of the boys who worked at the Inn, Stefan and Pyotr, also stood nearby, solemnly marking the occasion.

Goodbyes were hard.

"Don't forget us, Leelee," Oksana said.

"Never," Lily promised. "We'll always be friends."

"You must come to Europe to visit us," Morina said.

"Of course, and you to Vermont," Lily said.

"Love you," they said, in Ukrainian, Romanian and Bulgarian.

"Love you," Lily replied.

She hugged each of them again one last time, and also Stefan and Pyotr, and hoisted her duffel bag to board the ferry.

The Block Island Ferry was only the first stage of her very long travel day.

At Point Judith, Lily had to ask directions to get the 66 bus to Kingston, R.I. She walked about a half-mile to the bus stop, lugging her duffel bag, which got heavier with every step, and waited there twenty minutes before the bus arrived.

Her bus ride to the Amtrak station in Kingston took an hour.

Plus another hour waiting at the Amtrak station for the Northeast Regional train to South Station in Boston.

Plus once she was on the train another hour to get to Boston.

At South Station in Boston, she wolfed down a sandwich and coffee while waiting another forty-five minutes before boarding the Greyhound bus to White River Junction in Vermont.

Three hours later, by then late in the afternoon, Lily's bus pulled into the terminal in White River Junction.

Her mom was waiting for her inside the station.

"How was your trip?" Suzie asked, after she and her daughter hugged hello.

"Good," Lily said. "But I'm so tired. I can't wait to get home."

"I'll be glad to have you there," Suzie said. "Our house was very quiet without you."

Lily closed her eyes and Suzie concentrated on her driving as they climbed the onramp to Route 89, heading north.

A few minutes later, Suzie took Exit 1 off Route 89 onto Route 4, towards Tudorsville.

Feeling the car decelerate and turn, Lily opened her eyes and asked, "Any news about anyone I know?"

"No, I don't think so. Tudorsville's still the same."

Something in the reserved way that Suzie responded caused Lily to look at her. Usually her mom was much more talkative.

"Is anything wrong?" Lily asked.

"No, of course not."

"Mom, tell me."

"We'll discuss it when we get home," Suzie said.

They passed the sprawl of tourist shops, motels and restaurants in Quechee next to the bridge over Quechee Gorge, crossed over the bridge, and continued on Route 4 into Woodstock, slowed now by heavier traffic that was impeded by stop lights and pedestrian crosswalks, and then through Woodstock into Tudorsville.

Suzie parked in their driveway, and Lily grabbed her duffel bag from the back seat, ran to their front door, and didn't wait for her mother before going inside.

A moment later, Suzie heard Lily cry out, "Oh no!"

She found her slumped on the hallway floor.

"Why?" Lily asked.

"Let me…"

"The portrait is gone. You replaced it with a mirror?"

"Let me explain."

"How could you?"

"It was time for a change."

"You never asked me."

"I thought…"

"So you didn't care how I felt."

"Of course I care. I hoped you would understand."

"You knew what it meant to me. Still you did it."

"It had to go," Suzie said. "You have to let it go. It's not healthy, your relationship with that painting."

"How can you say that?"

"The way you looked at that man."

"I missed him so badly all summer. I couldn't wait to see him."

"It's just a painting, Lily."

"Where is it?

"I don't know."

"You're lying. You always hated it. If it wasn't for Dad, you'd have gotten rid of it long ago."

"I'm not lying, Lily."

"So where is it?"

"I sold it. The man who bought it took it away. I don't know where."

"Who is he?"

"All I know is that his name is Charles and he lives in Woodstock."

"I'll never forgive you, Mom," Lily said. "You'll be sorry."

"Please calm down so we can talk about this."

"I hate you."

Lily stomped up the stairs to her bedroom and slammed her door behind her.

Eleven

CHARLES FIRST BECAME AWARE of Miss Evelyn Billings' interest in his painting when a cream-colored envelope addressed to 'Mr. Charles P. Tucker' was dropped through his front door letter slot.

His name was handwritten on the envelope with the traditional cut and flourishes of a fountain pen.

The cover of the folded card inside was monogrammed 'EB' in gold lettering.

Opening the card, Charles read, "Miss Evelyn Billings requests a private viewing of your painting. Please call at your convenience."

No return address was provided, nor was one needed.

Charles was well aware that Evelyn Billings lived in a gracious Victorian mansion on Pleasant Street just around the corner from his house on Elm, that she was a member of Woodstock's pre-eminent Billings family and a first cousin of the Billings girl who married Laurance Rockefeller, grandson of John D. Rockefeller, co-founder of Standard Oil.

He found more about her on the Internet. A socialite in New York City during the 1930s, she was spotlighted in *Time*

Magazine as a "gloom-busting glittertante." During the Second World War she served as a nurse in England and then near the front lines in Italy and France. Her marriage in 1945 ended in divorce in 1947. The sculptor Willem Van Roos, her companion of forty years who died in 1996, produced a series of nudes said to be modeled on her that were on display in the Museum of Modern Art in New York.

In Woodstock, she subsidized the expansion of the town's public library; her Woodstock Heritage Trust paid for upkeep of the Woodstock Village Historic District and for repair of the town's covered bridge after destructive floods in 1998 and 2004; and, each year, her Evelyn Billings Scholarship Fund committed to pay four years of college tuition for two regional high school graduates, a boy and a girl.

Now 102, Evelyn Billings received continuous care at her home from trained nurses and other helpers.

Recently she'd developed an interest in the afterlife, in particular seeking any evidence for and against, although not to the extent of tolerating unctuous twaddle from the pink-faced sweater-wearing minister from her Episcopal church who droned on and on about prayer, and salvation, and the Holy Scripture, and the Kingdom of Heaven, until she had him evicted from her premises.

The young man who installed a new security system in Charles' home was attaching a camera and a motion detector in Charles' basement when he asked Buddy, who stayed there with him just to keep an eye on things, "Who's the guy in the painting?"

"His name was Ignatius Jones."

"Intense looking guy."

"He was a famous psychic a hundred years ago," Buddy said.

"No shit!"

"Yep," Buddy said.

"So this painting must be valuable."

"Not only valuable," Buddy said, elaborating for his appreciative audience. "It provides a channel to the spirit world. Mr. Tucker talks with Ignatius Jones through this portrait."

The young man, whose college tuition was paid by the Evelyn Billings Scholarship Fund, had heard about Miss Billings' interest in the afterlife. He passed his information about the portrait along to Miss Billings' staff.

Evelyn Billings wanted to see it.

Charles didn't need to be asked twice.

A woman who looked to be in her late twenties introduced herself as Sylvie, Miss Billings' personal caregiver. She led Charles to a large sitting room and asked him to wait there for Miss Billings, who would join him shortly.

Charles rested the painting, still in its box, against the side of his upholstered armchair, and took in the room's dark oak wainscoting, black marble fireplace, stained-glass window panes, museum-quality oil paintings of rivers, mountains, and other natural scenes, and lush Persian rug.

Evelyn Billings entered in a wheelchair being pushed by Sylvie.

She was tiny, very thin, and her face was deeply creased. Her wispy snow-white hair barely covered her skull. She had hearing aids in each of her ears. But her eyes were as sharp and as blue as a clear Vermont sky on a cold January afternoon, matched by her exquisite blue and gold silk kimono, and by the long blue cashmere wool scarf that was wrapped over her bony shoulders and chest.

"Mr. Tucker," she said, "I see that you brought the painting."

"I did, Miss Billings," Charles said, reaching for the box.

Miss Billings said to the young woman, "Sylvie, can you find us an easel for the painting?"

Sylvie returned with an easel.

"Set the painting up next to me," Miss Billings said to Charles.

Charles placed the painting on the easel.

"Quite wonderful," Miss Billings said, after looking at it silently for a few minutes. "Is it true that you can communicate with Ignatius Jones through this portrait?"

"Yes ma'am," Charles said.

Sylvie brought in a silver tray with an ornate Chinese porcelain teapot and two matching cups, and a plate of plain cookies, which she set down on a nearby table.

Miss Billings asked her to leave them alone until she was called. Sylvie left, softly shutting the door behind her, and Miss Billings said, "Now, Mr. Tucker, I want you to introduce me to Ignatius Jones."

Charles heard the voice of Ignatius Jones, "Take her hand."

He leaned towards Miss Billings and placed his hand gently over one of hers which was resting on the arm of her wheelchair. He could feel the bones and veins inside her hand's translucent skin. He took care not to place any weight on it.

Miss Billings' nurses, doctors, and other staff in her employ touched her often as required by their caregiving duties. But many years had passed since anyone took her hand out of kindness or personal regard. Those who might have done so, members of her family, were now mostly gone, except for a smattering of great nieces and great nephews from whom she received the occasional holiday or birthday cards.

The warmth of Charles' hand resting on hers caused Miss Billings to see him in a different way, as a good-looking man by and large, substantial, respectful, well-dressed, and a fellow resident of her beloved Town of Woodstock.

"Are you in contact with Ignatius Jones?" she asked, as she looked back and forth between Charles and the portrait.

"I am, Miss Billings. He is present with us now."

"What does he tell you about the afterlife?"

Charles seemed to listen to a sound that only he could hear, before replying, "First, of course, that there is an afterlife, as proved by the fact that he and I are communicating more than a century after he passed over."

"That's good to know."

"The way he describes it, spirits of the Departed are all around us, not just of humans, but of all beings."

"What about Heaven? Or Hell?"

"Ignatius Jones says not to believe any of that."

"God?"

"He has no awareness of a Supreme Being."

Evelyn Billings nodded, it was as she'd long suspected.

"What can I expect, Mr. Tucker?"

Charles paused, apparently listening. Then he said, "No less than anyone else, Miss Billings."

Charles reported on how people Miss Billings knew were doing on the Other Side, and on the love they felt for her. Fifteen minutes into their session, he could see that Miss Billings was tiring. She seemed to drift off, losing her focus. Rather than responding directly to his questions to clarify the messages that he was relaying, she replied vaguely, "I don't remember" or "I suppose so."

"We should stop for now," Charles said.

"Yes," Miss Billings agreed. "Time for a rest."

She pressed a button on a pendant that was suspended around her neck. A few seconds later, Sylvie entered the room.

"I need my nap," Miss Billings told her. "Mr. Tucker can show himself out."

As Sylvie began to turn her wheelchair around to push it out of the room, Miss Billings said, "Wait a minute. I have something more to say to Mr. Tucker."

"Yes, Miss Billings," Charles said.

"I want to do this again, with you and Ignatius Jones."

"Certainly, Miss Billings. Anytime."

"From now on, call me Evelyn."

"I will. Thank you, Evelyn. And please call me Charles."

"So be it, Charles. You'll hear from me soon."

Charles genuinely liked Evelyn Billings. A tough old bird. Funny. Smart. She said what she thought.

Also, she could be good for him financially.

Once a week, an invitation dropped through Charles' mail slot, "You and Ignatius Jones are kindly requested to visit." Each time, later that same day, Charles carried the painting to

Evelyn's house, was led by Sylvie to the sitting room where Evelyn awaited him in her wheelchair and where, before they started their session, she offered her hand for Charles to hold.

Each time, Charles relayed messages to Evelyn from Ignatius Jones about what she might expect on the Other Side.

In their fourth meeting, Evelyn said that she wanted to interact personally with Ignatius Jones.

"I know you're his Messenger," she said. "But I want to hear his voice for myself."

"And you should," Charles said.

"Will he talk to me?"

"We'll see. Let's try."

Charles set the painting on the easel so that Evelyn could look at it directly.

"Look into Ignatius Jones' eyes," Charles said. "Let yourself be drawn in. Don't resist."

Evelyn stared silently at the painting for five minutes or so, while her lips moved as if she were involved in an interior conversation. Then she murmured audibly, "thank you," and turned towards Charles.

"Did he speak to you?" Charles asked.

"He did, Charles. He told me that he'll be waiting for me when I pass over."

"Then I'm sure he will," Charles said.

"Thank you for introducing us," Evelyn said.

Several days later, when Charles' doorbell rang, he thought it might be Sylvie delivering another invitation to Evelyn's, perhaps this time by hand rather than dropping it through the mail slot.

Instead, a man was standing on his stoop. He looked to be in his thirties. He had short reddish hair, granny glasses, wore a blue suit and red tie, and held a leather briefcase. Unlike a missionary or fundraiser, he didn't offer an ingratiating smile when Charles opened his door.

"Yes?" Charles asked.

"My name is Cordell French," the man said. "My law firm manages the Billings Family Trust. I'm here to discuss your relationship with Miss Billings."

"What about it?"

In Charles' experience, lawyers brought nothing but trouble. He figured this one was no exception.

"May I come in?"

"We can talk out here," Charles replied, standing in his doorway. "What's on your mind?"

"Miss Billings is an elderly woman."

"I'm well aware of that."

"Her mental faculties…"

"Don't go there," Charles said. "She's as sharp as you or me."

"Yes, but concerns have been raised now that Miss Billings has instructed us to add you to her will as a beneficiary."

Evelyn did tell Charles on their last visit that she felt closer to him than to any of her remaining family members, whom she never saw and wouldn't recognize. She was grateful for his introduction to Ignatius Jones. But, she never mentioned putting him in her will, a detail that Charles would have recalled.

"News to me," Charles said.

"So you say."

Not even pretending to be polite.

Charles said, "Anyway, that's for Miss Billings to decide."

"We've checked your history, Mr. Tucker. It's not pretty. If this matter goes to court, I can assure you that any claims you might have on Miss Billings' estate will be rejected, and the estate will bring a counter-claim asserting that you exerted fraudulent influence on Miss Billings."

"So what do you want from me?"

"Sever your relationship with Miss Billings. Request that she remove your name from her will."

"Mr. French," Charles said, as he closed his door. "Go fuck yourself."

Sylvie answered the phone, "Billings residence."

"Sylvie, I need to talk with Miss Billings."

"We were going to drop off another invitation for later this week, Mr. Tucker. Can you wait until then?"

Charles deduced from Sylvie's response that the lawyers had not yet left instructions to block his visits, but they would do so soon enough after Cordell French, Esq., reported back.

"It would be better if we could talk today, Sylvie. I'll bring the painting. Can you arrange a time and let me know?"

Charles pulled Evelyn's wheelchair close to his armchair, and took her hand.

"What's the matter, Charles?" she asked.

"This morning a lawyer came to my house from the Billings Family Trust. He said you added me to your will."

"I intended that to be a surprise."

"Evelyn, you're very kind but we've only known each other for a short time."

74

"I don't need more time, Charles."

"The lawyer told me that the estate will claim that I influenced you. They'll contest the will."

"You've done nothing wrong," Evelyn said.

"I need to tell you about myself."

Charles told Evelyn about his career on Wall Street as the Pipster and about his other schemes.

"The point is, Evelyn, I have a long record of dishonesty."

Evelyn shook her head. "You're not a bad man, Charles."

"I've done bad things," Charles said. "But I've changed since Ignatius Jones entered my life. I have a purpose now, to bring others into contact with his spirit."

"You've achieved that already," Evelyn said. She pulled her hand free and grasped his hand in both of hers. They were warm but weightless, as insubstantial as butterflies. "I know now that Ignatius Jones will welcome me when my time comes."

"I'm sure he will, Evelyn, just as he promised. But I need to do more. I've got plans."

"Tell me about them."

"I'm going to establish a Center in his name where his portrait will be displayed and people can hear his words."

"What a wonderful idea!"

"I'll call it the Ignatius Jones Center for Spiritualist Discovery."

"How can I help?"

"Take my name out of your will."

"Why?"

"Because a controversy about your will might hurt the Center."

"Nonsense, Charles. Just tell me what you need."

"But then I'd be yet another person asking for your money."

"I do what I want to do."

Charles said, "Perhaps the lawyers would leave us alone if you made a gift directly to the Center instead of to me. Also if the gift were made while you're still with us and can explain your decision."

"I'm hanging on as long as I can," Evelyn said.

"I'm counting on that," Charles said. "I've grown very fond of you."

"I'll donate to the Center from one of my accounts. No need to bother the lawyers."

"If that's what you want, Evelyn. Please believe me that I'm not asking for your money."

"How much do you need?"

Charles knew the answer to that question. He and Murray had done the calculations.

"To purchase the land for the Center, and to build a place to house the portrait and a residence for our visitors, we've estimated two million dollars."

Evelyn pressed the call button on her pendant.

Sylvie opened the door into the sitting room, "Yes, Miss Billings?"

Evelyn said, "Sylvie, bring my checkbook for my account at Woodstock Community Bank."

Twelve

ACCORDING TO THE DEVELOPMENT PLAN for the Ignatius Jones Center for Spiritualist Discovery that was submitted to the Selectboard of the Town of Tudorsville, the Center would be built on the site of an abandoned farm on Route 100A.

The barn and farmhouse currently on the site would be demolished. A study center and a residence building would be constructed in their place. The field behind the buildings, down to the stream that demarcated the far end of the property, would be allowed to lie fallow, although the Center might decide later to plant locally appropriate crops such as hay or sweet corn.

The town was split on the proposed development.

Those in favor cited property rights and jobs. The old Pullman farm had failed, and was abandoned, and its two buildings were already derelict and looked like hell, so they'd be no loss to anyone if demolished. Also what kind of precedent would be set for other land holders if the town rejected a perfectly good proposal to develop the site? How would that affect property values? Tudorsville had watched development dollars flowing to the big ski resorts at Okemo and Killington and into neighboring already-rich Woodstock. Now it was Tudorsville's turn.

To those opposed to the development, it was too large, too ugly, too close, and too weird. Route 100A was a winding country road that didn't need any more cars. It was 'Scenic Route 100A' as advertised on its roadside signs, and it should be kept that way for tourists, the real life blood of the local economy, instead of getting cluttered up with ugly buildings. Also, while no one would ever seek to restrict anyone else's exercise of their religion, the notion of erecting a Center around a painting of a long dead psychic was strange, to say the least. One thing Tudorsville didn't need was a weird cult taking root in the town and messing with the minds of kids who didn't know any better.

A special meeting of the Selectboard was convened to vote on the development plan

The town's five Selectpersons presided at a long table at the front of the meeting room.

Charles was seated at a smaller table to the side of the Selectboard table, accompanied by Paul White of Green Mountain Engineering, out of Rutland, who'd designed the Center's drainage and septic systems.

Balding, thin, and wearing wire-rim glasses, Paul was known to town officials for his many projects over the years in Tudorsville, Woodstock, and elsewhere in the area, and put a respected local face on the development.

Interested citizens packed the room. They occupied all the seats, including some chairs brought in from other rooms, as well as the standing room in the back, the biggest turnout for a Selectboard meeting since the battle five years earlier over a supplemental tax to renovate the Woodstock/Tudorsville Regional High School.

Board Chairman Hank Boudreau invited Charles to speak first. "We've already read your proposal," he said, "so you can cover just the highlights."

Paul White propped up on the table a poster board showing the architect's drawing of the development. Charles recited numbers for the dimensions of the proposed buildings, capacity of the parking area, investment in buildings and landscaping, and the new septic system.

"We've met all of the Selectboard's requirements," Charles said. "We're bringing a very significant investment to the town and look forward to playing our part in this fine community. Mr. White and I will be glad to answer your questions about our proposal for the Center. With that, Mr. Chairman and members of the Board, I request that you vote to approve our proposal."

"Thank you, and now we'll open the floor for comments," Chairman Boudreau said.

Members of the audience lined up at the microphone to make their statements.

Wilt Schmidt, caretaker of historic Plymouth Notch, the preserved birthplace of Calvin Coolidge which was just two miles south of the development site down Route 100A, wrapped his large hands around the microphone. Wilt was a big man, built square like a lumberjack.

"I get it that the Pullman family had to sell their farm after Bruce died," Wilt told the Board members. "I don't blame them for that. I do object to planting these ugly buildings on the site and housing a spooky cult there so close to Plymouth Notch."

Wilt paused while some in the audience applauded and called out support, "you tell 'em, Wilt," and "hear, hear," and others booe'd, "not your business," "you're prejudiced," "socialist!"

Chairman Boudreau rapped his table with a wooden mallet.

"You'll all get your turns," he said. "Let the man speak."

"My basic point," Wilt said, "is that this development will degrade the experience of our visitors who drive past the Pullman farm to get to Plymouth Notch, so I respectfully request that the Board reject this proposal. We can do better."

Other residents who spoke from the floor hit essentially the same points either for or against the development, depending on the side they were arguing.

Chairman Boudreau then asked for comments from his fellow Selectpersons.

Selectwoman Doreen Marrone raised her hand.

"I do have something to add," she said. "It was at my church rummage sale that Mr. Tucker purchased the painting that has led to all this fuss so I know something about it. I doubt very much that it possesses the powers claimed by Mr. Tucker. It seems to me that if he believes his mumbo-jumbo, we should question anything else he tells us. But if he doesn't, then he thinks people in Tudorsville are not too smart and he's trying to fool us. Either way, I could never approve a plan to build a compound in our town for... *portrait worshippers.*"

The other members of the Board declined to add their comments, saying their views had already been expressed on the floor and didn't bear repeating, so Chairman Boudreau asked, "Would Mr. Charles Tucker care to respond before we vote?"

"Thank you, Mr. Chairman, and members of the Board," Charles said. "The Ignatius Jones Center for Spiritualist Discovery is not a spooky cult. We are an educational center.

We seek to attain greater understanding of the afterlife. Is that so strange? After all, 'Exploring the Afterlife' is next Sunday's worship topic at Ms. Marrone's church."

Several Selectpersons looked over at Doreen, who shook her head.

Seeing this, Charles asked, "Do I have that wrong, Selectwoman Marrone?"

"You got the topic right," she replied, "but in my church, we don't pretend to talk with dead people and we don't worship oil paintings."

"Nor do we," Charles asserted. "All I'm saying is that our interest in spiritual matters is not so different than your own. And concerning Plymouth Notch, I must remind the Board that Pullman farm is outside the historic district so we are not subject to historic preservation restrictions that Mr. Schmidt wants to impose on us."

"I didn't say you were," Wilt Schmidt called out from the audience.

"Settle down, Wilt," Chairman Boudreau said.

"Thank you, Mr. Chairman," Charles said. "I was just going to add that we intend to be a good neighbor even though we will not be located within the historic district. We'll do our part to maintain the Plymouth Notch that is treasured by all of us as patriotic Americans. I am hereby making a pledge to contribute generously to maintenance of its beautiful Union Christian Church where President Coolidge worshipped. On our visits there, we've noticed that its roof could use attention, as I'm sure Mr. Schmidt will agree."

Doreen challenged the other members of the Board, "Does anyone know anything about Mr. Tucker except that he lives in

Woodstock and he's a smooth talker? Shouldn't we learn more about him before approving this project?"

"That's a fair question," Hank Boudreau said. "Perhaps Mr. Tucker can enlighten us about his background."

"I didn't start with much," Charles said. His face flushed dark red and his high reedy voice quavered with emotion. "My parents were schoolteachers. They died while I was still in college. I had to work hard. Like anyone else, I faced setbacks along the way but I'm proud of what I accomplished in my business career in finance, in online services, and in telecommunications. Now that I have attained financial success, I've committed myself to spiritual growth for myself and to help others on that journey."

"That's all very touching but we should investigate his background," Doreen said. "What if he has a criminal record?"

Charles leaned towards his microphone, "Mr. Chairman…"

Hank Boudreau interrupted, "Doreen, we just need to decide on the merits whether to approve or reject this development. I don't believe personal attacks are called for."

Wilt returned to the microphone. "Just to clarify," he said. "I still oppose the development on Bruce Pullman's farm but if it has to go forward, I heard Mr. Tucker's offer to help us maintain our church and you can bet that I'll hold him to it."

"Sir, you have my promise," Charles said.

There was a lull, and Charles said, "Mr. Chairman, if I may?"

"Yes?"

"Are there questions for Mr. White, about drainage or septic?"

Paul White sat up straighter and tidied several sheets of paper in front of him, preparing to get into the details.

Hank Boudreau looked at his fellow Selectpersons. No questions there. He looked out at the audience. No one stood to approach the microphone.

"Guess not," Chairman Boudreau said. "We're confident Paul did his usual good job."

The Selectboard voted in favor of the development. Of the five Selectpersons, only Doreen Marrone voted No.

In general, happenings in Tudorsville held limited interest for residents of other towns. The greenlighting of the Ignatius Jones Center was no exception.

Woodstock's weekly newspaper, the *Vermont Standard,* relegated the story to a couple of column inches in the Local/Regional section below the fold on Page Three. No other papers or media picked up the story.

Evidently, readership of the *Vermont Standard* didn't extend to psychic mediums who knew Ignatius Jones' name and who might have spread news about the Center by word of mouth.

Thus, down in Boston, neither Dr. Frances Gourmelon nor Carter Haas at the MFA heard anything about it.

Thirteen

CHARLES SAT BEFORE his portrait of Ignatius Jones ready to transcribe the words of the great psychic.

"Let us begin," the voice said.

And so the *Book of Ignatius Jones* was written, word by word, line by line, chapter by chapter.

Even as began his transcription, Charles still harbored lingering doubts. *I must be crazy. I'm hallucinating. This is impossible.*

Perhaps it was wrestling with such doubts that fueled his ferocious headaches.

Perhaps so, because his headaches dissipated as he spent more time in Ignatius Jones' company taking down faithfully what he was told, becoming ever more certain that he was indeed Ignatius Jones' Messenger, and furthermore that the *Book of Ignatius Jones* as he was transcribing it presented the complete truth.

By the time the *Book* was completed, all of Charles' doubts were scoured from their dark crevasses in his mind.

The portrait of Ignatius Jones was Charles' most valuable possession and its subject, Ignatius Jones, owned him completely.

Murray had copies of the *Book* printed and spiral bound with a plain black cover.

Although at thirty pages the *Book* had the slender feel of a pamphlet, its lack of physical heft did not detract in any way from the revelations in its seven chapters:

Chapter One. Life continuous.
Chapter Two. Identity untethered.
Chapter Three. Aware everywhere and forever.
Chapter Four. Completing the circle.
Chapter Five. All spirits holy.
Chapter Six. Transferring to spirit.
Chapter Seven. My Portrait: Across the divide.

A *Special Note* on the inside facing page informed readers that the *Book* would be expanded over time to include additional chapters as they were dictated by Ignatius Jones and transcribed by his Messenger, Charles Philip Tucker.

Fourteen

It took a year to build the Ignatius Jones Center for Spiritualist Discovery.

Finally the hardhats and their trucks, dumpsters, and porta-potties were gone from the site of the old Pullman farm. Their work was done. The Center's two new buildings were fully constructed and ready for use.

The debate about the Center moved on from whether it should be built, since that was now moot, to opinions about the new buildings.

The Evelyn M. Billings Residence was praised by some for its resemblance to a resort dormitory in ski country, its steep roofline being an attractive and practical alpine design feature. It was condemned by others as typical of the colossal apartment eyesores you'd expect to see in a city like Burlington, and not on a scenic country road, at five stories taller than any other building in Tudorsville or in Woodstock for that matter.

The House of Spirits, right next to the Residence, was rated similarly as either an enhancement to the town or as a grotesque embarrassment. However, both sides agreed that its design was unique for the area, perhaps for all of Vermont: A windowless cube two stories high, encased in stubbly beige stucco, accessed through an octagonal all-glass atrium.

Today, the Center's sunny opening day, was a day for friends of the Center to celebrate.

The reflective glass of the House of Spirits' atrium flashed dozens of tiny suns.

The Center's ornamental bushes and trees bloomed with green leaves and new flowers.

Fresh gravel covered the driveway down from Route 100A, the turning circle in front of the two buildings, and the parking area out back.

A light breeze ruffled Charles' hair as he gripped his podium on the platform just outside the entrance to the Evelyn M. Billings Residence.

"Are we live?" he asked, tapping his mic.

Buddy gave him a thumbs-up from the audience of twenty or so townspeople and reporters from local media outlets.

"Welcome to the Ignatius Jones Center for Spiritualist Discovery," Charles said.

"Our House of Spirits, where a barn once stood, now houses our original and priceless portrait of Ignatius Jones. And just behind me is our magnificent new Evelyn M. Billings Residence, formerly a farmhouse, named after our generous benefactor Miss Evelyn Billings, whose memory we all cherish."

The audience applauded and Charles added, "But today we celebrate more than buildings. We celebrate the spirits of loved ones who have departed the physical world."

"Amen to that," someone in the audience called out.

Charles said, "Our new Center disproves the adage about the certainties of death and taxes, since here we will communicate with eternal spirits of those who have passed, and as a non-profit educational institution, we won't be paying taxes."

There were chuckles in the audience, led by Buddy, who guffawed robustly, slapping his knee.

Charles stretched his thin lips in a smile, and continued, "During my communications with the spirit of Ignatius Jones, he described for me the afterlife that awaits all of us, and I'm pleased to announce that I have transcribed his words in the *Book of Ignatius Jones* for all to read and contemplate."

Charles raised a copy of his *Book* high above his head and held it there.

"I hereby declare open the Ignatius Jones Center for Spiritualist Discovery."

Among those in the physical world who witnessed the ceremony, standing at the back of the audience. was a tall young woman with long blonde hair.

Lily Prestowicz had found the man named Charles who lived in Woodstock and who purchased the portrait of Ignatius Jones from her mother.

Fifteen

BY HAPPY COINCIDENCE, the International Spiritualists Convention, which was hosted each year in Hollywood, Florida, by the National Spiritualist Association, was slated to begin shortly after the opening day of the Ignatius Jones Center for Spiritualist Discovery.

This year, as in earlier years, the convention would offer numerous ground-breaking panels of experts providing fresh perspectives on topical spiritualist issues, insightful speeches by leading spiritualist practitioners, and exhibits by major vendors to the spiritualist community.

Charles called the number provided on the NSA's convention website.

A woman answered, "This is Janet. How can I help you?"

"My name is Robert Bartolo," Charles said. "Can you tell me your full name, please?"

"Janet Reed."

"Is that spelled R-e-i-d?"

"No, double 'e.'"

"Thank you, Ms. Reed. I'm VP Operations at Systems Secure, an online systems security firm that's been engaged by International World Travel, the NSA's travel partner."

"Yes?"

"It's kind of an emergency. We need to check with your attendees to make sure they've received the correct information about accommodations that the NSA's contracted for in the Hollywood area."

"We sent hotel reservations info out to everyone," Janet said. "I wasn't made aware of any problems."

"Well, maybe so, but International World Travel is getting panic calls from the hotels," Charles said. "Apparently a computer virus corrupted their servers. We need the attendee list in order to contact everyone right away so that we can fix things before people start turning up at the Convention with cancelled reservations."

"Attendee list?"

"Yes, ma'am, I need names, email addresses, street addresses, and phone numbers. Can you send the list to me right away? As I said, it's kind of an emergency."

Janet paused, trying to decide.

Charles said, "If you'd prefer, Ms. Reed, I can escalate to your NSA President. I figured Geoffrey was busy, with the convention coming up and all, and that we could handle it without bothering him. But if necessary, I'll call him. Not a problem for me. He's a good friend."

"No, that's alright," Janet said. "Where should I send the file?"

"Please send it to me at BartoloR@SystemsSecure.com," Charles said, spelling it out. "No space between Bartolo and R, and 'Systems' plural in SystemsSecure. I'll stay on the line."

About three minutes later, Janet Reed's email was received at the 'BartoloR' email address with an attached file of contact information for NSA's convention attendees.

"Got it," Charles said. "Appreciate your help."

As soon as Charles signed off, and the file was retrieved, checked, and saved, Murray cancelled the 'BartoloR' email account that had now served its purpose.

Using the NSA's list, Charles blasted an email to 4,486 registered attendees of the International Spiritualists Convention:

Dear Fellow Spiritualist,

More than one hundred years ago, shortly after the renowned spiritualist Ignatius Jones passed to spirit, the portrait was lost that he'd commissioned so that we could communicate with him after he passed.

Now it gives us great joy to report to you that his portrait has been found and that I, as its new owner, have communicated with Ignatius Jones on numerous occasions.

The Ignatius Jones Center for Spiritualist Discovery in Tudorsville, Vermont, is making the portrait available for spiritualists to communicate with Ignatius Jones and with other spirits for whom he serves as a willing channel.

You are cordially invited to visit the Ignatius Jones Center for Spiritualist Discovery. For more information, see our website at www.IgnatiusJonesCenter.org.

Charles Philip Tucker

Meanwhile, Buddy advertised staff openings at the Center on the Center's website and in the *Vermont Standard*:

The Ignatius Jones Center for Spiritualist Discovery in Tudorsville is seeking to hire: (1) two 'Protectors' who are physically strong and have demonstrated team loyalty, to ensure the Center's security and (2) two 'Spiritualist Helpers' who exhibit welcoming demeanors and exemplary virtue, to assist our visitors and to help the Messenger for Ignatius Jones in performing his duties.

Jobs for young people being scarce around Tudorsville, Buddy was swamped with applications. He scheduled interviews with thirteen applicants, five who were candidates to become Protectors and eight to become Spiritualist Helpers.

Of the five would-be Protectors, two were farm boys, one was working on a construction crew at the Okemo ski resort, and two were former stalwarts on the Woodstock/Tudorsville regional high school football team, now unemployed.

Buddy selected the two former football players, Jackson Kelly and Ricky Fotis.

Both met his criterion of large physical size.

He liked that Jackson Kelly showed proper deference, for example asking whether Buddy would prefer that he remain standing during his interview.

In Ricky Fotis, on the other hand, Buddy saw the potential of intimidating muscle. Ricky's clippings about his football games described how he dumped opposing football players so violently that they left the field on stretchers.

"Did you have any regrets about hurting them?" Buddy asked, as he scanned the clippings.

Ricky didn't blink his small eyes that were embedded in his massive face.

"No, sir. It was fun."

"You're hired," Buddy said.

Meanwhile, Charles interviewed the eight prospective Spiritualist Helpers. All were girls, since being female was an unstated prerequisite for the job.

Two were pudgy. Another showed attitude in the snippy way she responded to his questions. Of the remaining five candidates, he selected two.

Becca Clinton, slender, dark hair, brown eyes, had served as co-captain of the cheerleading squad in high school. Charles asked her, "What quality do you admire most in a person?"

"Loyalty," Becca said.

The other girl carried herself like a princess, five-foot-ten, physically fit, with fine light blonde hair tied back so that it tightened the skin on her high cheekbones. She had alert grey eyes, long eyelashes, and an engaging smile.

As soon as he saw her, Charles knew that she belonged in the Center. He didn't have to think about it. He just knew.

He glanced down at the sheet that Buddy had provided. "You're Lily Prestowicz."

"Yes, Messenger Charles," she said.

"Why does your name sound familiar to me?"

"You met my mother," Lily said. "Suzie Prestowicz. She sold you our portrait of Ignatius Jones."

Charles took note of the way Lily said *our* portrait.

"Yes, now I remember," he said. "We had a good discussion."

Lily's lips tightened. She had nothing good to say about that transaction.

"So you must be very familiar with the portrait," he said.

"It was hanging in our front hallway since I was little. My parents found it in Grandma Prudence's attic after she died."

"Grandma Prudence?"

"She died before I knew her. Prudence Prestowicz."

Grandma Prudence Prestowicz. Charles recalled Suzie's remark at the rummage sale that the painting was found in her mother-in-law's attic. At the time, he wasn't paying much attention to the woman's babbling. Now, he was curious. The painting disappeared from an apartment in Boston. How did it end up in Vermont?

He'd get Murray to research Prudence Prestowicz.

"What do you think about the painting, Lily, since you grew up with it?"

"The man in the portrait…"

Charles nodded, waiting.

"All I know is that he talks to me."

"You hear his voice?"

"Yes."

"What does he say to you?"

"I'd prefer…"

"That's alright, Lily. I shouldn't have asked."

"He makes me feel good," Lily said.

Sixteen

THE EMAIL'S SUBJECT LINE jumped out at Dr. Frances Gourmelon: *Portrait of Ignatius Jones.*

Someone named Charles Philip Tucker was inviting her, as a 'fellow spiritualist,' to visit the Ignatius Jones Center for Spiritualist Discovery where she could see the portrait.

Frances clicked on the link for the Center's website.

The Center offered a five-day program with daily access to the portrait and accommodations in its new Evelyn M. Billings Residence, all included for $4,950. On completing the program, each attendee would receive an official Certificate of Portrait Mediumship thereby becoming fully qualified to invite clients to the Center for exclusive private sessions with the portrait.

The website noted that fees for such private sessions could justifiably carry a very substantial premium, more than compensating for the cost of the program.

It was also noted on the website that the program would provide a memorable *communal* experience. "Our visitors will share semi-private rooms, help with chores, make their own beds, wash dishes, sweep the floors, clean the bathrooms, and tend the vegetable garden."

For Frances, communal living was not a selling point. She recalled, with a distinct lack of fondness, the commune in upstate New York where she was marooned for a year after college. Even then, she preferred her creature comforts.

Nevertheless, she had to see the Desmond Wilkins portrait of Ignatius Jones.

She reserved a slot in the Center's first five-day program.

To cover tuition and related expenses, she opened a new research project at her Institute for Psychical and Paranormal Research. As a non-profit, the Institute was required to allocate funds towards its research and educational mission. A project to explore the mystical properties of the portrait of Ignatius Jones would serve that purpose admirably.

Then she phoned Carter Haas at the Boston Museum of Fine Arts.

Her call went to voicemail. She left a message, "This is Frances. It's about the portrait of Ignatius Jones."

Carter called her back within five minutes.

"What have you found out?" he asked.

Frances had told him so many times that she had no news to report about the portrait, not even rumors, that eventually Carter had stopped pinging her for updates.

"Are you sitting down?"

"Yes."

"I've located the portrait."

Frances heard Carter inhale sharply.

"You okay?" she asked.

"More than okay," he replied. "Where is it?"

"In Tudorsville, Vermont."

"Where's that?"

"Near Woodstock. The place that's showing the painting is called the Ignatius Jones Center for Spiritualist Discovery."

"Any sign of Mr. Smith?"

"Maybe so, if his real name is Charles Philip Tucker."

Frances described the email she'd just received from Charles Tucker, and forwarded it to Carter as they spoke.

"I've signed up for the program at the Center," she said. "It's for psychics who want to see the portrait first hand. I'll get back to you once I've seen it."

"I'll hold my breath until then," Carter said.

He was already thinking about how best to celebrate the MFA's new Desmond Wilkins acquisition.

Frances knew someone in Tudorsville who'd have local knowledge of the Center.

Suzie Prestowicz had turned to Frances after her husband passed, and she loved gossip, both in the hearing and the telling.

As it turned out, Suzie was quite well informed.

"That Charles Philip Tucker has created quite a stir in our little town," she told Frances. "People say they're a cult. And their new buildings are as ugly as an oil spill. On the other hand, my daughter Lily works there."

"Little Lily! Can she really be old enough?"

"Eighteen. She's living in their Residence now. That's one of their rules. All staff must live on-site."

"What has Lily told you about the Center?"

"She's told me *nothing*. When she was hired, she had to promise not to talk about the place with anyone, not even family. They say it's for security. At any rate, she doesn't complain to me, which is a blessing."

"Have you heard anything about Charles Philip Tucker?"

"I've met him. We even talked."

"You met him?"

"At our church rummage sale when I sold him the painting. He was polite enough, although not too talkative. Nice clothes. He lives in Woodstock."

"Wait! You sold him the portrait of Ignatius Jones?"

"Had I known it was so special, I might have kept it. Although, to tell you the truth, Frances, it gave me the creeps."

"Oh, Suzie..."

"When I watched Charles Tucker carry it off to his car, I was thinking, *I just hope he doesn't change his mind.*"

Seventeen

AT THE CENTER of the stage in the Portrait Room in the House of Spirits, a structure shaped like a plank stood on one of its ends. It was about four inches thick, two feet wide, and six feet tall, and smooth and opaque like plexiglass.

Hanging about halfway up on this structure was the Desmond Wilkins portrait of Ignatius Jones.

Charles sat alone on the stage facing the portrait. His privacy with the portrait was assured, since he'd temporarily disabled the Portrait Room's video surveillance camera, and warned Buddy against allowing any intrusions while he was there.

When he locked eyes with those of the great psychic, the voice of Ignatius Jones came into his head as if he'd turned on a radio. It seemed that Ignatius Jones was just waiting on the Other Side for Charles to make contact.

Charles sensed now that the spirit of Evelyn Billings also was present in addition to the spirit of Ignatius Jones, and he basked in the warmth of her approval.

Ignatius Jones asked, "Do you serve without reservation as my Messenger?"

"Yes, Master Jones."

"Say it."

"Without reservation."

"Then you must show your commitment by wearing plain and humble clothing that enhances the power of my words."

"I will do so."

"Listen now to my wishes."

Charles listened.

Charles set about acquiring plain and humble clothing to suit his role as Messenger for Ignatius Jones, clothing such as worn by monks who subsisted on bread and water, who never spoke out loud except to pray and chant, who slept on hard beds in tiny cells and who served out their days studying sacred texts, isolated from corrupting worldly pleasures.

Charles found what he was looking for on an ecclesiastical costumes website: A plain brown robe with a large hood and large hanging sleeves; a rope belt for his waist; and simple leather sandals for his feet.

"What's with the monk's robe and Jesus sandals?" asked Murray, on seeing Charles in his new outfit.

"It's how the Messenger is dressed," Charles said.

"You look like you've taken a vow of poverty."

"My only vow is to Ignatius Jones."

"Charlie, I don't mind your costume, that's your privilege, but I didn't take any vows. Neither did Buddy. We're here for the money."

Buddy grinned when Charles appeared in their office in his brown robe and sandals, so as to be in on the joke, but now he spoke up to offer his support.

"I've got no problem with the way Charles looks," he said.

For the Center's newly hired Protectors, Charles chose military-style olive green cotton shirts and trousers, green cotton canvas belts with large silver chrome buckles, and black leather boots.

For the Spiritualist Helpers, he settled on white blouses, knee-length navy blue dresses, and white aprons, like suburban housewives wore in 1950s TV commercials, ladylike outfits that evoked chastity, cleanliness, and eagerness to serve.

All were dressed for duty when they lined up for Charles' inspection, with Buddy watching at Charles' shoulder.

Lily Prestowicz and Becca Clinton stood at attention, eyes forward like army recruits on parade review.

"Are you ready?" Charles asked them.

As coached by Buddy, Lily replied, "Yes, Messenger."

Charles looked at Becca.

"Yes, Messenger," she also said.

"What are your duties?"

"Assist our visitors," Becca said. "Help Buddy manage the Center. And help you, Messenger Charles, to fulfill your mission."

"Excellent," Charles said.

He turned next to Protectors Ricky Fotis and Jackson Kelly. Although Charles was five foot ten and well padded, each Protector towered over him and outweighed him by at least one hundred pounds.

Looking up at them, Charles asked, "Buddy has explained your duties?"

"Yes, Messenger," Jackson replied.

"Tell me."

"Secure the Center against intruders. Protect the portrait of Ignatius Jones. Trust Buddy one-hundred-percent and do what he says."

"Yes, and…?"

Ricky added, "Honor the spirit of Ignatius Jones and his words as you, his Messenger, have shared them with us in the *Book of Ignatius Jones*."

Lily raised her hand.

"Go ahead," Charles said.

"Every time I've been in the Portrait Room, the portrait of Ignatius Jones has been covered by a black cloth."

Buddy interjected, "That's to protect it in between sessions with Messenger Charles and with our visitors."

Lily didn't back off.

"When will we see the portrait without the cover?"

Charles clasped his hands inside the large hanging sleeves of his monk's robe and smiled benignly at the tall blonde girl. She had her own connection with Ignatius Jones. He was important to her, and if she heard his voice, she must have meant something to him. Possibly still did. Alienating her would be a mistake. Not just because that might displease Ignatius Jones, but also because he, Charles, had been thinking about her lately, her face, and her hair, although he intended nothing improper by it, given that she was just a teenager, and he was her boss.

"I'll invite selected staff to join me in the Portrait Room as a reward for outstanding work," Charles said. "Would that appeal to you, Lily?"

"Yes, Messenger," she replied. "Thank you."

After Charles returned with Murray and Buddy to their office, he said, 'One more thing..."

He got their attention, and continued, "From now on, false images of the portrait are prohibited."

"Not following you," Murray said.

"No cameras of any kind in the Portrait Room. That goes for everyone, all visitors and staff. No cameras. No photos."

"Why not?" asked Buddy.

"Because the portrait and its image are one and indivisible."

Charles sounded like Moses reading one of the Ten Commandments, albeit in a voice not as deep as Charlton Heston's.

"Could be good for us," Murray said, after reflecting a moment. "We'll sell more of our official reproductions, maybe at a higher price. Very clever, Charlie."

"Yeah, well, that's another thing," Charles said. "Stop selling the reproductions."

"Why? We're getting two hundred thirty dollars per."

"I can't allow people to claim they're communicating with Ignatius Jones through one of these reproductions."

"You think that's likely?"

"I won't give them the opportunity even though they'd be lying because Ignatius Jones only communicates through his original portrait that I bought and own, and that's hanging in the Portrait Room."

"So what's the problem, Charlie? They'll be exposed and that'll be the end of it."

"Their lies would reflect back on us."

"We printed a pile of posters," Murray said, still trying. "Let's at least sell the ones we have. We paid a fortune to get the best possible reproductions, maximum sharpness, great color, just like you wanted."

"We made a mistake. Burn them."

"Look, Charlie, the painting is great and all that, and we've got a thing going on here that we built around it, but it's not sacred. What's the big deal?"

Charles scowled: Murray was testing his patience. "When I'm listening to the voice of a man who died over a century ago, I'd say that's a big deal. And when I say no false images shall be permitted of the portrait, and that they dilute the authority of the original, you should accept that it's not just me telling you, it's Ignatius Jones. Alright?"

Murray fell silent.

Buddy asked, "What about the repros that we already sold?"

Murray cast a disgusted look at his colleague. Buddy talked too much.

"Get them back."

"What if the buyers want to keep them?"

"Offer them more money, double what they paid if necessary."

"And if they still refuse to sell?"

"Maybe our Protectors can persuade them."

"Hold on!" Murray exclaimed. "Are you telling us to threaten them?"

"Well, do what you can," Charles said.

"We've also got boxes of postcards," Buddy said.

Murray despaired. Why wouldn't Buddy shut the fuck up?

"Get rid of them too. No more images of the portrait. No reproductions. No photos. No postcards. Understood?"

"Got it," Buddy said.

"You good with that, Murray?" Charles asked, his voice casual, not in any way menacing.

"Yes," replied Murray.

Adding, after a beat, "Messenger."

Eighteen

IT DIDN'T GO UNNOTICED in Tudorsville that the Ignatius Jones Center for Spiritualist Discovery was recruiting young people to live and work on-site, dressing them in strange costumes, giving them weird titles, and making them pledge their loyalty to the Center's leader who set himself up as the 'Messenger' for a dead guy whose portrait they were worshipping.

Furthermore the young recruits were being ordered not to talk about the Center, not even with family or friends. Everyone knew that cutting them off from the outside world was the first thing a cult would try to do.

Doreen Marrone convened a meeting in the Bethel Congregational Church to discuss the situation.

People from all over town filled the sanctuary. They occupied every pew and stood along the sides and in the back. Not just everyday citizens, but also Tudorsville cops in uniform, and Doreen's fellow Selectboard members.

Doreen began the proceedings by announcing, "Our children are being brainwashed," and, "It's up to us to do something about it."

Then her fellow townspeople rose to denounce the Center as a pernicious cult, a den of spirit talkers, a seducer of children, a social and moral cancer, and a threat to Tudorsville's way of life that had to be stopped before it got out of control.

It felt good for everyone to blow off steam. No one actually planned to attack people or property. This was Vermont, after all. People realized, when they thought about it, that their own children who worked at the Center might get caught in the line of fire.

Doreen said, "Let's warn our children about cults. Get our teachers to talk about cults in school. And our pastors. Write letters to the *Vermont Standard*. The editor's a good friend and she'll add her voice to the chorus with one of her great editorials. She's here in fact. Raise your hand, Betsy, so people can see you."

A woman in one of the pews near the front raised her hand.

Someone shouted, "We need more than words! Let's burn the place down!" A couple of teenagers tried to get a chant going, "No cults! No cults! No cults!" But they were shushed by cooler heads in the room. "Don't be damn fools!"

The teenagers looked around sheepishly and then studied their cellphones, tuning out.

No one meant any harm.

Standing in the back of the sanctuary and wearing a hoodie so that he wouldn't be recognized, Buddy read the situation differently. He saw a mob working itself up to attack the Center, rural yahoos grabbing for pitchforks, crosses, and fiery torches.

He told Charles, "We're in danger."

"So call the police, get them out here."

"They're part of it," Buddy said. "I saw them at the meeting."

107

Charles said, "We have to defend the Center."

"Yeah, and since we can't call the police, it's up to us."

"Shit."

"We can do it, Charles. We just need the right kind of tools."

"Like what?"

"Like guns."

Charles hesitated. "Not sure I want guns around."

"They all have guns. Any fool who wants one in Vermont can get one. We can't defend the Center if they have guns and we don't."

"Still…"

"Look, Charles, you had to be there, to hear them screaming about cults, and how they'd burn us out. They were screaming for blood."

"Well, if there's no other way…"

"Not that I can see."

"I always knew it would come down to this," Charles said, like he was talking to himself, working it out. "We can rely only on ourselves. No one else."

"That's how I read it," Buddy said.

"So do it," Charles said. "Get what you need."

"If we have to use the guns, it will be in self-defense," Buddy said. "We'll have every right."

Late in the afternoon about three weeks after the meeting at the Bethel Congregational Church, Protector Ricky saw men walking along the stream at the far end of the Center's property, each carrying a rifle.

He called Buddy's mobile. "Intruders down by the stream!" he yelled. "They've got guns!"

Buddy said, "Get Protector Jackson and meet me at my office. Now!"

So they were under attack, as Buddy had expected they would be.

He passed leather gun holsters to Ricky and Jackson.

"Snap these onto your belts," he said.

Then he handed each of them a Glock 30 subcompact pistol, the ones they'd started using at target practice just a week earlier, which was just in time as it turned out.

"These are fully loaded," Buddy said. "Ten rounds. If you need more, I've got extra magazines in my bag."

"What about rifles?" Ricky asked. "Those guys are carrying rifles. I wouldn't want to come up against them with just a small pistol."

"For now, I'll carry the rifle," Buddy said, hefting his new Smith & Wesson semi-automatic. "You boys aren't trained on it yet. But don't worry. Whoever those guys are, they won't last long against this sucker."

Buddy led his troops on a path across the field down towards the stream.

The guys with rifles had dropped out of sight.

"Stay quiet," Buddy whispered to Ricky and Jackson. "No talking. Don't step on anything that'll make noise."

"What if they're waiting for us?" Ricky asked, whispering back.

"That's a chance we'll have to take," Buddy said. Striding across the field, his semi-automatic in hand and his men following just behind him, he was breathing hard, pumped by adrenaline, totally ready for battle.

Jackson whispered, "We don't know that they mean to attack us. They may just be hunters."

"So what?" Buddy replied. "They're trespassing. We have a legal right to shoot them."

"We'll get in a lot of trouble if we shoot guys just for trespassing," Jackson said.

"I'm ready to shoot them," Ricky said, lifting and aiming his Glock in the general direction of the stream.

Control, Buddy thought, recalling a mantra from his anger management sessions. *Stop. Think. Control.*

"Hold your fire until I tell you to shoot," he said, swallowing against the acid that was boiling up from his stomach.

They found the four guys lying on their stomachs on the grass, propped up on their elbows, holding their rifles ready to fire. They were aiming towards the woods on the other side of the stream, with their backs to the Center. They didn't see Buddy, Ricky, and Jackson coming.

"Drop your weapons!" Buddy shouted. "We have you covered."

"What the fuck?" one of the guys said, when he twisted around to see who was shouting. "Who the fuck are you?"

"Drop your weapons," Buddy repeated. "Or we'll shoot all of you right now."

Ricky collected their guns.

"Sit up so we can see you," Buddy said.

The four guys sat cross-legged on the ground while Ricky guarded them with his pistol.

Jackson recognized them. They were a couple of years behind him and Ricky at the high school, probably seniors now unless they'd dropped out. Farmer kids. Skin sunburned red-brown from working outside. Big kids, but not on the football team since they had to get home after school to help on their farms.

If the guys recognized him or Ricky, they weren't letting on. They just sat where they were told, still looking confused.

"What are you doing here?" Buddy demanded.

The guy who had twisted around replied, "Hunting beaver, wild turkeys, maybe a deer coming down to the stream if we get lucky."

"Didn't you see the No Trespassing signs?"

"We've always hunted along here. The Pullmans didn't mind."

"We mind," Buddy said. "We posted those signs for a reason."

Buddy took plastic handcuff ties from his bag and handed them to Jackson.

"Handcuff them," Buddy said.

"They understand now," Jackson said. "They won't come through here again."

"Need to teach them a lesson."

Then, to the guys, Buddy said, "Put out your wrists."

Ricky continued to cover them with his Glock while Jackson snapped plastic handcuffs on each of them.

"Stand up," Buddy said.

It took some effort for the guys to get to their feet with their hands handcuffed, but once they were standing, Buddy said, "We're going down to the edge of the stream."

Thinking that Buddy might still be planning to shoot them, Jackson asked, "Why down there?"

"You'll see," Buddy said.

He told them to stand next to a tree that was growing beside the stream.

Buddy said to Jackson, "We'll wait here while you get one of our bicycle cable locks."

Jackson looked puzzled, and Buddy added, "If that's okay with you."

"Yes sir," Jackson said.

Ten minutes later, Jackson was back with a cable lock.

Buddy directed the four guys to sit on the dirt facing the tree. Then he told Jackson, "Loop the cable between their wrists and around the tree, and close the lock."

When that was done, he announced, "Fine, we're done here. Time to head back to the Center."

"Are you just going to leave us here?" one of the guys asked.

"Would you rather we shot you?" replied Buddy.

"The black flies are crazy down here. We can't wave them off if our hands are handcuffed."

"You should have thought of that," Buddy said.

Two hours later, as darkness was falling, Buddy called the Tudorsville police to report that intruders armed with rifles had been captured on the Center's property.

Two cruisers arrived at the Center and four cops emerged, three patrol officers plus the officer in charge, a tall, thin, young-looking cop with a prominent Adam's apple, who identified himself as Sergeant Zach Lawrence.

Sergeant Lawrence said, "Take us to them."

The cops accompanied Buddy and his Protectors down to the stream.

Although they needed flashlights to follow the path through the field, they had no trouble finding the captured intruders since the guys were screaming, "Help! Fuck! Shit! Help!"

The light of the flashlights illuminated clouds of bugs that swarmed around the guys' heads and crawled on their faces like black poppy seeds with wings. Their foreheads, cheeks, necks and exposed skin on their arms blossomed with angry red swellings. Their eyes were swollen shut and their lips and ears were distended and leaking blood.

"Jesus!" one of the cops said. "Cut them loose."

Buddy opened the combo lock and pulled the cable free of the guys' handcuffs.

A cop snapped their plastic handcuffs using a cutter tool.

"Can you walk?" Sergeant Lawrence asked.

"Yeah," the guys said, as they staggered to their feet.

"We'll take you to a hospital," the Sergeant said.

"I want them charged with trespassing," Buddy said.

"We'll see about that. You put these boys' lives in danger, leaving them down there. As it is, I'm considering charging *you* with assault, maybe kidnapping."

113

"They were carrying rifles on our property. We have a right to defend ourselves."

"We were just hunting," one of the guys said.

"We didn't know that."

"We won't forget this," the guy said to Buddy, adding, "Asshole."

Sergeant Lawrence asked, "How long were they tied up?"

"Maybe a few hours," Buddy replied, glaring at the guy who called him an asshole. "Did you hear him threaten me, just now?"

"Next time, sir," Sergeant Lawrence said, looking at Buddy like he was dog vomit, "you call us if you see someone you're worried about. You hurt someone, you'll regret it."

Buddy stood with Protectors Ricky and Jackson watching the police cars drive off with the four guys.

"You did well," Buddy said. "I'm proud of you."

"Too bad we didn't get to do any shooting," Ricky said.

"Next time, Ricky."

Jackson said, "But the cops warned us not to harm trespassers."

"Fuck them," Buddy said. "We have every right to defend ourselves against intruders."

"Including to shoot them?"

"We can do *anything* we need to do in self-defense."

Charles returned to the Center later that evening, having missed all the excitement, and Buddy gave him a full report.

"So they claimed they were just hunting," Charles said.

"Yeah, but that's bullshit," Buddy said. "They were scoping us out, testing us, seeing how we'd react. Today was just the beginning. They basically said they'd be back, right in front of the cops."

Charles leaned forward, picturing the scene that Buddy described.

"It's as we've been told," Charles said. "Ignatius Jones warned that we'd face enemies."

"He was right about that."

"We have a duty to protect the portrait and the Center."

"That's what I told the cops but like I said, they're not on our side."

"I made that commitment to Ignatius Jones."

"Which is why you're his Messenger," Buddy said.

"Good thing you got the jump on the intruders."

"Yeah," Buddy agreed. "We only had handguns against their rifles. We would have been out-gunned."

"So get what we need to win, next time."

"Assault rifles."

"If that's what it takes," Charles said. "Our enemies are leaving us no choice."

Nineteen

THE LOON LAKE INN appeared on the outside much as it did when it was built in 1840, a classic New England white frame hotel shaped long and narrow like a landlocked wooden ship, three stories high, with dormers jutting up from its steep roof, a covered veranda gracing its entire length in front, and flowers cascading from pots that hung down from the slanted roof along the veranda's outer edge.

Rocking chairs on the veranda were unoccupied when Frances arrived at the Inn shortly after lunch on a warm early September day, the afternoon before her week-long program at the Ignatius Jones Center. She figured that the other guests were still out for lunch or otherwise enjoying the late Vermont summer.

The springs squeaked on the Inn's screen door as she pulled it open to enter the reception area. Martyn Zimmer, Innkeeper, formerly from Zurich, was standing behind the counter. He greeted her with a big smile.

"Welcome back," he said, reaching behind him for Frances' room key. "Room 23, as requested."

Room 23 was furnished as Frances liked, with typical Vermont understatement, a king size bed, two bedside tables with reading lamps, an antique wooden bureau, and a ceiling fan. Frances propped open her window to let in fresh air. Outside, she could see Loon Lake glistening in the afternoon sun.

After getting settled, she wandered back downstairs into the Inn's common area. As usual, it was cool and shaded since its windows looked out onto the covered veranda.

Everything in the common area seemed the same as on Frances' earlier visits, the well-used easy chairs and sofas, the bookshelves crammed with old books in worn hardback covers, the old floor lamps, and coffee tables, and assorted magazines from months and years earlier.

With one glaring exception: The artwork hanging above the stone fireplace.

For as long as Frances could recall, the oil painting over the fireplace depicted a traditional Vermont tableau of cows grazing in a pasture. Now, in its place, was a poster showing the Desmond Wilkins portrait of Ignatius Jones. Below the reproduction, were the words, "Ignatius Jones Center for Spiritualist Discovery, Tudorsville, Vermont."

The full-color reproduction of the painting revealed a virtuosic depth and intensity that Frances hadn't appreciated from the old black-and-white photographs.

Even so, she thought the cows were more suitable for a Vermont country inn.

"Can I get you anything?" Martyn asked, as Frances steamed towards him at the reception counter.

"You've hung new artwork over the fireplace," she said.

"I purchased it from the Ignatius Jones Center," Martyn replied. "A nice touch, don't you think, given all the excitement?"

"Very nice, but what does it have to do with the Inn?"

"Quite a lot, as it happens. Ignatius Jones visited here when he was staying with friends at their farm just up the road. He liked to play billiards downstairs and to relax on the veranda with his drink and cigar."

"You never mentioned this before."

"Everyone wanted to hear about our other famous visitors like Calvin Coolidge and Henry Ford. I didn't realize how significant Ignatius Jones was, until they built the Center."

"Ignatius Jones on a farm," Frances said. "I never thought of him that way."

"The farm was owned by a top Boston family, their way to reconnect with Nature, although of course their hired hands did all the work. I suppose that when Ignatius Jones had his fill of Nature, he liked to come to the Inn. Also…" Martyn stopped, blushing suddenly.

"What?"

"Gentlemen were known to entertain lady friends in our rooms. Mr. Jones joined in this practice when he required a degree of privacy that was unavailable on the farm."

"His way to reconnect with Nature," Frances said.

Next morning, Frances recognized several of the other guests having breakfast in the Loon Lake Inn dining room, which was decorated country-style with striped wallpaper, filmy white cotton curtains on the windows, and white tablecloths and flower cuttings on the tables.

Lisbeth Smythe, who was sitting alone at one of the tables, waved hello. Frances smiled and waved back. An elegant woman with a café au lait complexion and startling green eyes, Lisbeth's career began as a storefront psychic serving the African-American community in Providence, Rhode Island. She broadened her base of followers through a weekly column in the *Providence Journal*, and became even more widely known when she launched her own late-night FM radio program, *Psychic On Call*, which was picked up on a national network feed for broadcast in over two hundred radio markets.

Also sitting alone, and giving Frances a quick nod and smile, was Samuel Fisher, from Oxford, UK. Plump and bald, he spent much of the year on tour to cities around the world for private mediumistic sessions with clients. During one of his visits to Boston, Samuel had contacted Frances and they enjoyed a pleasant dinner together at the Copley Plaza, a courteous gesture that she appreciated.

There were other solitary diners as well who looked serenely comfortable eating alone. Frances assumed they were fellow practitioners. She saw herself in them. She understood implicitly how they experienced their worlds, both physical and spiritual, and she expected to see them again later that morning when they all signed in at the Ignatius Jones Center for Spiritualist Discovery.

Frances picked a two-seater table in a corner where she'd have a good view of the room.

A waitress approached with a glass carafe of coffee in each hand. "Regular or decaf?"

"Neither," said Frances. "Just black tea with milk, please, and for breakfast, I'll have orange juice, two eggs over easy, bacon very well done, and an English muffin with grape jelly."

Suzie Prestowicz bustled through the dining room door and located Frances after a quick scan of the room.

"Do you mind if I join you?" she asked.

"Of course not," Frances said. "Take a seat. Do you normally come here for breakfast?"

"No, I came to see you."

Suzie greeted the waitress by name, "Good morning, Billie, dear," and accepted her offer of coffee, regular, with milk.

"Well, I'm glad you came," Frances said. "It's always nice to see a friendly face."

Suzie leaned forward towards Frances. "There are people at the other tables watching us," she said, in a lowered voice. "Are they here in Tudorsville for the same reason you are?"

"I expect so."

"I'm upset about Lily," Suzie whispered, keeping her eyes on Frances, not looking around.

"I thought she had no complaints."

Assuming that the other psychics were listening, Frances avoided mentioning the Center and Suzie picked up on her cue.

Suzie replied, "She was angry with me for selling the… *you-know-what*. That's why she applied for the job."

"To get close to it again?"

Suzie nodded. "I didn't realize that when I got rid of that damn thing I was also losing my baby girl. It's not healthy. She's too attached to it. We tried, when she was younger… we brought her to a psychologist. Which was useless, the psychologist just said she had a vivid imagination. She's such a bright girl. She should go to college instead of hanging around Tudorsville."

"Have you told her what you think?"

Suzie gave Frances a look, like, *Are you kidding?*

"And?"

"She says she'll make her own decisions."

"Maybe she's old enough now at eighteen," Frances said. "I thought that I was, at that age."

"People in town are worked up about... the place. They held a meeting at my church about it. You helped me when John passed so I know there are things about spirits that I don't understand, and I'm not prejudiced about what goes on there, not like others in town, but then our boys were caught on the property and they were treated so badly, and I asked Lily..."

Frances broke in so that Suzie could take a breath, "What did she say?"

"Nothing, she just went silent. The way she cut me off left a bad vibe, like there really is something going on." After a pause, Suzie muttered, "Maybe I was imagining it. I just don't know, anymore. Please talk to her, Frances. Find out what you can."

"I'll try. But she may not agree to talk."

"She will, if you ask her. You have your ways. Anyway, I'll leave you now to enjoy your breakfast."

"You don't have to go."

"I have to open my store and I'm already late."

Suzie came around to Frances' side of the table, planted a kiss on her forehead, and then rushed out of the dining room.

Twenty

ONE AFTER THE OTHER, cars turned off Route 100A, crunched down the gravel driveway, and stopped in the turning circle in front of the Evelyn M. Billings Residence.

There, Buddy greeted each visiting psychic medium with a genial, "Hi, my name is Buddy," and "Welcome to the Ignatius Jones Center for Spiritualist Discovery."

Protectors Ricky and Jackson helped to unload each car, and then took its keys and drove it to a parking area behind the building.

Frances watched her rental disappear with Ricky at the wheel.

She said to Buddy, "I'll want my car keys back."

"No problem," Buddy said. "When you're ready to leave, one of our Protectors will bring your car here and he'll return your keys to you then."

"Protectors?"

"We call them Protectors because they're responsible for our security at the Center."

"They look like militia in their soldier uniforms."

"Don't worry, Dr. Gourmelon, their only concern is to protect the Center."

"To protect the Center from what?"

"From those who don't understand what we do here," Buddy said. "Maybe we can discuss this at another time, Dr. Gourmelon. There are other visitors…"

"Okay," Frances said. "So, where do I go next?"

"One of our Spiritualist Helpers will show you."

Buddy gestured to Lily to join them.

Frances saw a self-possessed young woman – attractive, tall, blonde – walking towards her with a big smile.

"Hello, Dr. Gourmelon," the young woman said. "I'm Lily."

Frances grasped Lily's outstretched hand in both of hers.

"I've heard so much about you from your mother."

"As I have about you. Also from my mom."

"We must talk later after everyone is settled."

"I'd like that."

Lily extracted her hand and reached down for Frances' suitcase. "I'll lead you to your room."

She showed Frances into her room on the second floor, a suite comprising a common area, a bedroom with two twin beds, and a bathroom.

"You're the first to stay in this room," Lily said.

It did have a new-room freshness, plus a scent of pine from its pine flooring, its pine wood furnishings in the living area and bedroom, and in the bathroom, a wire basket of pine chips perched on the window sill.

All of the windows faced the back of the property, overlooking the Center's untilled field, the stream at the far

123

edge of the field, and dark green woods on the other side of the stream.

Becca Clinton entered the suite accompanied by Lisbeth Smythe.

"Hello again, Frances," Lisbeth said. "I asked Buddy to put us together, being that we're fellow New Englanders. I hope you don't mind."

Frances had long admired Lisbeth's ability to increase public awareness of her gifts as a psychic medium. She'd watched Lisbeth emerge as a respected member of their profession in Providence and nationally. Now they'd get to know each other better.

"To the contrary, my dear," Frances said. "I'm delighted."

Becca excused herself in order to help other new arrivals.

Lily said, "I've also got to go but before I do, I'll tell you what happens next. About one hour from now, at ten-thirty, all visitors will convene in the Residence Meeting Room."

"Which is where?" Frances asked.

"On the first floor. Go down to the front and someone there will guide you to it. You'll meet Charles Philip Tucker, Messenger for Ignatius Jones. Then shortly after noon, at twelve-thirty, visitors are invited to the Center Café, also on the first floor, where lunch will be served."

"What happens after lunch?" Lisbeth asked.

"Your program schedule will be provided during your meeting with Messenger Charles."

After a pause, when neither Lisbeth nor Frances spoke, Lily asked, "Do you have any more questions for me?"

"I need a key to our suite," Frances said.

"Me too," Lisbeth said.

"The doors have no outside locks so there's no need for keys. The Center is a trusting community. Everyone's belongings are quite safe."

Lisbeth looked skeptical. "No locks?"

"At night, if you want, you can bolt your door from the inside before going to sleep."

Frances said, "Also, there's no phone in the room."

"We don't have phone lines in visitors' rooms. No Internet access, either, in case you're wondering. Messenger Charles wants to keep outside distractions to a minimum."

Frances and Lisbeth had no further questions.

Lily smiled. "We'll see you at ten-thirty."

"She seems to like it here, at least," Lisbeth said, after Lily left.

Frances nodded. "She's an impressive young woman."

Lily did seem more cheerful than Frances had expected. Perhaps Suzie was imagining things, as she herself said.

After a few minutes of good-natured milling about, each of the twenty visiting psychic mediums found the seats in the meeting room that were labeled with their name cards.

Frances' seat was in front, close to the stage. She had to squeeze herself into it since space was tight under its integrated lift-up table top, like a seat in a middle-school classroom. This resemblance was intentional. Charles figured that classroom seats in the meeting room would help to foster a teacher-pupil relationship between himself and the visiting psychic mediums. Also the Center got a great price on the seats from Murray's supplier, which specialized in items that leaked out of the Boston school department's inventory.

Charles made his entrance through a door at the back of the stage, dressed in his plain and humble monk's robe and sandals. He held in front of him a copy of the *Book of Ignatius Jones*.

Chatter ceased in the room as all eyes faced front.

"Welcome to the Ignatius Jones Center for Spiritualist Discovery," he said.

This was the moment he'd worked towards ever since finding the portrait at that rummage sale. Since then, following the guidance of Ignatius Jones, he conceived of the Center; befriended Evelyn Billings; fended off the Billings' lawyers after she passed; instructed the architects; navigated the town's approval process; managed the contractors; staffed the Center; and reached out to psychic mediums around the country, who were now assembled before him in a meeting room of the Ignatius Jones Center for Spiritualist Discovery, his creation.

"My name is Charles Philip Tucker. I am Messenger for the spirit of Ignatius Jones."

Frances wondered why Charles Tucker was dressed like a monk, unlike the photos on the Center's website showing him in an open necked cotton shirt, pressed khaki trousers, and leather loafers. And why was he thrusting his book in the air like a mega-church pastor blandishing his Holy Bible? Did he think that he was anointed in some fashion by Ignatius Jones? If so, Frances felt disinclined to grant him the deference that he might expect. She'd never been good disciple material.

"Please lift your table tops," Charles said. To be fair, Frances thought, his voice sounded normal enough, high pitched, but businesslike. "Underneath you will find a schedule for the program during the rest of the week, your personal copy of the *Book of Ignatius Jones*, and a large manila envelope with a metal clasp and your name printed on the front. Does everyone have these items?"

Affirmative murmurs floated throughout the room.

"So let's start by introducing ourselves. Tell us your names, where you're from, and why you've come to the Center."

In addition to Lisbeth Smythe and Samuel Fisher, there was Edgar Delacroix from Tulsa, a very large man who, like Frances, had trouble squeezing into his seat, and Carla Monson from Honolulu, and Dr. Katherine Brown from Albany, author of a classic study on spiritualism in the Middle Ages and by far the oldest person in the group, who had entered the meeting room using a walker, and Angel, from San Francisco, and Marina Levitt, a psychic from Tucson with big blonde hair, and Lin Wang from Brooklyn, New York.

There was also Tammy Bell, from Philadelphia, who observed pointedly that unlike most other people in the room, except of course for Messenger Charles, she already knew a great deal about Ignatius Jones, having written a thesis about him at the Universal Spiritualism College in Bala Cynwyd, PA. She was big shouldered and matronly in her tweed jacket and plain dress and sensible shoes. She spoke with a twinkly little-girl voice and a superior smile. "I'm so very grateful to Messenger Charles for making all of this possible."

Tammy wasn't one of Frances' favorite people.

During an interview on a Boston radio station, Tammy remarked that Boston, which she called Beantown, ranked in the second-tier for spiritualism after New York City, Chicago, and Philadelphia, a slur that Frances could neither forget nor forgive.

Tessa Pruitt from Anchorage, bright eyes, freckles on her cheeks and nose, told the group that she'd just graduated from college and as a graduation present, her parents and aunts and uncles chipped in to pay her fee for the program and her travel costs to the Center.

She said she'd always been sensitive, even as a child.

"At first, I didn't know what was happening to me. I was so depressed. I even thought about taking my own life to escape from the voices I was hearing. Then I learned about psychic mediums and I realized that I had a gift and could use it to serve others, and I knew what I wanted to do."

After Tessa finished, there was quiet in the room, until Lisbeth said, "Good on you, girl!" and Frances and several others clapped to show their support.

When her turn came, Frances said, "I live and work in Boston, where Ignatius Jones also lived and worked, where his portrait was painted, and where he passed to spirit. I'm looking forward to connecting with our greatest practitioner through the portal that he created for us so long ago, when he made Boston the worldwide hub for leading spiritualists that it still is today."

Take that, Tammy Bell!

After all the introductions, Charles said, "Now for your schedule: It's very simple. Each morning you will participate in discussion groups on the *Book of Ignatius Jones*. You'll go to the meeting room in the House of Spirits where the chapter you select is being discussed. Okay so far?"

Tammy called out, "Yes, perfectly clear, thank you, Messenger Charles."

Tessa asked, "Will we have to take a test for our Certificate of Portrait Mediumship?"

"No test," Charles replied.

"Great!" Tessa exclaimed, causing several in the room to chuckle.

Charles continued, "And each afternoon, starting this afternoon, will be devoted to your sessions with the portrait of Ignatius Jones, also in the House of Spirits, in what we call the Portrait Room."

"That's why we're here," Tessa said.

"Indeed," Charles said. "Now, to get everything started, I'll read to you the words that I transcribed for Chapter One of the *Book of Ignatius Jones*."

Twenty One

CHARLES OPENED his *Book* where he had inserted a blue ribbon as a bookmark, and began reading:

Chapter One. Life Continuous.

My physical life was ended by bullets fired by William Price, my close friend and trusted colleague.

1 My spirit departed my body amidst chaos and lamentations.

2 And my spirit was merged with a great light that is everywhere and that illuminates everything, a light that contains the spirits of all those who have passed since the beginning of time, of all species that have ever inhabited Earth.

3 And the light has within it all colors, hues, and shades, each containing spirits of different species.

4 Including our fellow human beings.

5 And creatures that lived on land on farms and in forests, mountains, and deserts.

6 And also the spirits of birds and insects that flew in the air and of creatures in our oceans, lakes and rivers.

7 For spirits of human beings this light is as bright as the sun.

8 Except for human beings who inflicted cruelty on others, and who betrayed others, as I was betrayed by William Price, their spirits remain trapped forever in unremitting darkness.

9 Spirits of human beings that are contained in the light remain near to those who have known them.

10 As I remain near to those who know and follow me.

11 And to those who contact me through my portrait.

12 And to pilgrims who come to hear my words, who will increase to become a multitude.

13 And to my Messenger who transcribes my words so that they are shared with others in the physical world.

Charles closed his *Book*.

"Any comments?" he asked.

Tammy Bell spoke first.

"So beautiful," she said. "Every word matches what I know personally from my own contacts with the spirit world."

Then Lisbeth said, "Well I, for one, am tired of hearing how the bad part of the Other Side is dark, and the good part is bright and white. Why not the other way around?"

"I transcribed these words as I received them from Ignatius Jones," Charles said. And then, a bit stiffly, "You can ask him why during your sessions in the Portrait Room."

Dr. Gourmelon raised a hand encrusted with multicolored gemstones. Her face shone with guileless curiosity, eyebrows raised.

"Yes, Dr. Gourmelon."

"Please forgive me, Messenger Charles," she said.

"For what?"

She beamed at him, not looking at all contrite.

"I'm asking only because I want to learn."

"Go ahead."

"How did you become Messenger for Ignatius Jones?"

"Do you doubt that I am, Dr. Gourmelon?"

"I would never doubt that, Messenger Charles."

She clasped her hands on her seat table, a student eager for his instruction. The woman was mocking him. He already regretted admitting her to the program.

Charles said, "Ignatius Jones spoke to me after I brought his portrait into my home. He told me that I would serve as his Messenger in order to create the *Book* that I now hold in my hand."

"And you accepted this task?"

"When I heard his voice, I knew that it was what I was here to do."

Angel asked, "How can we be sure that what you've written in the *Book of Ignatius Jones* are his words and not just imagined by you?"

"You can believe it or not," Charles said, pulling up his hood so that it shadowed his face. He shoved his hands inside his robe's large sleeves and padded off the stage through the door at the back.

Buddy Choate took his place. "My name is Buddy," he said, with an easy gap-toothed grin. "We all met when you arrived this morning."

Tammy trilled, "Hello, Buddy!"

"Hello Ms. Bell," Buddy said. "I've been assigned by Messenger Charles to inform you about our rules, as he has received them from Ignatius Jones."

Buddy took a piece of paper from his shirt pocket, unfolded it, and started reading.

"Rule One: No unapproved visits to the Portrait Room in the House of Spirits."

"Rule Two: No touching the portrait of Ignatius Jones."

"Rule Three: No photographs of the portrait. This means no cellphones, cameras, or other picture-taking devices are allowed inside the Portrait Room. Prior to entering the Portrait Room, all visitors must store any such devices in the envelopes that have been provided to you. A Protector will collect your envelopes when you enter the Portrait Room and return them when you leave."

"Rule Four: Respect the words of Ignatius Jones by respecting his *Book* and by honoring his Messenger, who receives his words and shares them with us."

There was silence in the room and then Samuel Fisher said, "These rules aren't mentioned on your website."

"That's why I'm telling you about them now."

Tessa said, "Some of us might want to take photos of the portrait of Ignatius Jones to help us remember the experience and to show people back home. What's the harm?"

"I can't answer that," Buddy said. "I just enforce the rules. I suggest that you follow them."

"Or else what, Buddy?" Frances asked.

This was not how Buddy had envisioned his part of the meeting. He hadn't expected the visiting psychics to balk at rules passed down from Ignatius Jones.

"Or else you may be expelled from the program," said Buddy, keeping his voice calm as he'd practiced so many times.

Tessa said, "It would be so unfair to expel someone for just taking a photo."

"I agree with Tessa," Frances said.

Tammy jumped in, "Most of us believe that the rules Buddy read to us are very reasonable despite what *some* people may think. If you break the rules, you have to face the consequences, just like Buddy says."

That's more like it, thought Buddy.

"Thank you, Ms. Bell, for saying it better than I was able to."

Twenty Two

CHARLES HEADED to the Portrait Room directly from his meeting with the visiting psychics.

The meeting had not gone as he'd planned. He could deal with the Center's external enemies. He hadn't expected skepticism from the Center's visitors. Did it reveal shortcomings in his performance as Messenger? Should he interpret their skepticism as a threat to the Center's future?

Staring at the man in the portrait, he said, "I transcribed your words. I created a Center for you to communicate with your followers. I have defended your portrait against all attackers. But now I'm unsure. Am I failing you? Have I misunderstood my role?"

He heard Ignatius Jones' voice, "You are on the right path."

"What more can I do?"

"I will guide you."

What Charles saw then was the blonde hair, and face, and body of Lily Prestowicz.

He was not surprised to see her.

His dreams about Lily Prestowicz had become more frequent and more disturbing.

They were feverish dreams in which her body was available to him and he took her, again and again, frenzied couplings that brought him no relief, while she looked right through him as if he were invisible, and her body, slicked with sweat, remained opened to him, and he couldn't stop, until he woke up.

The voice of Ignatius Jones said, "She is mine. You will complete us."

Now Charles knew what Ignatius Jones wanted next from him, and he would do his part.

"I will," he said.

Twenty Three

THE TWENTY PSYCHIC MEDIUMS filed into the House of Spirits glass atrium and joined a line to enter the Portrait Room.

Protectors Jackson Kelly and Ricky Fotis were stationed at the Portrait Room door to collect their cellphones and cameras.

When Frances got to the front of the line, Jackson said, "Your envelope, please, Dr. Gourmelon."

Frances handed it to him, and he placed it inside the 'G' slot in shelves next to the door.

Ricky watched her intently, looking suspicious. "Is that everything?" he asked.

"Yes, Protector Ricky," Frances said. "I don't have any more cellphones or cameras with me at the moment."

Ricky didn't appreciate the way Dr. Gourmelon talked to Messenger Charles that morning, nor the way she contradicted Buddy in front of everyone, nor her snarky tone just now when she said 'Protector Ricky.' He took a little extra time staring at her before letting her pass.

Messenger Charles sat on the stage with his back to the program participants as they came into the Portrait Room.

Once they were all seated, the overhead lights in the room dimmed except for the floods illuminating the painting and Charles said, without turning around, "Welcome to the Portrait Room. I am now in contact with Ignatius Jones. Your presence here pleases him."

Frances had eyes only for the painting. The man in the portrait compelled her total attention as if commanding her, "Behold me! Do not avert your eyes!" It seemed from the force of his gaze that he was trying to burst out of the canvas to reach her. Apparently he had the same unsettling effect on the others in the Portrait Room. Everyone stayed quite still, saying nothing, and waiting.

Charles finally turned to face the Center's visitors.

"Protector Ricky will call your name when it is your turn," he said. "Each visitor will be given fifteen minutes with the portrait of Ignatius Jones while the rest of you meditate silently on the spiritual experience that you anticipate having when you come down here. The order of your sessions will be different each afternoon. Not knowing when your name will be called is like life itself and thus also part of your experience with the portrait. Once you have completed your session, you will leave the Portrait Room. The remainder of your afternoon is free time for you to do what you wish. Any questions?"

"What do we do when our names are called?" Tessa asked.

"Come down to the front where I am now. Sit in this chair, facing the portrait. Look into the eyes of Ignatius Jones and hear his voice."

Silence in the room.

"Any more questions?"

Silence.

PORTRAIT OF IGNATIUS JONES

"No? Okay, I'll leave you now with Ignatius Jones."

On his way out, Charles told Buddy, "I'll wait at my house until they're done. Don't call me unless there's a problem."

"Okay," Buddy said. "But why? I figured you'd prefer to stay with the portrait, to protect it."

"I don't want to watch while others interact with Ignatius Jones. It'll make me uncomfortable. Can you handle it?"

"Sure," Buddy said. "We've got video surveillance. And anyway, our visitors won't do anything stupid."

During Tessa's entire fifteen minutes, she sat silently in front of the portrait, staring at it.

The room lights blinked, and she rose to leave the Portrait Room.

No one said anything.

Frances caught Tessa's eye as she climbed the stairs. Tessa winked, and smiled, and continued on her way out.

When her turn came, Frances took the chair on the stage and she looked into the eyes of Ignatius Jones. She heard a voice in her head much more clearly than the usual ambiguous impressions from the Other Side. "Do you know who I am?"

"Ignatius Jones," Frances replied, silently.

The voice said, "Are you ready to meet your lost children?

"I am," Frances replied.

She felt the touch of their tiny hands, forever innocent. She heard cackling laughter, and her four girls, MingMei, Jeannie, Minal, and Pamela, chatting with each other. One of them, she thought Pamela, asked, "Frances, is it time for us to go home now?" Frances replied, "Soon, my darlings." And the boys, Warren and Malcolm, were jostling in the background, until Warren, or possibly Malcolm, bumped into her, and she said, as she had so many times before, "Settle down, my darlings."

Frances was a professional. She didn't shout, or leap up. She sat in her chair, facing the portrait, without exhibiting anything but intense concentration.

But, internally, at her core, she exulted over the confirmation that all she'd believed about spirits was true.

That night, Tessa Pruitt tiptoed into her bedroom. It was dark in the room and Tessa had to feel her way to her suitcase to find her pajamas.

Her roommate Tammy Bell was already in bed with the bedroom lights off.

"Do you mind?" Tammy said. "I'm trying to sleep."

"Sorry," Tessa said. "I'll try to be quieter."

"Do try," Tammy said.

They didn't speak again until Tessa finished fumbling in the dark and slid under her covers.

"You know," Tammy said, "you talk too much."

"What?"

"In our meeting today with Messenger Charles and then again with Buddy."

"I don't think…"

"What you think doesn't matter, Tessa. You have a lot to learn before anyone cares about your thoughts."

"I do have a lot to learn," Tessa said, hoping to placate her irritable roommate.

But Tammy wasn't finished.

"So few of us are authentic psychic mediums," she said. "The rest are fakers."

"I suppose so."

"Take Frances Gourmelon, for example. I've heard stories about how her clients feel cheated by her readings."

"I never heard that."

"You wouldn't, would you, being up in Alaska, not exactly in the thick of things?"

"Still, I try to keep up," Tessa said.

"Frances has been sued for fraud on more than one occasion. She's had to settle with her clients, pay them to keep everything quiet."

"So how did you hear about it?"

"I have my sources, Tessa. Anyway, I'm only telling you this to give you friendly advice about picking your friends. You don't want to get too close to Frances Gourmelon."

"I like Frances," Tessa said. "And Lisbeth Smythe"

"Lisbeth is another one cut from the same cloth," Tammy said. "Of course, most of *her* clients wouldn't be all that discerning."

"What do you mean by that?"

"You know what I mean."

"Frances took my side today, which I appreciate," Tessa said.

Tammy said, "She wasn't doing you any favors, little Tessa. For my part, I choose the side of Ignatius Jones and of his true Messenger, Charles Philip Tucker. You'll choose that side for yourself as well if you know what's good for you."

After Lisbeth and Frances turned off their book reading lights, Lisbeth asked, "Did you hear his voice?"

"I did," Frances said. "I'm sure of it."

"Me too," Lisbeth said.

They lay in the dark for a few minutes, thinking.

Frances said, "I'm not quite ready to accept that Charles Tucker is his Messenger."

"Yeah, they didn't tell us about that on their website."

"Nor do I get his robe and sandals. I mean, he can wear what he wants, but why a medieval monk?"

"Definitely creepy," Lisbeth agreed.

"Not to mention dressing up those boys as soldiers and calling them Protectors, and dressing the girls as TV housewives," Frances said.

Lisbeth said, "The portrait, and Ignatius Jones, they're just what I hoped when I signed up to come here, but I'm getting a weird feeling about Charles."

"And Buddy," "Frances said. "With his talk about rules and how he'll enforce them."

"He started off friendly enough when he greeted us this morning."

"He was trying to intimidate us at the meeting. I get it that they have to protect the portrait but even so, I agree with Tessa about taking photographs."

"I like Tessa," Lisbeth said. "She reminds me of myself when I was starting out."

"Me too," Frances said. "But she was up to something in the Portrait Room."

"What…?"

"I don't know. She winked at me on her way out."

142

"Maybe she was just being friendly."

"Maybe so."

"I hope you don't snore," Lisbeth said.

"Wake me if I do," Frances said. "How about you? Do you snore?"

"No complaints from my husband. Although he knows better than to complain so I can't be sure."

"I'm not good at keeping complaints to myself."

Lisbeth said, "You have my permission to wake me up."

Lisbeth's breathing was steady and quiet, not a problem, although Frances stayed awake anyway. She had a lot to think about.

Today Ignatius Jones brought her babies to her. For that, she was deeply grateful. And his presence in the Portrait Room was undeniable, giving proof to the story about him and his portrait.

And yet, he responded only with riddles to each of her questions:

Question: "How did you invest your portrait with your spirit?"

Answer: "As I describe in the *Book of Ignatius Jones*."

Question: "But you give no details there."

Answer: "You must find meanings in my words."

She had so many questions. What was it like to be Boston's preeminent psychic during the 1890s? When he passed over, did he meet the spirits with whom he'd previously had contact? Was it true that Charles Philip Tucker was his Messenger?

She'd try again to get answers during her next sessions in the Portrait Room.

Twenty Four

BUDDY WAS REVIEWING the day's videos at the console in the video monitoring room when he noticed an anomaly in the video file from the Portrait Room.

He replayed it to double- and triple-check.

There was no doubt.

Charles would not be pleased.

Buddy hurried to Charles' office. It was empty. Next he tried his own office that he shared with Murray, and found Charles there.

Charles and Murray stopped talking when he rushed in.

"What's going on?" Charles asked.

Buddy blurted it out, "One of the visitors took pictures in the Portrait Room. We caught it on our video surveillance. She must have sneaked in a second phone after handing in her first one at the door."

"Who?"

"Tessa Pruitt, from Anchorage."

"Are you sure?" Murray asked.

"The video camera that's behind the portrait caught her holding a camera-phone at her waist. She was aiming it at the portrait. I printed out a frame capture that shows her in the act."

Buddy handed copies of his evidence to Charles and to Murray.

"Guess our surveillance system worked," Murray said. "Let's take her aside. Demand to see her cellphone. If we find photos of the portrait, tell her to delete them, watch her do it, and then warn her against trying this again. We'll make it clear that we're sure to catch her."

Charles was looking at the frame capture that Buddy handed to him. "We can't let her off so easily," he said, in a flat expressionless voice like he was just stating an obvious fact. "She defied a rule given to us by Ignatius Jones. Arrange a general meeting tomorrow morning. Get everyone there."

"And then what?" Murray asked.

"We'll expel her from the Center," Buddy said. "She had fair warning."

"Bad for business," Murray said. "She'll blog about it and other psychics will think twice about coming here."

"I told them what would happen," Buddy said. "We can't go back on it now."

Charles said, "I'll think on it."

A notice to assemble in the Residence Meeting Room was slid under everyone's door before daybreak.

At breakfast, Spiritualist Helpers Lily and Becca repeated the same information at each of the tables in the Center Café, "Special Meeting at nine-thirty in Residence Meeting Room."

"What's this about?" Frances asked.

"I don't know," Lily said. "But everyone has to attend."

145

Buddy stood on the stage watching the psychics as they filtered in. He stood ramrod straight, chin out, shoulders pressed back, his thumbs hooked in his green canvas belt on either side of his silver chrome belt buckle. It was a Protector's belt, which complemented the rest of his uniform for this Special Meeting, including a Protector's olive-green shirt and trousers, and polished black leather boots.

"He looks like Mussolini," Frances muttered to Lisbeth.

Once shuffling and chatter in the room died down, he got right to business without any opening pleasantries.

"A person in this room has broken Rule Three against taking a photograph inside the Portrait Room."

He let that sink in, and then, "We know that person took pictures of the portrait of Ignatius Jones."

"You must be mistaken," Lisbeth said. "We all handed over our phones and cameras at the door."

"No mistake. The person was caught on our surveillance video. I am giving that person an opportunity now to confess."

No one moved.

"I won't draw this out. Tessa Pruitt, please stand up."

Tessa stood beside her seat. She'd gone pale and her hands, holding the back of her seat, were trembling. *She looks terrified*, Frances thought. *Poor girl*.

"Do you admit that you took photographs in the Portrait Room?"

Tessa didn't respond, and Buddy repeated, "Do you admit it?"

Finally she replied, so softly that Frances could hardly hear her, "I admit it."

"Even while you realized that you were breaking a very clearly stated rule?"

"Yes."

"Speak up. What rule is that?"

"Against taking photographs of the portrait."

"And you're aware the penalty for breaking that rule is to be expelled from the program?"

"Yes." She brushed tears from her eyes and cheeks with the back of her hand. "I'm sorry."

Frances said, "I think that's quite enough, don't you, Buddy?

"We're not finished here, Dr. Gourmelon."

"Tessa apologized. You've made your point."

"Not yet."

Turning back to Tessa, Buddy asked, "Have you shared your photos with anyone else?"

"I didn't share them," Tessa said.

"Is that the absolute truth, Tessa?"

"Yes."

"Come here."

Tessa joined Buddy on the stage.

Buddy moved close to her, invading her space. She looked straight ahead with her nose inches from his chest.

"Give me your camera phones now, all of them, so that we can delete the photos."

Tessa extracted a cellphone from her purse and another from her back pocket, and handed both of them to Buddy.

"Do you have any other devices that can take pictures?"

"No."

147

"We'll return these phones to you when you leave the program. Do you have a problem with that?"

"How will I communicate with my family or my friends?"

"You can use the landline phone in our Residence office."

"Okay."

"Also you need to give us your computer devices."

"I'll have to go back to my room to get them."

"No, you won't."

Protector Ricky brought forward several items which Buddy laid on a table. "We have here an iPad, a laptop, and a thumb drive. Do these belong to you, Tessa?"

"Yes, I think so. How did you…?"

"Protector Ricky took them from your room at my request. Surely you don't object, Tessa, do you?"

Tessa glanced out at the others in the meeting room. Mostly they looked embarrassed, or sympathetic, except for Tammy, who was watching her inquisition with a chilly smile. The foolish girl had ignored her warning to pick the right side. Now she would pay, and she had only herself to blame.

"You could have asked me," Tessa said, finding some defiance.

"Yes, but you can understand why we might want to check for ourselves, can't you?"

"I suppose so."

"We'll hold onto these until you leave the Center. Now return to your seat. Messenger Charles will deal with you shortly."

Buddy strutted out of the Meeting Room.

The room was dead quiet. Tessa wiped her cheeks with the back of her hand. Frances rose to hand her a tissue. Tessa accepted it, mouthing a silent "thank you."

Charles glided onto the stage, his eyes deep in shadow under his raised hood.

"Tessa Pruitt," Charles said. "Please stand."

Tessa once again rose to her feet.

"You are found to be in violation of Rule Three which specifically prohibits taking photos in the Portrait Room. You have admitted breaking this rule. Is that correct?"

"Yes."

"You may address me as Messenger Charles."

"Yes, Messenger Charles."

"You promised Buddy that you did not share the photos with anyone, is that correct?"

"Yes, Messenger Charles."

"Are you lying to us now, Tessa?"

"No, I'm not lying."

"Because you can't hide the truth from Ignatius Jones."

"I am not lying, Messenger Charles."

"Come here and swear it on this *Book of Ignatius Jones*."

Tessa joined Charles on the stage. She placed her hand on the *Book* that he was holding.

"I swear that I didn't share the photos."

"So be it," Charles said, pulling the Book away from her hand. "I will allow you an opportunity to repair what you have done. Tessa, are you prepared to accept this opportunity?"

"Yes, Messenger Charles."

"A meditation room has been prepared for you. You will receive your lunch and dinner there. You will not speak with anyone during your meditation time. You may have with you only your *Book of Ignatius Jones* and paper and pencils which will be provided for you to record your reflections on what you have done. You may return to your own room at eight o'clock tonight. Do you accept my decision?"

"I do, Messenger Charles."

"You may leave us now."

She looked as tiny as a child as Protector Ricky led her out.

Frances caught up with Charles in the hall.

"Messenger Charles, may I have a word?"

"What is it, Dr. Gourmelon?"

"Is it necessary to treat Tessa Pruitt so harshly? All she did was take some photos."

"She violated the rules."

"Are they so important, these rules?"

"These are not my rules. They are given to us by Ignatius Jones. So yes, they are so important."

"Ignatius Jones says no photos?"

"He warned against reproductions of his portrait that could be used in false readings."

"Even so, the Center sold a reproduction that I saw hanging in the Loon Lake Inn."

"That was a mistake. We are correcting it."

"Messenger Charles, I believe that you are making another mistake. I must warn you of the perils of hubris."

"Thank you for your warning, Dr. Gourmelon. Is that all?"

"No."

"What else?"

"The way that Buddy spoke to Tessa, it was excessive. He was bullying her."

"He was doing his job."

"We're here as your guests, Messenger Charles. We're not inmates, and Buddy is not our warden."

"Buddy's job is to protect the portrait."

"Against being photographed?"

"We're talking in circles, Dr. Gourmelon. Protecting includes respecting the words of Ignatius Jones. If you or Tessa Pruitt disagree with that, you're free to leave the Center at any time. Is that what you want?"

Charles had her there and Frances knew that he knew it. She wanted more sessions with Ignatius Jones, like they all did. She had questions that only he could answer. She hadn't yet talked with Lily, as she promised Suzie that she would. She had only just arrived. For lots of reasons, she wasn't ready to leave.

"Not right now," Frances said.

"Then you'll have to excuse me," Charles said, ending their discussion. "I must go. I have things to do."

Twenty Five

MURRAY STARTED WITH Tessa's second cellphone, the one she'd carried into the Portrait Room. He found and deleted three photographs of the portrait.

Reviewing her outgoing emails on that phone, he discovered that the photographs were emailed to 'Mom' with a message, "See attached photos."

So Tessa had lied about sharing them.

Which was fine with him. It was just a painting, after all, and taking its photograph wouldn't steal its essence, despite Charles' edicts on the topic.

Not a big deal, Murray thought, although he'd have to report what he found to Charles and to Buddy.

He copied Tessa's contact files, phone logs, texts, and emails from each of her cellphones.

He copied her client records from a folder on her PC labelled "Psychic Tessa Pruitt" including their credit card numbers. He also copied a file labeled 'Financial,' which provided Tessa's ID names and codes that she'd devised to help recall her passwords to access her bank account, her credit cards, online merchants, and her blog.

The same ID names and password codes were stored on Tessa's iPad. Just for completeness, Murray copied them as well.

Her thumb drive was blank. Evidently she brought it with her as a back-up storage device.

If Tessa complained about the Center in her blog, he could access her blog to change or delete her negative comments. Maybe he'd post his own comments under her name, just to stir things up. In any case, he could make quick money selling the bank and credit card information to a contact in Romania.

For now, Murray decided, he'd keep to himself that he'd made copies of Tessa's files.

That night, around eight-thirty, there was a knock on the door to Frances' and Lisbeth's suite.

"Can I come in?" Tessa asked, speaking just above a whisper.

"Sure," Frances said. "How was your meditation?"

"I thought I would go crazy," Tessa said. "I read the *Book of Ignatius Jones* so many times, and it's very inspiring and all, but then I had nothing to do for hours. I tried to channel Ignatius Jones. I tried to imagine his portrait but nothing came."

"Sounds like jail," Lisbeth said.

"That's how it felt," Tessa said. "When I had to go to the bathroom, they sent one of the Spiritualist Helpers with me to make sure I did my business and then returned without making a run for it."

"I asked Charles why you were treated so harshly," Frances said. "He told me that the rule against photographing the portrait comes directly from Ignatius Jones."

"That's just the thing," Tessa said. "During my session with Ignatius Jones, I felt that he approved of my taking pictures."

"Makes you wonder whether Charles is speaking for Ignatius Jones or just for himself," Lisbeth said.

Tessa said, "I need to ask a favor. You were so nice to me, Frances, and I don't want to get you in trouble, but I need to talk to my mom and I don't want to make the call in the Residence office where they'd be listening."

"Of course," Frances said. "You can use my cellphone. Make your call in our bedroom while Lisbeth and I occupy ourselves out here in our sitting area."

Although their bedroom door was closed, the wall was thin enough that Frances and Lisbeth could hear Tessa's side of the call.

"Hi, can I speak to Mom?"

"Yes, everything's fine. Is she there?"

"Mom, I got into trouble today."

"No, I'm fine. It was because of the photos that I took of the portrait."

"They found out."

"They have a rule against it."

"I know. I lied. I didn't know what to do."

"If anyone asks, say you know nothing about it."

"Yes, but just tell them that, Mom. Please. It's important."

"They were going to expel me from the program, but…"

"I know we paid a lot of money. They didn't…"

"Mom, let me finish. They didn't expel me. They put me in a meditation room for the day."

"It's just a room. It did have a window. But the door was locked, like a cell."

"They did let me out to go to the bathroom."

"Also, they took away my phones and my computer. I'm calling on a friend's phone."

"I'll get them back when I leave. No, I'm okay, Mom, I just wanted to let you know."

"The portrait of Ignatius Jones is just what I hoped. I was in contact with his spirit."

"I heard his voice. I felt him with me."

"No, I'm sure of it. I've never felt anything like it."

"Yes, it's worth it. I still believe that."

"Bye, Mom. Love you."

Tessa re-joined Frances and Lisbeth. "You probably heard everything," she said.

"There's not much soundproofing in these rooms," Frances said.

"Well, there's one good thing about my bad behavior," Tessa said. "I've got a private room now. Tammy doesn't want to room with me anymore and she moved out, and Buddy says no one else wants to be my roommate."

Frances said, "Trust me, you're better off without her. If you get lonely, you're always welcome to visit with me and Lisbeth."

"Right," Lisbeth said. "And Tessa, you take care, now."

Twenty Six

NEXT MORNING, AFTER BREAKFAST, Frances wheeled a cart around the Center Café to collect trays, dishes, and utensils that were left on the tables and on the returns counter.

She pulled her loaded cart into the kitchen, backing through the swinging door from the Café.

Lily was alone in the kitchen, with her hair pulled back and wearing an apron to protect her Spiritualist Helper outfit. She worked methodically, rinsing the dishes and utensils and placing them in the dishwasher.

Frances wiped the trays clean and stacked them for re-use at lunch.

Protector Jackson came into the kitchen.

"Can I help?" he asked. He looked towards Lily, who was absorbed in her work at the sink and dishwasher and didn't reply.

"We're almost done, Jackson," Frances said, "but thank you."

"Sure, alright," Jackson said, sounding deflated. He turned to leave the kitchen after stealing another glance at Lily.

"That was nice of him," Frances said to Lily.

Lily nodded. "We try to help each other."

Frances stayed to dry the pots and bowls that Lily washed by hand.

Lily pressed the dishwasher's Start button, and Frances moved nearer to her and asked, in a low voice and keeping her back to the video camera over the kitchen door, "Can we talk now?"

"We need to dump our trash," Lily replied. "I'll show you where it goes."

She handed Frances a bulging black plastic trash bag and led her out of the kitchen's back door to a dumpster. "Drop it in there," she said. Then, followed by Frances, she doubled back to an alcove being used to store a wheelbarrow, shovels, rakes, and other property maintenance equipment.

"There's no video into this alcove," Lily said.

"So dumping the trash was just to get us out of the kitchen," Frances said. "Good thinking."

"Jackson showed me this place," Lily said. "But we have to be quick. Becca will tattle if she doesn't see me for a while."

"Why would she do that?"

"We're supposed to report on anything out of the ordinary."

"What's going on here, Lily? All this surveillance?"

"Buddy says we need it because plots can be hatched anywhere."

"Do you believe that, Lily?"

"It's what Buddy says."

"There's a story going around that some boys were mistreated after being caught on the property."

Lily looked silently at Frances.

"Is that true?"

Still no response.

"Are you not saying anything because it isn't true, or you're not allowed to?"

Finally Lily replied, "There's nothing I can say."

"And the way they bullied poor Tessa just for taking pictures, why would they do that?"

"I really can't... "

"Okay, Lily, sweetheart, let's change the subject," Frances said. "Suzie told me that the portrait means a lot to you."

"I grew up with the man in the portrait. For as long as I can remember, he comforted me, made me feel safe."

"Ignatius Jones."

"I didn't know his name at the time."

"He communicated with you."

"I heard his voice."

"You were upset with your mom that she sold it."

"She never told me that she planned to sell it. She did it while I was away. When I came home, it was gone."

"She wanted it out of her house, Lily."

"It's my house too. She should have told me. Whatever. It's too late now."

"Your mom is disappointed that you chose not to go to college."

"I know."

"She said you would have been accepted at your first choice school."

"There's no point in discussing it. This is where I belong now."

"Have you spent time with the portrait now that you're here?"

"Not yet. Messenger Charles told us that if we do our jobs well, he'll invite us to join him in the Portrait Room when it's not reserved for visitors."

"You'd be alone with Charles?"

"I guess so. Maybe. Why?"

"I notice things, Lily. I've seen Charles watching you."

"That doesn't mean anything, Dr. Gourmelon."

"You're an attractive young woman. Just because he dresses like a monk…"

"I'd be more nervous if he really were a monk," Lily said, with a quick smile. "I can take care of myself."

"Lily, as your mother's friend, I must tell you I have a strange feeling about this place. She's worried for you and so am I."

"Well, don't be."

"You don't have to stay here."

"When my mom sold the portrait, I didn't know what to do. Then I heard about the Center, that the portrait was here. I *do* have to be here with it, Dr. Gourmelon."

Lily looked at once both so sad and so resolute that Frances couldn't help but get teary eyed. "My dearest Lily."

"We need to get back," Lily said.

Twenty Seven

LISBETH NOMINATED Frances to lead their group discussion on Chapter Seven of the *Book of Ignatius Jones.*

The others in the group, Samuel, Tessa, Angel, and Tammy, concurred, although Tammy wasn't happy about it, being the only true authority in the room on Ignatius Jones.

Frances accepted, and to get their discussion going, asked Samuel to read the Chapter aloud.

He read:

Chapter Seven: My Portrait Across the Divide.

On the first day, I commissioned my portrait to be painted by Desmond Wilkins.

1 I told him to render my image truthfully as if I were present on the canvas.

2 I set aside the second day, and the next five days, for him to do his work.

3. On these days, I left my house on Beacon Hill and crossed Boston Public Garden to his house on Commonwealth Avenue.

4 And each day I sat motionless for an hour in his studio as he labored to capture my image on canvas.

5 On the seventh day, he presented his handiwork to me and I deemed it satisfactory.

6 I revealed his handiwork to my benefactor William and to his sister Melissa and they both deemed it satisfactory.

7 I accepted his handiwork as My Portrait.

Frances said, "It's interesting that Ignatius Jones showed the portrait first to William Price, whom he describes as his benefactor."

"Because he points out in Chapter One that William Price was also his murderer?" Lisbeth asked. And then, answering her own question, "But I guess back when the portrait was commissioned, he didn't anticipate that."

Angel said, "He says he also showed the portrait to Melissa Price, William's younger sister. How old was she at the time?"

"Fifteen," Tammy said. "I researched the history for my thesis. The portrait was completed in 1896, and she was born in 1881, so she was fifteen."

Frances said, "There's more about Melissa in the next part where Ignatius Jones invests the portrait with his spirit."

Samuel continued reading:

8 After I felt the presence of the Departed and received their messages for my followers, I was beseeched by my followers, "How will we manage when you have passed?" and I had naught to tell them.

161

9 Melissa asked, "How will I manage when you have passed and are no longer here to comfort me?" and I had naught to tell her.

10 She said, "You must become one with your portrait so that after you have passed, I can meet you in your portrait and be comforted," and I promised her that I would.

11 And I took hold of my portrait in my hands for a day and a night, and I willed my aura to join with the paint and the canvas, and my portrait and I become one, forever."

12 And I told my followers that after I passed to the Other Side, those who possessed the gift of sensitivity could meet with me through my portrait.

13 And I promised Melissa, as I promised others whose company I shared, that I would be available to her always through my portrait, so that she could be comforted, even after I passed to the Other Side.

"What do you think Melissa means when she says Ignatius Jones was comforting her?" Frances asked. "Given that she was only fifteen."

"Not sure we want to go there," Samuel said.

Angel said. "We know what happened later between them."

Recalling what Lily had told her about how the man in the portrait made her feel when she was growing up, Frances said, "It could have an innocent explanation, that he made her feel safe, for example."

"In any case, Ignatius Jones isn't embarrassed about it since these are his own words," Lisbeth said. "According to Messenger Charles, at any rate."

"Messenger Charles ought to know," Tammy said.

Lisbeth said, "He credits Melissa with the idea that he should invest the portrait with his aura. So he respected her opinion even then."

Tessa said, "She would have been twenty-two in 1903, when Ignatius Jones was shot by her brother."

"Obviously," Tammy said.

"I didn't write a thesis like you did, Tammy," Tessa said. "But I did take the time to do Internet research before coming to the Center."

"Yes, well, Internet research makes you an authority, does it?"

Pointedly ignoring Tammy's gibe, Frances asked Tessa, "What else did you find about Melissa?"

"There were society articles that mentioned her in the old *Boston Evening Globe*. They said she was very beautiful with long blonde hair like white gold. But she dropped out of sight after giving birth to a daughter a month after Ignatius Jones passed to spirit."

"Her daughter also being Ignatius Jones' daughter," Frances said. "Or so William Price believed."

"So, no more reports in the *Globe* about Melissa after her daughter was born?" asked Lisbeth.

"Not until her obituary in 1918 when she passed in the flu pandemic."

"What about Melissa's daughter?"

"Just a birth notice that gave her name as Sarah Price."

Samuel read on:

14 Since I passed to the Other Side, those still in the physical world feel my presence and hear my voice.

15 And they are in contact with their Departed, through me.

16 And my Messenger receives my words for my Book.

17 As I promised, Melissa and her descendants, and others and their descendants, are comforted whenever they look upon my portrait and feel my presence with them.

Lisbeth asked, "Who are these 'others' that he keeps mentioning?"

Tessa said, "Their names didn't surface in my Internet search."

"What about you, Tammy?" asked Frances, finally turning in her direction. "Do you have any information on other descendants?"

Tammy shook her head. "No."

"Even so," Frances said, "his own words imply that Sarah Price may not have been his only child."

"Anyone can speculate," Tammy said. "For example, if he did have other descendants, I believe that my own ancestry might track back to one of them."

"Why do you think that?" asked Frances.

"Because Ignatius Jones and I have shared a special closeness ever since I first learned about him when I was introduced to spiritualism."

"Awesome!" Tessa said.

Frances said, "So let's talk now about how we're connecting with Ignatius Jones in the Portrait Room."

Tessa said, "No matter what Buddy or Messenger Charles say, he was not displeased about my taking pictures of his portrait."

"So now you know better than Messenger Charles," Tammy said, her voice dripping with scorn. "You think it's up to you whether to accept what he tells us."

"I'm just telling you what I heard," Tessa said.

"You lied before. Why should we believe you now?"

"That's enough," Frances said.

"Since you brought it up, Frances, what did *you* hear from Ignatius Jones?" asked Tammy. "I read in the *Spiritualist Testifier* that you're always searching for your babies on the Other Side. Did he lead you to them?"

"He did," Frances said, matter-of-factly.

Samuel said, "I must have missed that article. What are you talking about?"

Lisbeth said, "I don't think this is the time…"

"I don't mind talking about it," Frances said. "I owned a child care center. I rented a van for an excursion. It crashed. Six little ones in my care passed to spirit. Tammy is right. Since then, I've never stopped searching for them."

Silence in the room.

Lisbeth said, "Ignatius Jones brought me into contact with my brother. I lost him when I was just a kid and he was in high school, and he in the wrong place when fools with guns came around. I hardly knew him. He told me that he's proud of his little sister."

More silence.

Angel said, "The portrait doesn't do anything for me. Back in my own place, at my table with my lights and candles, I'm in touch with spirits all the time. So far, I'm very disappointed."

"Maybe you don't believe in it the right way," Tammy said.

"And what would that be?" Angel asked.

"That's not for me to say," Tammy replied. "You should ask Messenger Charles."

Tessa asked her former roommate, "How about you, Tammy? Does Ignatius Jones speak to you?"

"Of course he does," Tammy replied, with a lemony smile. "But what he tells me is none of your business. And anyway, Tessa, you wouldn't understand."

Twenty Eight

CHARLES PROCESSED Murray's report that Tessa Pruitt had emailed copies of her photos to her mother.

To Murray, he seemed surprisingly unperturbed. His face stayed blank, his eyes as dead as stones, as he listened and then considered what he'd heard.

"So she lied when she swore with her hand on the *Book* that she didn't share the photos."

"Looks that way," Murray said.

"Can we get them back?"

"Her mom will keep copies for herself no matter what she says. They're out there."

Buddy lost it.

"Fuck Pruitt and fuck her mom!" he barked. "She'll pay for this. We'll make her an example for the others. You don't disrespect the *Book* and Messenger Charles and get away with it."

Protector Jackson, who had come to the office to review the schedule for the day, was staring at Buddy, stunned.

"What do you have in mind, Buddy?" Murray asked.

Charles took charge. "Murray, you and Jackson can leave us now. Buddy and I will decide what we're going to do."

"Shouldn't I be involved?"

"No, you've done your part. We'll let you know."

Charles watched from the window as Murray drove up the gravel driveway and turned right on 100A towards Woodstock.

"Why are we excluding Murray?" Buddy asked.

"Because he'll raise objections," Charles said. "We'll keep this between us."

"Fine with me."

"Will Jackson be a problem? He was standing here listening."

"I don't think so. We didn't say anything really."

Charles said, "This time I want Pruitt gone, out of here."

"So we'll expel her like we should have done in the first place."

"No, she'll cause problems afterwards if we just expel her. Murray's right about that. And we'd have to deal with dramatics from the others who watch her leave."

"Like Gourmelon."

"Like her, especially," Charles said.

Buddy said, "So, we want Pruitt gone, no dramatics, no noise from her about it later."

"Right. Any ideas?"

"We'll expel her after midnight when everyone is asleep. We'll keep her quiet as we escort her out to her car. No one will hear. Next morning, we'll let it be known that she left without telling anyone because she was ashamed."

"What about later? How do we stop her from posting complaints about us in her blog?"

Buddy was working out his plan as he talked. "The thing is," he said, "she'll be despondent about leaving the Center and about letting down her family who helped to pay her costs to come here. So despondent, she may choose to take her own life, like she told us she thought about doing earlier when she was depressed."

Charles said, "She *may* choose?"

"Next morning when tourists are admiring the rapids in Quechee Gorge, they'll discover that a horrible tragedy has occurred."

"So she'll be dead?"

"Tragically, yes."

Charles thought about it, and said, "She swore falsely with her hand on the *Book*. Ignatius Jones warned us, *Defend my Book against defamers and blasphemers*. He was warning us about Pruitt."

"I agree."

"She's a blasphemer. She has dishonored Ignatius Jones. For that, she has to be punished."

"That's how I see it."

The time for deliberation had passed. Pruitt's flagrant disdain for the *Book* had to be confronted before it became a cancer in the Center, undermining all that they were trying to build. As Messenger, Charles would not, could not, shirk his responsibility to call Tessa Pruitt to account. He asked Buddy, "So, how will we do it?"

"You sure you want to know the details?"

"Yeah, Buddy. The details. How else can I decide whether your plan will work?"

"We'll tell Pruitt that we'll return her toys when we get to the parking lot at Quechee Gorge, far enough away from the Center so that we won't cause additional offense to Ignatius Jones. Ricky will go with her, in her car, following me driving in one of our cars."

"Why would she agree to that?"

"We'll wake her up very early in the morning just after midnight when she's groggy and not thinking clearly. She's alone in her room since Tammy Bell moved, so no one else will know. She'll find out after she gets into her car that Ricky is joining her. He'll make her behave. After we park at Quechee Gorge, we'll check that no one's around, and Ricky will toss her off the bridge. Next morning the police will find her car there with everything in it, and her body on the rocks below the bridge, a clear case of suicide."

"Will Ricky play his role in this?"

"He does what I say. We see things the same way. Also, he takes it personally that Pruitt took her photos while he was on duty in the Portrait Room. He'll enjoy watching her flapping her arms on her way down to the rocks."

"So no witnesses, a verdict of suicide, and no blowback."

"That's the plan."

Charles liked what he heard. It should work. And Pruitt would get what she deserved.

"Do it, Buddy."

After Murray returned from Woodstock, he asked Buddy what he and Charles had decided for Tessa Pruitt.

"Haven't decided yet," Buddy said, busying himself with papers on his desk.

Murray knew the signs; Buddy was hiding something.

"We can't hurt her, Buddy, you do know that, right?"

"Sure."

"You don't lay a hand on her."

"Don't worry about it. We'll handle it."

"No bullshit, Buddy. Nothing physical. Do you understand what I'm telling you?"

"Of course I understand."

"Keep me posted on whatever you and Charles decide."

"Will do. Meanwhile, you can help by organizing an excursion for our visitors tomorrow morning."

"Why?"

"Whatever we decide for Pruitt will require preparation and I don't want them around."

Psychics were observant. Buddy needed them safely away while he and Ricky rehearsed removing Pruitt from her room, escorting her to the parking area, and getting her into her car. He didn't want anyone around when he and Ricky drove to Quechee Gorge to scope out the parking area and the bridge. He promised Charles that every step of the plan would be checked and practiced, except for the last step, tossing Pruitt off the bridge, since they didn't have another body to work with. They'd just have to imagine how that would go. No need to worry about that. Ricky could throw her over the railing with one hand.

"Just give me a couple of hours," Buddy said.

Twenty Nine

"OUR SPECIAL TREAT," Murray explained, as he handed out flyers at breakfast: "See historic Plymouth Notch. Meet out front at nine-thirty for the minibus. Back by lunch. No charge."

Frances had visited Plymouth Notch many times and never tired of it.

It cast a calming spell on her, this small cluster of wood-framed buildings perched on a rise above the road, surrounded by fields and hills. Nothing of note had happened there since a pre-dawn morning in 1923 when, by the light of a kerosene lamp, Vice President Calvin Coolidge was sworn in as President by his father, a notary public. It was a quiet place well off the beaten path, populated mostly by the elderly ladies who managed the Florence Cilley General Store and the Wilder House Restaurant, a crew of artisanal cheese makers in the Plymouth Cheese Factory, a few old guys in plaid shirts who hung around the Wilder Barn museum, and other elders who sold tickets to the Coolidge family homestead.

On its busiest summer days, there might be four or five cars parked on a clearing across from the cheese factory, next to a pasture where sheep were munching grass and occasionally

172

lifting their heads to contemplate the gawkers on the other side of their fence.

After dismounting from the Center's minibus, several of the visitors meandered across the road to the Plymouth Cheese Factory, where they could witness Vermont granular curd cheese being made from the milk of local cows. Others peeled off to see the Coolidge family homestead and the Union Christian Church.

Having already seen these sights, Frances strolled down the road past the church to the general store, where she planned to stock up on Vermont Pure Maple Syrup Candy.

She found Lily already in the store in conversation with a white-haired lady behind the counter.

"Dr. Gourmelon," Lily said, when Frances entered, "I'd like to introduce you to Mrs. Veysey, who was my fourth grade teacher in Tudorsville Elementary School."

"Pleased to meet you," Mrs. Veysey said. Her thick-lensed glasses reflected the store's ceiling lights, and she wore a

173

shapeless granny dress, but she spoke with a loud voice as if she were still managing unruly fourth-graders.

"Don't you think our Lily has turned out well?" she asked.

"I do."

"Although she should have gone to college rather than working at that awful place."

"I agree about that, as well," Frances said.

"Are you one of the psychics we've been hearing about?"

"I am."

"So you can read my mind, I suppose."

"Well, I do know what you're thinking now."

"And what might that be?"

"Is the fat woman going to buy anything or just stand there blabbing?"

Lily laughed and Mrs. Veysey protested, "I was thinking nothing of the sort."

"However," she added, "let me know if there is anything here that you would like."

Frances pointed to a large box of Vermont Pure on the shelf behind her.

As she was counting out change, Mrs. Veysey said, "That Center of yours is not all bad."

"Not all bad?"

"They did give us money to repair the roof on our church, as they promised."

"But not all good either."

"Well, it's not for me to say but they're a cult, aren't they? With their precious book and their odd ideas about that painting that Lily's mother sold to them after it was hanging for years in her house, doing no one any harm."

"They're right about the painting," Lily said.

"If you say so, dear."

"It's true, Mrs. Veysey," Lily insisted. "The man in the portrait, if you look into his eyes, he speaks to you. You can hear his voice. It's much more than just a painting."

"Sure it is," Mrs. Veysey said. "And now I hear their leader Charles Tucker wears a robe and sandals. He wasn't dressing up like Jesus Christ when he got the town to allow him to build on the Pullman farm, I can assure you. Nowadays, when people ask Wilt Schmidt or Hank Boudreau about the Center, they hide their heads, as they should."

"Who are Wilt Schmidt and Hank Boudreau?" Frances asked.

"Wilt's the caretaker here of the President Calvin Coolidge State Historic Site. He spoke against the development until they waved dollar bills under his nose for our church. Whereas Hank Boudreau just wasn't paying close enough attention. He could have done something about it, being on the Selectboard, but ended up voting for their permit. Now that Charles Tucker is showing his true colors, people who fought against his development don't mind saying, 'told you so.' But I'm just a grumpy old lady, so what do I know? What do you think of the Center, Dr. Gourmelon?"

"What Lily says about the painting is true," Frances replied. "That may seem strange to some people, but of course, when you examine anything closely enough, it can seem strange, don't you agree?"

"It *is* strange," Mrs. Veysey said.

Frances was out of the store and half-way across the road to the Wilder House Restaurant when she heard footsteps. She turned around and saw Lily hurrying to join her.

As they walked together towards the restaurant, Lily looked at Frances like she wanted to say something and Frances was tempted to stop, to ask what was on her mind, but by then they were at the Wilder House and Lily stepped ahead to grab the screen door and hold it open for Frances to enter.

Menu choices were handwritten in chalk on a blackboard behind the counter.

Frances requested the rhubarb crumble topped with vanilla ice cream, plus a cup of coffee.

The lady at the cash registered looked inquiringly at Lily, and Lily said, "Just coffee for me, please."

"No crumble and ice cream?"

"No, thanks," Lily said. "I'm trying to be good."

The lady asked Frances, "Are you also paying for your beautiful daughter?"

"I'm not…" Lily began.

"Sure," said Frances, and handed the lady cash.

Lily held the door again for Frances as they walked out to join Tessa and Lisbeth at a picnic table on the grass behind the restaurant.

Tessa was asking Lisbeth about her radio program, and then then they got on to chatting about using the Internet to attract clients for psychic readings, the pluses and minuses of social media, and tips for website design.

176

Frances mostly listened, and Lily also sat quietly, looking out at the view of fields, a small pond, and a farmhouse in the distance.

Finally, during a lull in the chit-chat between Tessa and Lisbeth, Lily said, "I've always loved it here. So peaceful."

She sounded more wistful that one might expect of someone who was still only eighteen years old, and Frances asked, "Lily, sweetheart, are you alright?"

"I'm fine," Lily said. "It's just that this place is so quiet, it's almost like a church."

"Amen to that," Lisbeth said.

Lily said, "I have to tell you something."

"What is it, my dear?" Frances asked.

"Promise not to let anyone know that I told you."

"Of course," Frances said.

"I could lose my job."

"We won't, Lily. You can tell us anything."

Lisbeth and Tessa nodded. "Anything," Tessa said.

"It's about you, Tessa," Lily said.

"Maybe Lisbeth and I should leave you two alone," Frances said.

"No," Tessa said. "Please stay."

Then, to Lily, Tessa asked, "What about me?"

"They know you shared your photos of the portrait."

"Oh no!" Tessa's face turned grey-green like she was about to be sick. "How?"

"They checked your cellphone and found the emails you sent with the photos attached."

"Where did you hear this, Lily?" Frances asked.

"I can't tell you that."

Tessa asked, "So what happens now?"

"Messenger Charles and Buddy are really angry that you lied about sharing the photos despite what you swore on the *Book of Ignatius Jones.*"

"I can't take another day in the Meditation Room," Tessa said.

"If they send you back to the Meditation Room it will be for longer than just one day," Lily said. "They're planning to make an example of you."

"Why?" Lisbeth asked, reaching to grasp Tessa's hand. "What will that achieve?"

"They believe Tessa must be punished for what she did and as a warning to others."

Tessa said, "My mom could tell them she's deleted the photos."

"They won't believe her," Frances said. "Lily, we need to know, would they hurt Tessa?"

"I don't know about Messenger Charles, but I'd be worried about Buddy."

"Buddy doesn't seem all that scary to me," Lisbeth said.

Lily said, "Something happened at the Center, that you asked me about, Dr. Gourmelon."

"About the boys?"

Lily nodded. "Just after the Center opened, some boys trespassed onto the property. Jackson said that Buddy was ready to shoot them. Jackson wouldn't tell me the details. I heard from people I know in town that afterwards the boys had to be brought to a hospital."

"Maybe he *is* a bit scary," Lisbeth said.

"Dear Lily," Frances said. "Why didn't you tell me this earlier?"

"I couldn't. But now, it's different. I'm worried for Tessa."

"I've heard enough," Frances said. "Let's call the police."

"What would we tell them?" Tessa asked. "We heard from a source we can't reveal that Messenger Charles and Buddy are angry at me and maybe they'll do something to me but we don't know what?"

"Tessa," Frances said, reaching across the picnic table for her other hand, the one that Lisbeth was not already holding. "For your own safety, you've got to leave the Center."

"But I can't just leave. They have my car keys, and my other stuff, my cellphones, my PC, my iPad. Also all the money it cost me and my family to send me here would be wasted."

"Right now you should think about your safety, not what it cost you to get here."

Lily said, "Your stuff is being kept in a locked filing cabinet in the Residence office. Buddy carries the key with him except when he leaves the Center, when he gives it to Ricky."

Tessa said, "If I tell them I want to leave, they have to return my stuff and let me go, right?"

"Lily's told us they want to make an example of you," Frances said. "They may come up with reasons why you can't leave right away."

"Now you're scaring me," Tessa said. Her voice broke, "What am I going to do?"

Frances said, "We'll get outside help to force them to let you go safe and sound."

Collecting herself somewhat, Tessa said, "I don't want to get you involved, Frances. This is my fault. And Lily, thank you so much, you've already done more than enough."

"I don't mean outside help from any of us," Frances said. "I mean from Ignatius Jones."

Lisbeth warned, "We've got company."

"You and I will take this up later," Frances told Tessa.

"I've got to go," Lily said, standing up from the picnic table. "Please don't…"

"We won't, Lily," Frances said. "Thank you."

Tammy Bell was tramping across the grass towards their picnic table. She had split off from Samuel, Angel, and Becca as the four of them were walking up the road towards the parking area.

She nodded to Lily as they passed each other.

"Well, well, what have we here?" Tammy asked, with a milk-curdling smile.

"We're enjoying the view and the restaurant's outstanding rhubarb crumble," Tessa said. "You should try it."

Tammy looked past Tessa to the other two at the table, "Becca says you have ten minutes to get back to the minibus."

"We'll be there," Frances said.

"You were so deep in conversation," said Tammy. "Have I missed anything important?"

"Not at all," Lisbeth said.

"Just enjoying the view and the rhubarb crumble, like Tessa told you," Frances said.

Thirty

BEFORE RETURNING to the minibus, Frances stopped in the Wilder Barn, a museum of farm implements that were in use on Vermont farms until the mid-1900s.

Frances saw no one else in the barn when she entered. The only sound she heard was the scuff of her shoes on the wood floor. Dust particles hung suspended in streams of sunlight that poked in through a couple of windows and the cracks in the barn's wooden walls.

The items in the Wilder Barn were functional, and rugged, made of wood, iron, and leather; an iron plow, a buggy with cracked leather seats and wooden wheels, a corn sheller with a hand-crank, a horse-pulled hay rake.

For Frances, their simplicity and plainness of purpose brought back an earlier age. She sensed the spirits of the people whose hands had gripped these utilitarian tools and stained them with their sweat as they extracted meager livings out of their rocky hillside farms. These were people who made do with what they had, and what they lacked, they did without.

She noticed a horse-drawn sleigh that stood out from the other items because of its ornate brass metal work. According to the card posted in front of the sleigh, it was donated to the Wilder House museum by 'Price Farm' in Tudorsville.

A thickset man entered the Wilder Barn.

He had steel-grey hair, and wore farmer's denim overalls and a peaked cap embossed with 'Justin Boot Company.' He saw Frances and walked towards her, apparently cycling through a checklist: Large woman with curly grey hair, check! Wearing a muumuu, check! Gemstones on fingers, check! Only person in Wilder Barn, check!

"You're Dr. Gourmelon, I presume," he said.

"I am indeed," Frances said.

"I'm Wilt Schmidt," he said. "Hildy Veysey said I might find you in here,"

"How...?"

"She was watching from the store. She keeps an eye on things."

"I recognize your name," Frances said. "Mrs. Veysey told me about you."

"Did she?"

"You're the caretaker of the historic site."

"Yes, that's me."

"Do you and your wife live here in Plymouth Notch?"

Frances surprised herself, sometimes, by the words that flew out of her mouth. Now, already, she was checking Wilt Schmidt's marital status!

"I do live here in the caretaker's cottage, but alone. My wife died."

"I'm so sorry, Wilt," Frances said, touching his arm. "I shouldn't have…"

His arm felt like the limb of a giant oak, and his hands and fingers were those of a man who worked outdoors regardless of weather, making things, fixing things, keeping things going.

"No, that's alright," Wilt said. "What else did Hildy tell you?"

"She said you were fighting the development of the Ignatius Jones Center, and then changed your mind."

"When Charles Philip Tucker waved dollar bills under my nose."

"Yes."

"Did she mention that our church needed a new roof?"

"She did. And that you hide your head when folks bring up the topic."

"Doesn't stop them from sharing their opinions. People around here are riled up about the Center."

He didn't elaborate. He just stood silently beside Frances looking at the exhibits. It was taking him a while to get to the reason that he had sought her out. She thought, *He's shy, for such an imposingly large man.*

She didn't need to check her watch to know that she'd soon have to board the minibus back to the Center.

To move things along, while Wilt was deciding how to broach whatever was on his mind, Frances asked, straight out, "What can you tell me about those boys who were caught on the Center's property?"

"You heard about that?"

"Only the headline."

"Just local boys hunting along the stream. I did that myself when I was younger. They didn't mean any harm."

"But they did have guns."

"For hunting. Not to shoot people."

"I heard that they were treated badly after they were caught."

"A big mistake," Wilt said. "People in town are upset. And the boys are angry. They were humiliated. We haven't heard the last of this, unfortunately."

He paused a beat. Then, getting finally to the point, he said, "Hildy tells me you're a psychic."

"Yes."

"I've never met a psychic, until now."

"Well, here I am, Wilt," Frances said, giving him a big smile. "What do you think? Do I pass?"

Again she surprised herself. She might as well start batting her eyelashes at the man.

"Well, you do make a strong impression," he said.

Something in Frances' expression caused him to add, "I mean that in a good way."

"Glad to hear it," Frances said. She did care what the big man thought of her, she realized. *Maybe we've met in our earlier lives*, she thought. *I need to get out more*.

"So, Wilt, do you have any questions about what I do as a psychic?"

"Is it true that you hear voices when you look at that painting?"

"I do hear the voice of Ignatius Jones, the man in the portrait, and I'm not the only one who does."

In Wilt's opinion, psychics ranked in terms of honesty alongside carnies and big-tent preachers, but Frances Gourmelon did seem a forthright, intelligent, and likeable woman. He wanted to believe that she wouldn't look him in the eye and flat-out lie.

"What does Ignatius Jones say about life after death?" he asked.

"Are you asking because of your wife?"

"Yeah, maybe."

"Have you heard from her since she passed?"

"No. And I don't expect to. I've got to be honest with you. I don't believe in that sort of thing."

"Many people don't," Frances said, touching his arm again.

Wilt pressed on, "What about the book that Tucker is selling on his website, do people in the Center really believe that it's sacred, like the Holy Bible?"

"Charles seems to think so."

"What about you?"

"Still making up my mind."

Finally, Wilt couldn't help himself asking, "Dr. Gourmelon, are you serious about all this?"

"Please call me Frances," she replied.

"Sure," he said. "Frances."

"And to answer your question, I'm serious about the portrait. As for the book, I'm still thinking about it, as I said."

Wilt went silent again.

"Now I have a question for you," Frances said.

"Shoot."

"Do you know anything about the Price Farm that donated this sleigh?"

Wilt thought for a moment, and then said, "No, but you might check with Hildy. She's our local historian."

"I'll do that, Wilt, thank you," Frances said. She laid her hand on his arm a third time, as a good-bye gesture, and let it rest there for a few extra seconds. Frances was not too old to appreciate a solid, well-formed man, and she liked what she saw in Wilt Schmidt.

"Pleasure to meet you, Frances," Wilt said, touching the brim of his Justin Boot Company cap.

Now Frances had yet another stop to make before returning to the minibus.

"Back again," Mrs. Veysey said. "Are you here for more Vermont Pure?"

"I haven't eaten them all yet," Frances said. "I'll pick up more on my next visit."

"So you're just coming to say good-bye. How nice."

"Yes, and also to ask you a quick question. Who were the Prices of Price Farm?"

"I knew them, of course. A Boston family."

"Are there any Prices still living there?"

"The last Price who lived on the farm was Prudence Price. When we were kids we called her Prudie, and the name stuck. She died about fifteen years ago."

"Prudie."

"She didn't care that we called her that. In her eyes, we were just country ragamuffins. We couldn't be expected to have good manners. Of course, her married name wasn't Price, although she told anyone who'd listen that she came from the Price family."

"So she was married," Frances said.

"She was. Poor Prudie had a lonely childhood, being schooled at home. The other Prices mostly stayed down in Boston. She had a lot of time on her hands and then she was getting on in years. One thing followed another, and eventually she fell for their farm manager."

"What was her married name?"

"Prestowicz," Mrs. Veysey said. "Her son, John, was Lily's father."

Standing by the minibus door, Spiritualist Helper Becca said to Lily, "We've got everyone on board except Dr. Gourmelon."

"I'm sure she's on her way," Lily said.

"Two more minutes and then we'll leave without her," Becca said. "It's not fair to the others, making them wait."

"I'll go look for her," Lily said. "Won't take long to find her in a place this small."

"I saw you talking with her and the others. Buddy warned us…"

Lily bristled. "So I suppose now you'll tell him…"

"Never mind, she's coming now," Becca said, looking down the road towards the general store where Frances was walking towards them. "Let's get on."

Frances clambered on board.

"Sorry I'm late," she said.

Becca, in the front row, glared at her. Lily, sitting beside Becca, was staring out of the window.

Tammy, in the aisle seat across from Becca and Lily, caught Frances' eye and tapped her wristwatch with her forefinger.

Farther back, Tessa and Lisbeth looked inquiringly at Frances but she shook her head, and mouthed silently, "Later."

There was a vacant seat beside Samuel Fisher. The driver must have been watching her in his mirror because as soon as she was safely down in the seat, the minibus lurched forward.

"We weren't waiting all that long," Samuel whispered. "A bunch of us were stocking up on cheese at the Cheese Factory. We got on just before you."

"Good to hear," Frances whispered back.

"Did you get lost?"

"More like I got found."

"That's alright then," Samuel said.

Frances called Suzie Prestowicz as soon as she got back to her room at the Center.

"Tell me about your mother-in-law, Prudence Prestowicz," she said.

"She died a long time ago. Have you been in contact with her spirit?"

"That's not why I'm calling. Didn't you tell me you found the portrait of Ignatius Jones in her house?"

"After she died, yes. In her attic."

"Did she ever say anything to you about it?"

"Nothing. She never mentioned it. But John knew it was there. He went straight for it after Prudence died."

"I met Hildy Veysey today in Plymouth Notch. We were on an outing and Lily introduced us."

"Lily was in her classroom. As was I. Two generations of our family."

"She said Prudence's maiden name was Price."

188

"That's true, although Prudence wasn't her real first name."

"It wasn't?"

"We found out when we did the paperwork after she died. Her given name was Sarah."

"Sarah Price."

"Yes. But why the interest in her now?"

"Because the daughter of Ignatius Jones, the man in the portrait, was named Sarah Price."

"Oh my!"

"In 1903, when Ignatius Jones was shot by William Price, William's younger sister Melissa was pregnant with Sarah. Ignatius Jones was assumed to be the father. Maybe the Price family protected Sarah from scandal by raising her on their farm in Tudorsville well away from the bright lights of Boston and by letting her and everyone else believe her name was Prudence."

Suzie said, "If Ignatius Jones is Prudence's, or Sarah's, father, and she is Lily's grandmother, then Ignatius Jones would be Lily's great-grandfather."

"So it seems," Frances said.

"Frances, you've got to promise me, don't tell Lily."

"Doesn't she have a right to know?"

"If she finds out that she has a blood connection to Ignatius Jones, she'll never leave the Center. Promise me, Frances."

"If you say so," Frances said. "You're her mother."

Thirty One

TESSA SHOVED HER CHAIR BACK away from the portrait, and lurched to her feet.

She started up the stairs to leave the Portrait Room. Her face was pale.

Frances put out her hand to stop her. "Tessa! What's wrong?"

"I'd rather not say."

"Will you wait for me outside the Portrait Room?"

"Yes," Tessa said. "Please hurry."

Protector Ricky called down to Tessa that she had to leave the Portrait Room so that the next session could get underway.

When Frances' own time with Ignatius Jones ended and she rose to leave, the other psychics who remained in the Portrait Room could see that her normally cheery expression was unusually grim.

Tessa was waiting for her in the hallway, shuddering, and looking miserable.

Frances asked, "What upset you in there, Tessa?"

"Ignatius Jones said that something terrible was about to happen to my mom."

"Tessa, my dear, I don't want to alarm you but Ignatius Jones also let me know that your mom needs you."

"Oh no!" Tessa cried out.

"You must go home to Anchorage as soon as possible."

"Are you all right, Ms. Pruitt?" asked Protector Jackson, who was standing at the door to the Portrait Room.

"Thank you, Protector Jackson, but I'll handle this," Frances said. And then to Tessa, "You must leave right away. You can catch a flight out of Burlington."

"But I can't go until I've earned my Certificate," Tessa said, choking back tears.

"Your mom is more important," Frances said, putting her arm around Tessa's shoulders and drawing her close. She asked Protector Jackson, "Is Buddy in the office?"

"I believe so, Dr. Gourmelon," Jackson said.

Frances and Tessa found Buddy alone in his office.

Frances asked, "Where is Messenger Charles?"

Buddy's lips couldn't quite pull off an amiable grin. He'd just been congratulating himself on his plan for Tessa Pruitt and thinking how well his rehearsal had gone that morning with Ricky while the psychics were away touring Plymouth Notch. He hadn't expected to see Pruitt materialize in his doorway. That she was accompanied by Gourmelon compounded his unease. Had they discovered his plan? Bloody psychics! Could they really read minds?

"He's away at the moment," Buddy said.

Which was as Frances expected, since she'd learned that Charles preferred to wait at his house in Woodstock until visitors were gone from the Portrait Room.

191

"Then we'll talk with you, Buddy," Frances said. "Tessa was warned by Ignatius Jones that her mom is in danger. During my session with Ignatius Jones, I received the same message. Tessa needs to leave the Center right now so that she can get back home to Anchorage to help her mom."

Buddy turned to Tessa and she nodded her agreement. "I'd so much prefer to stay the rest of the week to get my Certificate, but I have no choice. I've got to put my mom first."

"Well, I don't know..." Buddy began. "Let's wait until Messenger Charles gets back."

"There's no time," Frances said. "Tessa can still catch a flight out of Burlington if she leaves now. Please return her phones and other things to her now. Also her car keys."

"I don't have that authority," Buddy said.

"Then get Messenger Charles on the phone."

"This is his relaxation time. He doesn't want to be disturbed."

Tessa began to weep in frustration, tears streaming over her cheeks and dripping from her nose.

Frances leaned over Buddy's desk, blocking his light.

"Last chance, Buddy. Or I'll call the Tudorsville Police and we can discuss it with them."

Buddy recalled the nuns at St. Juanita Catholic Academy where he was exiled to learn self-discipline, an experience that still produced sweat-drenched nightmares. He could still hear them threatening to tell his foster parents about his transgressions, thereby surely consigning him to hell on earth as well as in the hereafter.

More than anything he wanted to strike the insufferable woman who was leaning across his desk, looming over him, invading his space. He longed to see her shock at what she'd unleashed, the fear on her bloodied face, and the crash of her body onto the floor. *Control*, he thought. *Stop. Think. Control.* Pruitt was in the office with them. She'd be a witness, and Sergeant Zach Lawrence and the TPD might not buy his side of the story, how she was asking for it.

Buddy felt that his head would explode, but he had to let Pruitt go.

"Alright, alright, don't get yourselves in a twist," he said.

He unlocked a filing cabinet drawer and retrieved Tessa's PC, iPad, thumb drive, and two cellphones.

He held them out in her direction. "Here, take your stuff."

"Thank you," Tessa said, with a meek sniff.

"And her car keys," Frances said.

"I've told you already that only staff can drive on the Center's premises. We'll bring her car around to the front."

Tessa was waiting with Frances and Lisbeth at her side when Protector Jackson drove her car to the front door of the Residence.

Buddy hurried out to join them.

"We all wish the best for you and your mom," he said, almost sounding sympathetic. "Safe travels."

"Thank you so much for everything, Buddy," Tessa said, as she lifted her car keys from Jackson's outstretched hand.

Thirty Two

"YOU LET HER GO," Charles hissed. "What about your plan?"

"I'm not happy about it either," Buddy said. "I had to. Otherwise Gourmelon said she'd call in the police."

Murray asked, "What plan?"

Buddy glanced at Charles and got nothing there, still just a blank stare. He replied to Murray, "We were going to expel her tonight."

"And she got away before you could do that?"

"Yeah."

"We're better off," Murray said, "like I told you before. Otherwise she'd have posted nasty blogs about us."

"No, she wouldn't," Buddy said. "We had that all worked out."

"How?"

"Never mind."

"Tell me, Buddy," Murray said.

Buddy shook his head, and glanced again at Charles.

"Because she'd be dead." Charles said. "She was going to commit suicide off the bridge at Quechee Gorge."

Murray looked at each of his longtime associates and didn't recognize them.

"You were planning to murder Tessa Pruitt? Because she lied about sharing some photographs?"

Charles asked, "Do you have a problem with that?"

"You mean do I have a problem with spending the rest of our lives in prison?"

"You knew nothing about it."

"No one would believe that! Have you both gone totally fucking insane?"

"She profaned the *Book of Ignatius Jones*. She's a defamer and a blasphemer."

"Charlie, get a grip. It's just a book."

Charles slammed his hand on his desk. "It's not *just a book*. It contains the words of Ignatius Jones, transcribed by me, his Messenger."

"There would have been witnesses," Murray said, "evidence she wasn't alone on the bridge at Quechee Gorge, finger-prints, police all over the place. Ricky would have been questioned, and he'd only last five minutes before he confessed and pointed fingers. And apart from all that, how would it look for the Center if one of our first visiting psychics committed suicide?"

The three of them took stock: Murray, alarmed; Charles, fuming; and Buddy, embarrassed, not because his plan was lacking, which it wasn't, but because he failed to execute.

Charles breathed in deeply, getting back in control.

He said, "We need to re-group."

Buddy said, "I bet she was warned that we'd deal with her."

Charles asked Murray, "Who else knows we found out she shared her photos?"

"Only Protector Jackson. He was here in the office when I told you and Buddy."

"You told no one else?"

"No."

Buddy said, "Jackson and Lily talk to each other."

"So?" asked Charles.

"Becca saw Lily talking with Pruitt, Gourmelon, and Lisbeth Smythe in Plymouth Notch this morning."

"So, Jackson to Lily to Pruitt?"

"Could be," Buddy said. "And Gourmelon came with Pruitt to my office, don't forget."

He couldn't shake the image of the fat psychic leaning towards him over his desk, blocking his light.

"Yeah," Charles said. "I'm not forgetting."

"Take it easy," Murray said. "You're not going to push Dr. Gourmelon around like you did Tessa Pruitt. We might as well close the Center if she comes out against us. And anyway, what would you do to her? Send her to the Meditation Room?"

Charles said, "Gourmelon undermined me at our first meeting."

"Her time at the Center will soon be over and then she'll be on her way. Let it go, Charlie. Move on."

Charles recalled then what Ignatius Jones said, that his followers would "increase to become a multitude." Soon they would fill all the rooms and floors in the Residence, and then also rooms and floors in new buildings yet to be constructed.

Memory of Gourmelon's brief time in the Center would fade, and before long, vanish completely.

"Okay," he said. "On Gourmelon, we'll move on. We'll be rid of her soon enough."

"What about Jackson and Lily?" Buddy asked. "Should I interrogate them?"

"No," Charles said. "For now, just keep Jackson at arm's length. Assume he can't be trusted. As for Lily, leave her to me. I have plans for her."

That night, Frances' cellphone buzzed with an incoming text.

"Now in Boston. Thx for your help and letting me stay overnight in your place here. Leaving tomorrow for Alaska. Love to you, L, & L. Tessa."

Frances texted back, "Love to you too. Keep us posted."

Lisbeth was on her bed reading when Frances handed her the cellphone to show her Tessa's message.

"Good for her," Lisbeth said. "Your story worked, Frances."

"It wasn't all fiction," Frances said.

"So her mom…?"

"No, we invented the part about her mom. But during my session with the portrait, Ignatius Jones did tell me, 'She is in danger.'"

"He was warning about Tessa?"

"I assume so."

"Well, you got her out of here safely, and that's what counts," Lisbeth said.

Thirty Three

LILY STEPPED SIDEWAYS to avoid Buddy in the hallway. He moved in the same direction, blocking her.

"Got a minute?" he asked.

"Yes, sure, Buddy."

"Are you happy here?"

"Yes. Why?"

"You were seen in Plymouth Notch talking with our visitors."

"I thought you wanted me to accompany them on the outing."

"What were you talking about?"

"They had questions about Plymouth Notch."

"Like, what kind of questions?"

"About its history. Also, whether I had been there often since I grew up right next door in Tudorsville."

"What did you tell them?"

"That I visited there on school trips and later by myself after I got my driver's license."

"Did you talk about anything else?"

"What do you mean?"

"Like about the Center?"

"No."

"Wasn't it strange that just after Tessa Pruitt arrived back here from Plymouth Notch, she announced that she had to leave?"

"I don't know, Buddy."

"Was it because of something you told her?"

"Didn't she say she received a message from Ignatius Jones that her mom needed her?"

Lily returned Buddy's stare directly. She refused to get rattled. She held her ground even though he was close enough for her to smell the tuna fish sandwich he'd had for lunch.

Buddy backed down.

"Yeah, well, I was just wondering. As long as you did nothing wrong."

"No, I didn't."

"I'm glad to hear it."

"Why?"

"Because Messenger Charles will receive you this evening in the Portrait Room. You'll meet him there after dinner."

Protector Ricky smirked as Lily approached the door to the Portrait Room.

"Your big date," he said.

"Open the door, Ricky."

"Not yet, honeybuns. I need to check your purse for cellphones, cameras, recording devices."

"I know better than that, Ricky."

"Doesn't matter. Buddy says no exceptions. Hand it over."

Ricky rummaged through Lily's purse, pushing around her wallet, keys, a glasses case, a package of tissues, a mirror, a hairbrush, and loose change.

"Now empty your pockets."

"Ricky, give me a break!"

"Or would you prefer that I patted you down?"

"You wouldn't talk like that if Jackson were here."

"That's what you think. Don't kid yourself about what he'd do about it. Maybe we'd both pat you down together. A full-body pat-down. Would you like that?"

When Lily didn't answer, Ricky said, "But Jackson isn't here, is he? Empty your pockets."

When Lily entered the Portrait Room, all she saw was the portrait of Ignatius Jones. His eyes drew her in, pulling her closer.

She hardly noticed Messenger Charles standing beside the portrait, watching her approach the stage.

Lily reached to touch the portrait as she had done so many times before.

Charles shoved her arm aside.

"Are you mad?" he shouted. "No one touches this painting."

"I'm sorry," Lily said, abruptly brought back to the reality that she was here, now, in a room with Messenger Charles. "I was… overcome."

"Sit here," Charles said, indicating the chair in front of the portrait. He stood directly behind her. She could feel the heat of his body on her neck.

"Tell me what you see in the portrait," he said.

"I see Ignatius Jones."

"And?"

"He's asking me to meet him on the Other Side."

Lily suppressed a shudder when Charles placed his hands on her shoulders. She exiled to a distant corner of her consciousness her awareness of the Messenger's hands. She felt only the loving presence of Ignatius Jones. As she gazed into his eyes, she heard his voice, as she'd heard it all her life in her front hallway, "I'll always be here for you, darling Lily."

Charles massaged her shoulders, squeezing and releasing with his fingers, thumbs, and palms.

Lily flowed with Ignatius Jones through a garden, a lagoon, a fragrant pine forest. They were together under a canopy of stars and the moon and a warming Sun. It was all that she'd dreamed of, and it was worth everything.

Charles' hands moved down from her shoulders towards her chest.

"You will be my partner," Charles said, cupping his hands on her breasts, massaging them. He pressed himself against her, swaying his body against hers, but she felt only the presence of the man in the portrait.

She was guided to a tatami mat that was stretched out on the floor below the portrait. She didn't recall seeing it earlier. She was lowered gently onto the mat, and Ignatius Jones' Messenger was unbuttoning her blouse. She raised herself to make it easier for her skirt to be removed, and then her underwear. As she was entered by the spirit-become-flesh, her body was suffused with heat and light.

Afterwards, when she opened her eyes, Lily saw Messenger Charles staring down at her from his chair in front of the portrait.

"Welcome back," he said.

Lily realized that she was naked below her waist. She stood, unembarrassed as Messenger Charles watched her, and pulled on her clothes.

"What just happened…" he said.

"It's fine," Lily said, cutting him off.

"No, Lily, what I mean to say is that I have chosen you to become my partner."

"I don't know," Lily replied.

"Do you want to visit again with Ignatius Jones?"

His high-pitched voice grated on her ears like the whine of a mosquito.

"Yes."

"I'm giving you the opportunity to become my Consort, Lily. This is a great honor."

"I know. But…"

"We will meet here with the spirit of Ignatius Jones, as we have just done, joined in body and in spirit."

"May I think about this, Messenger Charles?"

"Of course you may. I hope that you'll make the right decision."

His meaning was clear.

Accept, and she'd be invited back to the Portrait Room.

Refuse, and Ignatius Jones would be lost to her forever.

"I will respond soon, Messenger Charles," Lily said.

"Until then, Lily, no one else needs to know."

"I won't tell anyone."

"Not your mother. Not Dr. Gourmelon. Not Protector Jackson. No one."

"No one."

"Until next time, then."

"May I go now? I need to change."

Thirty Four

NEXT MORNING at breakfast, Lily was so busy chasing one task or another that Frances was unable to catch her attention. It seemed that she rushed off whenever she saw Frances approaching.

At first, Frances wanted only to exchange a quick hello and how-are-you. Being shunned changed that. Now she was determined that she and Lily would have another talk.

Frances lurked in the kitchen beside the swinging doors, standing off to the side so that she wasn't visible from the dining area.

When Lily pushed through the swinging doors and saw Frances, she spun around to leave.

Frances touched her arm. "Wait."

"Oh, hi," Lily said, looking sheepish, like a shoplifter caught with bulging pockets. "I'm in a terrific hurry."

"Darling child," Frances said. "What's wrong?"

"Nothing, Dr. Gourmelon."

"Sweetheart, I'm a psychic. I can tell there's a problem."

Lily turned her back to the kitchen's video camera and lowered her voice to a whisper. "We just can't talk right now."

"Shall we go to…?" Frances jerked her head towards the kitchen back door."

"No. Not again."

Frances kept her voice low but her tone was urgent, and insistent. "You and I will talk, Lily, one way or another."

Lily said, "We can talk when I bring clean towels to your room."

"When?"

"We make the rounds mid-morning after everyone has left for their discussion groups."

"I'll wait for you."

Frances heard a soft knocking on her door.

Buddy was standing in the hallway, holding neatly folded bath and hand towels.

"Fresh towels," he said, with a good-guy grin.

Frances glanced into the hallway to check whether Lily was there.

"You look surprised to see me," Buddy added. "Were you expecting someone else?"

"Where's Lily?"

"I'm her substitute. We both thought it best."

"Why, Buddy?"

"You harassed her this morning."

Buddy's grin widened as his erstwhile tormenter sputtered, "That's outrageous and you know it."

"I know no such thing."

"I wasn't harassing Lily."

"She says differently."

"Why shouldn't she chat with me or anyone else?"

"Lily has her instructions."

"What are you hiding, Buddy?"

"Nothing."

"Well, then, why…?"

"If you must know, Messenger Charles will soon grant her new responsibilities at the Center."

"What kind of responsibilities?"

"That will be announced in due course."

"I'm not satisfied," Frances said. "I must insist on talking with Lily to find out from her what is going on."

"No can do," Buddy said. "She doesn't want to talk to you."

Thirty Five

THAT EVENING, Lily rejoined Charles in the Portrait Room.

He instructed her to remove her 1950s housewife's outfit, her calf-length skirt, and shirt, and underwear. She handed each of these items to Charles, and he draped them neatly on the chair. Then she lay on her back on the tatami mat in front of the portrait.

"Look at the portrait, Lily" Charles said. "Receive Ignatius Jones."

The man in the portrait gazed at her and she was warmed by him, with no need for the light blanket that Charles had left folded beside the tatami mat. She reached towards the portrait and felt herself flowing towards it. She heard the voice of Ignatius Jones, "Come to me Lily. You have nothing to fear. I'll be here for you always."

Warm scented oil was massaged gently on her breasts and then lower down, persistently, searchingly, and she moved in response, surrendering to the pulsing sensations in her body until finally she shuddered and cried out.

Messenger Charles said, "Have you considered my proposal?"

"Yes."

"You understand that you are chosen as my Consort not by me, but by Ignatius Jones."

Lily nodded.

When she looked at Messenger Charles, she didn't see the old man whose jowly face was purpled by his recent exertions. She saw Ignatius Jones.

And it was *his* voice that she heard when Charles said, "I want you to accept my proposal."

Sitting up on the tatami mat, Lily pulled the blanket over her to combat the sudden chill crawling on her skin.

"I do accept," she said. "I will become your Consort."

Thirty Six

THE LIFE-SIZE fiberglass pig ensconced on four stubby legs on the sidewalk outside Suzie's Wool Store was shiny white with large pink and green polka dots, and as round as it was tall.

It was one of the trademark pig sculptures stationed all over Tudorsville and depicted in the town's tourist brochures. Each was painted uniquely to suit its owner's fancy. Aubuchon Hardware dressed its pig in Old Glory with a blue head, two white stars for eyes, and red and white stripes circling its torso and legs. The pig in front of the Loon Lake Inn was bright pink, to stand out against the Inn's green lawn in the summer and its white snow in winter.

Frances patted Suzie's polka-dotted pig on its glassy smooth head, and entered the store.

"Why Frances, what a surprise!" Suzie said, from her post behind a counter.

She had just rung up the purchase of another customer, a plain no-nonsense woman with short brown hair.

The customer said to Frances, "You're one of those *psychics* at the Ignatius Jones Center."

"I am indeed," Frances agreed, equably. "How did you know?"

209

"I was talking with Hildy Veysey."

"Let me guess. She described me as a big woman wearing a muumuu."

"More or less."

"Where are my manners?" Suzie exclaimed. "Let me introduce you both. Frances, Dr. Gourmelon, this is my friend Doreen Marrone."

Frances extended her hand. Doreen took it warily, but her handshake was firm.

"Hildy told me that you talked about Prudence Price," Doreen said.

Out of the corner of her eye, Frances saw Suzie shake her head: *Don't tell her about Ignatius Jones and Lily.*

Frances said, "I was curious about a sleigh in the Wilder Barn. Its card said that it was donated by the Price Farm in Tudorsville. Wilt Schmidt suggested I ask Hildy what she knew about it, and Hildy told me about Prudence Price."

"We all called her Prudie," Doreen said. "No offense, Suzie, being that she was your mother-in-law, but the woman put on airs. She grew up here, and married here, and lived here until the end, but she always acted like she was a sophisticated lady from Boston who was just visiting us country folk."

"That's okay, Doreen," Suzie said. "You're right about Prudence. She could be a real pill."

"The Prices *were* a prominent Boston family," Frances said.

"So Prudie told us many times," Doreen said. Then she added, looking curiously at Frances, "Hildy got the impression that Wilt was quite taken with you."

Frances felt a blush warming her already rosy cheeks.

"Just small-town gossip," Doreen said. "Might be something in it though. Wilt's wife was also... full-figured, poor thing."

Suzie intervened. "Doreen, that's none of our business, is it?"

"No, of course not," Doreen said. "Anyway, after Wilt switched sides on the Center I don't put much stock in anything he says."

Frances said, "I take it that you're not a big fan of the Center."

"It's an abomination," Doreen said. "We should never have allowed it. It's a cult, isn't it, talking to the dead, bowing down before a painting? And now they're coming after our children."

"They are?"

"You must have heard about those poor boys they tortured."

"You mean the boys who were hunting?"

"They tortured them," Doreen repeated, glaring angrily at Frances and Suzie both. "There'll be a reckoning for that, mark my words."

To change the subject, Suzie turned to Frances, "Do you have news for me?"

"I'm not sure," Frances said, glancing at Doreen.

"Time for me to go," Doreen said. "Pleasure to meet you, Frances. And Suzie, we'll talk later, yes?"

After Doreen left, Suzie locked her door and reversed her door sign to indicate that her store was closed.

"So what's going on?" she asked.

"Buddy Choate, a manager at the Center, told me that Lily is about to take on new responsibilities."

"What new responsibilities?"

"I don't know," Frances said. "He wouldn't tell me."

"What does Lily say?"

"Nothing. She dodged me at breakfast. When I finally got hold of her, she said we could talk later when she brought fresh linens to my room but then Buddy came instead."

"How did she seem to you?"

"She was anxious when I saw her after breakfast."

"Was she frightened?

"I don't know. But she seemed different than when we talked earlier."

"Why did Buddy come to your room instead of Lily?"

"He claimed that I was harassing her."

"But that's nonsense!"

"Of course it's nonsense! As Buddy well knows. He was smirking when he said it."

Suzie's face flushed and her voice broke as she asked, "What's happening to my daughter, Frances?"

"I'll keep trying to find out," Frances said.

Back in the Residence, Frances ran into Tammy Bell.

She was dressed in a nun's habit, a brown tunic with large sleeves, a white apron draped over it both in front and back, a black wool belt cinched at her waste, and sensible black leather shoes.

"Why the new costume?" Frances asked.

"Haven't you heard?"

"Heard what?"

"I was appointed by Messenger Charles as the Center's first Psychic Guide. I'm Sister Tammy now. I've been given a special mission to recruit pilgrims to come to the Center."

"You mean more visitors, like us?"

"No, *pilgrims*. Not psychics who just drop in for a week-long program. Pilgrims will join the Center and live here, permanently, building the community."

"What will they do during the day, in addition to building the community?"

"They will study the teachings of Ignatius Jones as brought to us by his Messenger."

"Well, recruiting people to live here is an important responsibility for you," Frances said.

"I agree," Tammy said. "Messenger Charles has granted me a great honor."

"So you dress like a nun?"

"While I'm at the Center. To show my commitment."

"You'll fit right in beside Charles in his monk's robe."

"Aren't you the cranky one, Frances? Are we having a bad day?"

"No, I'm just curious about how you'll do your recruiting."

"I've already started. I was interviewed this morning on a radio station in Philadelphia. Some listeners contacted the Center. They said they heard me speak about Ignatius Jones as my spirit guide and about Messenger Charles as my brother in spiritualism."

Frances winced, and Tammy said, "Don't scoff. For many people, joining the Center will add meaning to their lives."

"I'm sure you're right about that," Frances said. "By the way, have you seen Lily around here, recently?"

"Spiritualist Helper Lily has been selected."

"Selected for what?"

"She will become Consort to Messenger Charles."

"What?"

"Didn't you know that either? It's amazing that Dr. Frances E. Gourmelon is so out of the loop."

"Well, thank you for telling me," Frances said. "Sister Tammy."

"You're so welcome. Although just between us, I don't know what Messenger Charles sees in her. She doesn't have much to offer, in my opinion."

"It's not for us to judge," Frances said, solemnly.

Tammy's smile showed total forgiveness and love as befit her new station. "No, you're so right, Frances, we all must trust in Messenger Charles, mustn't we."

Thirty Seven

MURRAY PREFERRED to give Charles the benefit of the doubt.

It was Charles who purchased the portrait at the church rummage sale. He conceived of the Ignatius Jones Center for Spiritualist Discovery. He got Evelyn Billings to donate the money to build it. His *Book of Ignatius Jones* provided doctrinal authority for the Center's selling message. And his monk's outfit was a masterstroke of showmanship.

True, he did go too far with his persecution of Tessa Pruitt and his demented plot with Buddy to have her killed, but these errors inflicted no lasting harm thanks to Pruitt's timely departure.

What Murray could not abide, however, was Charles' plan to make Lily Prestowicz his so-called Consort.

Evidently, the girl had some sort of hold over him, the nature of which was easy to imagine, but she was still only a teenager, hardly suitable for a grown man like Charles Philip Tucker.

Plus the inconvenient fact that she was a direct descendent of Ignatius Jones, as Murray discovered when Charles had him research the history of Lily's Grandma Prudence. With that pedigree, and her privileged position at the elbow of Messenger

215

Charles, the girl might imagine that her status in the Center was elevated even to the extent of becoming comparable to his.

The door to Charles' office was closed. Murray knocked twice.

"What is it?" he heard Charles ask.

"It's Murray."

"Just a minute."

Murray could hear bustling and muttering. Finally, after cooling his heels for several minutes too many, Murray knocked again.

"What?"

"Should I come back later?"

"No. Hang on."

Charles' door opened and Spiritualist Helper Lily Prestowicz emerged. Confirming Murray's worst fears, she didn't avert her face and scurry off. Instead, she met his eyes without apology. She was taller than Murray so when she got closer, she actually looked down at him, like a blonde Teutonic princess encountering a lowly clerk in her counting house.

"You can go in now," she said.

Charles leaned back in his chair. "What's up?"

"What's going on, Charlie, with you and the girl?"

"What do you mean?"

"Were you fucking her just now?"

"You're talking about my future Consort," Charles said. "Watch your tone."

"You didn't answer my question."

"If you must know, we were selecting the clothes that she'll wear as my Consort. We were debating creamy white versus daffodil yellow when you interrupted us."

"You need to consult me on big decisions and I would rate this Consort notion of yours as a big decision."

"Buddy has no problem with it, last time we talked."

"The girl has no concept of why we built the Center, which, in case you've forgotten, was to make money."

"I'm well aware."

"You don't need to make her your Consort in order to fuck her."

"Be careful, Murray."

"She's eighteen years old, for Christ's sake."

"Yes, and she communicates with Ignatius Jones as if they're family, which they are, as you found out."

"So, is she another Messenger?"

"I'm the one and only Messenger, but what's true is true."

"You're losing me, Charlie. As long as I've known you, you've been in charge of your emotions. You've been smart. No entanglements. Now comes this teenager and all bets are off."

"I don't need to explain myself to you."

"You and the girl, it won't go over well with the good people of Tudorsville."

"Lily has consented to become my Consort. She's of age. It's going to happen and they can't stop it. Nor can you."

Back in his office with Buddy, Murray said, "We need to do something about Charlie and Lily Prestowicz."

Buddy grinned and shrugged his shoulders. "Doesn't bother me."

"You'll be bothered soon enough when your former Spiritualist Helper starts ordering you about."

"The way I see it," Buddy said, "if I keep her happy, she could prove useful. Like an ally."

"What if she tries to freeze us out?"

"She'll learn that would be a mistake."

"How will she learn that, exactly?"

"There are ways," Buddy said, vaguely.

"Jesus."

"Calm down, Murray. As a friend, I've got to tell you, Charles is getting concerned about your loyalty. Between you and me, that's not a good thing."

"He's our partner in a business venture. He can call himself Messenger all he wants. That doesn't make him our leader."

"He *is* the Messenger," Buddy said.

"You believe that?"

"Yeah, I do."

Murray shook his head, and Buddy added, "I'm telling you as a friend, things are changing around here and you're gonna have to get into line."

Thirty Eight

FRANCES SENSED THAT she was being watched during her breakfast with Lisbeth at the Center Café.

She turned her head slightly. Murray was staring at her from several tables over.

He stopped by their table on his way out of the Café.

Laying his tray down beside Frances, he asked, "Have you ladies enjoyed your time at the Center so far?"

"Some good, some bad," Lisbeth said.

"How about you, Dr. Gourmelon?"

"I agree with Lisbeth," Frances replied.

"Well, I hope you both find more good than bad during the rest of your time here," Murray said.

After he left, Frances noticed a scrap of paper on the table where Murray's tray had been. On it was scrawled, "Call me," plus a phone number.

Frances went outside to make the call.

"You got my note," Murray said.

"Yes."

She assumed Murray was recording their call.

"Can't talk here," he said. "Can you meet with me outside the Center?"

"What's going on?"

"I'll tell you when we meet. I'm heading out shortly as I usually do this time of day to pick up supplies. Can you leave a bit later? Meet me at Quechee Gorge?"

"Why not closer to us, in Tudorsville, or Woodstock?"

"I'd be recognized in either of those places. Quechee Gorge is only ten minutes out of Woodstock on Route 4. We can talk there."

"I know it well," Frances said.

"There's a diner near the bridge called the Quechee Diner. Let's meet there at eleven o'clock."

The Quechee Diner was easy to find. It was a vintage diner car with 'Quechee Diner' painted in red under its windows across almost its entire length, bracketed before and after by 'Booth Service' in smaller arched letters.

Frances found Murray standing beside his car in the diner's parking lot.

"Before we go in," Murray said, "walk with me to the bridge. I want to show you something."

"I've already seen Quechee Gorge," Frances said.

"Still, please join me, Dr. Gourmelon. It's a short walk. You'll understand why, when we get there."

Murray leaned against the iron railing at the edge of the bridge's pedestrian walkway. Far below, the Ottauquechee River churned over black rocks between the steep cliffs on either side of the gorge.

"What do you want to show me?" Frances asked.

"Tessa Pruitt was going to commit suicide here by jumping into the gorge."

"Tessa had no intention of committing suicide."

"She didn't know she was going to do it. Luckily for her, she left the Center before Protector Ricky could throw her over this railing."

"How do you know this, Murray?"

"Buddy and Charlie told me about their plan after she left. They said she broke the rules and then she lied with her hand on Charlie's sacred book. She dishonored Ignatius Jones. So she had to be punished."

Frances looked at Murray, speechless.

"I know you believe me, Dr. Gourmelon. You're a psychic. You know when someone is telling the truth."

Frances did believe him. But that didn't mean she trusted him.

"You work with Charles and Buddy," she said. "You're their partner. So why are you confiding in me? Are you trying to threaten me?"

"Let's go back to the diner and I'll explain," Murray said.

The diner had six booths plus eight stools at the counter. It was still early for lunch so Frances and Murray had their pick of booths. They took the one nearest the door, where Murray thought they'd be less conspicuous than in the booths towards the middle. Frances didn't argue the point, although anyone who entered would surely notice the large woman in a purple muumuu sitting opposite a smaller man with furrowed brow and a goatee.

The Quechee Diner waitress brought a pot of coffee to fill the mugs that were already on the table. Frances asked also for a slice of the diner's 'world-famous' cherry pie. Murray said all he wanted was the coffee.

The waitress returned with Frances' cherry pie. "Anything else I can get you?"

"Nope, thanks," Murray said.

He watched the waitress leave. He leaned towards Frances, and asked, in a low voice, "You've communicated with Ignatius Jones, right?"

"I have."

"Through his portrait?"

"Yes."

"So he's really there?"

"I believe so. Why are you asking?"

"Because he's driving Charlie batshit crazy."

"What makes you think that?"

"Look at him. His robe, his sandals, and carrying his holy book everywhere."

"He's dressing the part."

"Before all this, all Charlie cared about was how to make a buck. He dressed like a guy in a country club. He enjoyed the good life. He ridiculed any kind of believer, saw them as suckers. Now, he's changed."

"Did he have relationships with women?"

"If you mean like Lily Prestowicz, he had women around but he never got emotionally involved. He's not married. Never lived with anyone. I've known the guy for years. We've been partners on a number of things. I don't understand him anymore. I'm telling you, he's possessed."

Frances asked, "So, again, Murray, why are you confiding in me?"

"Because you and I share interests in common."

"We do?"

"Look, I partner with Charlie for the money, right? I've put two years into the Center. Now I stand a good chance of ending up with nothing. Or less than nothing, if he commits a crime like murdering one of our visitors and I'm implicated. And if you care about Lily, Charlie's insanity should concern you too."

Murray was rotating his coffee cup, which he'd emptied. Their waitress came by. "Would you like a refill?"

Murray said no, covering his cup with his hand.

She asked, again, "Can I get you anything else?"

"No, give us a moment," Murray replied.

"We're all set, dear," Frances said. "Just the bill, please."

The waitress placed their bill on the table.

"My treat," Murray said.

He handed ten dollars to the waitress to cover their bill plus a tip that was reasonably generous, but not too memorably so. "Just a little while longer," he told her.

"No hurries," the waitress said, bustling off to attend to a family of four who were occupying another one of the booths.

Murray looked so distressed that Frances reached across the table and touched his hand. Also, his fiddling with his empty coffee cup was getting on her nerves.

"You believe in spirits," he said.

"Of course."

"Do you agree with me that Charlie could be possessed, somehow, by Ignatius Jones?"

"I haven't come across possessions before. People call their priests for possessions, not their psychics."

"But it's possible?"

"Anything is possible."

"So, we've got to break the spell."

"We?"

"You," Murray said. "I'll help."

Frances shook her head. "I'm not an expert on breaking spells."

"You just told me you've communicated with Ignatius Jones. Can't you tell him to release Charlie, for Lily's sake?"

"Murray, we don't tell spirits what to do. They operate by their own rules which are different than our rules in the physical world."

"So don't tell him. Try to reason with him, find out why he's controlling Charlie, and try to resolve his issues."

"I wouldn't know where to start," Frances said.

"Think about it, at least. There must be a way. Not for me. For Lily."

"About Lily, where is she?" Frances asked. "I haven't seen her at the Center since yesterday morning."

Thirty Nine

SUZIE WAITED on the sidewalk in front of her store for Frances to pick her up.

They drove to Woodstock, and parked on Elm Street across from Charles' house.

Frances pressed Charles' doorbell. She heard movement inside. She glanced at Suzie, who was staring at the door. She'd heard it too.

Lily opened the door. She wore a white cotton robe and her white-blonde hair hung down over her shoulders. She didn't look glad to see them.

"Why are you here?" she asked.

Frances replied, "Lily, dear, may we come in?"

"Messenger Charles doesn't allow visitors."

Suzie said, "I'm not 'visitors.' I'm your mom."

"This is Messenger Charles' house."

"You're only eighteen," Suzie said. "That old goat is not right for you."

Her voice cracked and she had to stop, to get control over it.

"Mom, I've made up my mind," Lily said.

"Do you love him?"

Lily didn't answer.

"Are you sleeping with him?"

"Mom…"

"That's not an unreasonable question, considering..."

"I won't…"

"Then why his Consort?" Suzie demanded. "Why doesn't he ask you to marry him?"

"Messenger Charles is already married. His wife is an invalid. She's been in a coma for years. Charles is paying for her care in a nursing home."

"Such a kind man," Suzie said, with a derisive snort.

"Yes," Lily replied.

"You believe him?"

"He showed me her picture. He told me I could meet her, if I wanted."

"What did you tell him?"

"That I trusted him."

Suzie could only shake her head, and Frances asked, "Is Charles here?"

"I'd rather not say."

"Will you deliver a message to him for me?"

Lily nodded.

By now, Frances had located the video surveillance camera embedded artfully in the base of the porch light hanging over the front steps, where Murray had told her to look.

She said to Lily and to the video camera overhead, "Charles will have to answer to me if any harm comes to you. Can you tell him that, my dear?"

"That kind of message you'll have to deliver yourself, Dr. Gourmelon."

"When will we see you back at the Center?"

"I don't know."

Suzie said, "This is all because I sold the portrait, isn't it? You still blame me."

"Mom, that's in the past. I'm doing what's right for me now."

They had to get Lily away from the house. Once they were out of range of the video surveillance, Frances could tell her that Charles lied about being married. She might even tell her about Charles' plan to murder Tessa Pruitt, but only if she were sure that Lily would then immediately leave Charles' house and the Center. Otherwise, it would be too dangerous for Lily to know.

"Walk with us to Bentleys," Frances said. "It'll only take a few minutes. It's just up the street. We'll get coffee, maybe ice cream."

"I know where Bentleys is," Lily said. "I can't. Not now. I need to study my *Book of Ignatius Jones*."

Suzie asked, "So after you're done studying, can you come home with me for a quick visit?"

"I don't know, Mom."

Suzie's voice broke again. "We need to talk, Lily, please."

"Messenger Charles has told us to rid ourselves of past entanglements. Soon pilgrims will join us and live with us in the Center. We must clear our minds so that we can help them to understand the words of Ignatius Jones."

Frances asked, "Has Charles told you to shun your mom?"

Glancing at her mother whose cheeks were wet with tears, Lily said, "I don't think that's necessarily what Messenger Charles means."

"Will I be invited to your ceremony?" Suzie asked.

"I don't know. Messenger Charles may keep it just between us in the Portrait Room."

"So, just the two of you," Suzie said.

"And Ignatius Jones."

"Doreen was right," Suzie said, alternating between ranting and weeping as Frances drove her back to her store. "The man is nothing but trouble. Him and his crazy cult. And now they've sucked my daughter into it."

"Not much of a cult," Frances said. "Basically just Charles and one or two others."

"But Lily said they're expecting pilgrims who'll live at the Center. You've got to do something, Frances. Please. All this stuff about the portrait, and spirits, that's your field."

When Frances didn't answer, Suzie said, "I'll pay for your time. I'll be your client."

"No need for that," Frances said. "The Institute is covering my costs. Sort of a special project."

"But you'll help?"

"I have to get back to Boston. My clients need me there."

"Please, Frances. I'm begging you."

Forty

PROTECTOR JACKSON appeared beside Frances' car as soon as she came to a stop in the Residence turning circle.

He looked perplexed.

"Is something the matter, Jackson?"

"You're Lily's friend," he said. "I'm worried about her."

"Would you like to talk?"

"Yes, please," Jackson said.

Just as Lily had done, when they were in the kitchen after lunch, Jackson handed Frances a filled thirty-gallon plastic garbage bag, while carrying two bags himself, and led her out of the kitchen's back door. After they tossed their bags into the dumpster, he ducked into the alcove, and she followed.

Jackson's bulk occupied much of the available space. Frances had to stand near to him to stay clear of the back-door camera's line of sight, which forced her to crane her neck upward to meet his eyes.

"Tell me what's worrying you, Jackson," she said.

"Lily doesn't answer my texts."

"Were you close to her?"

"I thought so but now she's shut me out."

"Have you been told…?"

"About her becoming Consort to Messenger Charles? I wanted to ask her about it." He stared down at Frances. "You saw her, Dr. Gourmelon, didn't you? You were coming back from seeing her when you dropped off your car."

"I can't discuss that," Frances said, adding, "I can tell that you care for her."

"She went with the smart kids in school while I hung out with the jocks, so we never got together. I thought I'd have a better chance here. Guess I was wrong."

"Things can change," Frances said.

"I want to help her," Jackson said. "I'll do anything."

"Then stay here and look out for her when she returns to the Center."

Dropping his voice to a whisper, Jackson said, "This place isn't safe for her, or for any of us."

"What do you mean?"

"You heard about the boys we caught on the property, how Buddy tortured them? Everyone in town knows, they're not going to let that go."

"What will they do?"

"Probably something really stupid. They're not bad guys but they're seriously pissed."

"Did you tell Buddy?"

"He's expecting them. He says we'll shoot them when they cross onto our property. He says we can shoot them legally because we posted signs that give fair warning, 'Trespassers Will Be Shot,' and he's buying more guns, like assault rifles."

"Have you called the police?"

"No. Buddy doesn't trust the cops."

"So Buddy is preparing for battle."

"He is."

"That's nuts, Jackson."

"I don't want Lily here when it happens."

Decision time.

Frances had an Institute to run back in Boston. She had clients there who needed her. Appointments booked. A waiting list.

She'd almost completed her week-long program at the Ignatius Jones Center for Spiritualist Discovery. She'd spent amazing time with the Desmond Wilkins portrait of Ignatius Jones, the greatest psychic medium who ever lived, and heard his voice.

She could now provide Carter Haas with her report about the painting that he so eagerly awaited.

Soon she, Lisbeth, and her other fellow psychics would all go their separate ways.

She had no reason to stay around any longer.

Except that she had to do something about Lily. The girl was about to become Consort to a man who would commit murder for lying about sharing a few photographs. Suzie, Jackson, Murray, each had pleaded with her to get involved.

Frances couldn't just walk away and wash her hands of the place.

Not yet.

She said to Jackson, "Did you mean it when you told me that you'd do anything for Lily?"

"Yes."

"Then I have a request."

"Anything."

"Contact those boys. Ask them to be patient for a while longer."

"What if they ask me why?"

"Promise them that their time will come, that it won't be too long from now, and that they'll be very satisfied with the result."

"What are you planning, Dr. Gourmelon?"

"I'm still working it out. But whatever I do, I can't do alone."

"So I'll be involved?"

"Yes, Jackson, I'm sure you will."

"And the boys?"

"Them too," Frances said. "If they're patient."

Buddy watched the video of Gourmelon and another woman talking with Lily on Charles' front steps. Then he called Murray. "You've got to see this."

Buddy replayed the scene.

"This is a video from yesterday morning," Buddy said.

"Interesting," Murray said. "Wonder what they're up to."

"Should we tell Charles?"

"I don't know, Buddy. They didn't say anything that should concern us."

"Even Gourmelon's 'message' for Charles?"

"I doubt that would worry him."

"What about the other woman, Lily's mother? Because of what she said about Messenger Charles and Lily?"

"Well, she is Lily's mother, after all."

"Yeah, but how did she and Gourmelon find out that Lily was at Charles' house?"

"Maybe Lily called her."

"Maybe," Buddy said, not sounding convinced.

"She might just have phoned to tell her, 'I'm at Messenger Charles' house, so don't worry about me,' and then they turned up."

"So look at this other video," Buddy said.

Recorded just after lunch, it showed Protector Jackson and Dr. Gourmelon carrying garbage bags out the back door of the kitchen. Another camera, just outside, showed them dropping the bags into the dumpster. Then they walked off-screen. It was several minutes later before the kitchen camera picked them up again, coming back in.

"Where were they?" Buddy asked. "Do you think they were talking?"

"You mean, about Lily?"

"Yeah," Buddy said. "I don't trust Jackson, after the Jackson-Lily-Pruitt thing."

"One more reason to keep a close eye on him," Murray said. "Also on Lily. If we catch them together, maybe we can get Charlie to rethink his plans."

"You hate this Consort business, don't you?"

"You should too," Murray said.

Forty One

GRADUATION DAY at the Ignatius Jones Center for Spiritualist Discovery.

Nineteen psychic mediums were assembled in the Residence meeting room.

As Messenger Charles called their names, he handed a Certificate of Portrait Mediumship to Spiritualist Helper Becca, who delivered it by hand to its designated recipient.

Each Certificate was signed, "Charles Philip Tucker, Messenger for Ignatius Jones."

When the ceremony was concluded, Tammy called out, "Thank you, Messenger Charles!" She led a smattering of applause that rippled through the meeting room.

Charles bowed his head to acknowledge the applause.

"No, thank *you*, Sister Tammy, our first Psychic Guide, for recruiting our first pilgrims."

Tammy blushed.

Charles continued, "…two couples, plus a child with one of the couples, who will arrive here next week."

"I'm just getting started, Messenger Charles," Tammy said.

"Ignatius Jones notices all that you've done, Sister Tammy," Charles replied. "We are counting on our Sister and

Brother Psychic Guides to build our community. Sister Tammy has shown the way."

Frances Gourmelon raised her gemstone-encrusted right hand.

"Yes, Dr. Gourmelon?"

"How can I become a Psychic Guide like Sister Tammy?"

"Is that what you want to do, Dr. Gourmelon?" asked Charles, well aware that she was watching him like psychics do, *reading* him.

"Yes, very much so," she said, nodding emphatically.

Charles had been counting the days, hours, and minutes until the woman's departure. Extending her association with the Center was the last thing he wanted. But he replied, as pleasantly as he could pretend under the circumstances, "Then of course we'll welcome you as one of our Psychic Guides, Dr. Gourmelon."

"I'm so glad," she said.

"Please arrange to meet with me personally to discuss what's involved in making this commitment."

"I will, thank you, Messenger Charles."

"One final announcement," Charles said, "I'm delighted to report that Spiritualist Helper Lily has consented to become my Consort."

Frances felt several in the group looking at her. She didn't change her expression of serene attentiveness to what Messenger Charles was saying.

Their meeting and week-long program at an end, the visiting psychics extricated themselves from their seats, certificates in hand.

Frances followed Charles out of the meeting room.

"Messenger Charles," she said. "Is this a good time for us to have a word?"

"Perhaps later, Dr. Gourmelon, I'm just heading out…"

"Won't take but a minute."

"Fine," Charles said. "Let's go to my office."

Sandalwood-scented smoke twirled up from joss sticks in a ceramic bowl on the floor next to Charles' desk.

"Take a deep breath," Charles said. "It improves receptivity."

Frances pretended to breathe in deeply, trying not to gag.

"Aaah," she said. Then, "I know you're very busy, Messenger Charles. I promise that I'll be quick."

Charles clasped his hands inside the large sleeves of his monk's robe and rested them on his stomach. He leaned back in his chair. "Please go ahead."

"I meant what I said at the meeting. I do want to become a Psychic Guide."

"Well, then," Charles said, through clenched teeth, "I'll share this happy news with my team."

He tapped a number on his cellphone.

"Murray, can you come to my office? And tell Buddy to join us as well."

Murray's eyes widened when he saw Frances sitting in Charles' office. She greeted him with a placid smile.

"To what do we owe this pleasure?" he asked.

"Dr. Gourmelon wishes to become a Psychic Guide," Charles said.

Looking appraisingly at Frances, Murray said, "We're fortunate to have you on board, Dr. Gourmelon."

"Where's Buddy?" Charles asked.

"He should be here any minute. He was working with Protector Ricky to install another video camera out back behind the kitchen. He found a blind spot in our system."

Murray didn't look in Frances' direction as he relayed this information, but his message was clear: The alcove behind the kitchen was no longer safe.

Buddy entered Charles' office. When he saw Frances, he looked quickly at Murray, whose face remained blandly uninformative, and then asked Charles, "What's up?"

"Dr. Gourmelon wishes to join us as a Psychic Guide."

"Is that so?"

"Yes. Buddy. And we're just about to discuss with Dr. Gourmelon what that involves. So, Murray, why don't you do the honors?"

"Sure," Murray said. He turned towards Frances. "Your mission as a Psychic Guide is to spread the word about the Center to those who seek greater meaning for their lives so that they'll consider joining us here as pilgrims."

"That's exactly what I want to do," Frances said.

Murray said, "Obviously your desire to become a Psychic Guide is not about money…"

"…certainly not," Frances confirmed.

"…but you will be compensated. You will be given a share of the income that we realize from each pilgrim who joins us as a result of your efforts."

"What income do you expect from them?"

"They'll each make a voluntary contribution for housing expenses. Beyond that, each also will contribute to the Center according to his or her means. Those who have high-paying occupations may allocate to the Center a share of their income, like a tithe. If they come from wealth, they may donate a portion of their assets. We'll arrange these details with them on a case-by-case basis."

Buddy said, "Also I'm expecting the pilgrim men to help to defend the Center."

"What about the pilgrim women?" asked Frances.

"They'll take care of the Center's children, things like that."

"I've got only one more question," Frances said. "Will I have to wear a nun's habit like Sister Tammy's?"

"That's entirely up to you."

"Then, I'm ready."

"However, on our side, we still have some issues," Charles said. "A few days ago, you questioned my decisions. You warned me about hubris. You even seemed unsure about me being Messenger for Ignatius Jones. So what's changed?"

Frances said, "I admit, we did go through a rough patch during my first days here."

Buddy said, "That's one way to put it."

"And I regret that very much, Buddy."

"So what changed?" Charles asked, again.

"After Ignatius Jones brought me into contact with my darlings, I realized that I had to share with others such wonderful experiences. When I asked what I could do, Ignatius Jones told me that I should play my part to bring pilgrims to the Center."

"What do you think, Murray?" Charles asked.

"I think we should take Dr. Gourmelon at her word," Murray replied.

"What about you, Buddy?"

"I guess so," Buddy said.

He was staring at Frances the way a cop eyes a vagrant flaunting an expensive watch.

"Then, I'll administer your oath," Charles told Frances. "Place your right hand on my *Book of Ignatius Jones*, and repeat after me, 'I, Dr. Frances Gourmelon, do solemnly swear to honor the words of Ignatius Jones and to honor Charles Philip Tucker as his Messenger.'"

Frances repeated these words, with her hand on his *Book*.

"And to undertake faithfully my mission to recruit pilgrims for the Center."

She repeated these words as well, and Charles said, "I hereby appoint you, Sister Frances, as a Psychic Guide in the Ignatius Jones Center for Spiritualist Discovery. Welcome to our community."

"Thank you, Messenger Charles," Frances said. Her eyes were tearing, and Murray handed her a tissue from Charles' desk.

"Are you okay?" he asked.

"I'm so delighted to become part of this community," Frances replied. "I get emotional sometimes."

She did think Charles looked impressed by her watery eyes, one benefit, at least, of the scented smoke in his office.

After Frances left, Charles asked his two colleagues, "Now, what do you think, for real?"

Murray said, "I'll believe her when she sends pilgrims our way."

"Buddy?"

"I don't trust her for shit."

"Me neither," Charles said.

Murray asked, "Then why are you going along with her scheme, whatever it is?"

"Because I want to catch her in the act," Charles said. "Then we'll deal with her."

"Yeah, payback time," Buddy said.

"Something to look forward to," Murray said.

Forty Two

FRANCES PULLED OVER to the side of Route 100A after departing the Center. She texted Murray, "11:30 at Q.Diner?"

Her cellphone beeped with his return text a minute later, "See you there."

This time, Frances arrived first. She was waiting next to her car in the parking lot when Murray drove in.

Once they were settled in their booth by the door, Frances said, "I'm not a big fan of the smoke in Charles' office."

"Nor am I," Murray said. "Charlie says Ignatius Jones wants us to burn joss sticks throughout the Center. The guy is nuts."

Frances asked, "Do you still want me to help?"

"Yes."

Looking Murray straight in the eye, she asked, "Can I count on you."

"You can count on me. You have my word."

"Buddy glanced at you when he joined us in Charles' office and saw me there. What was that about?"

"We'd just come from watching videos of you with Lily at Charlie's house in Woodstock, when you went there with Lily's

241

mother, and of you and Jackson. You left the kitchen together and didn't return for what seemed like a long time."

"And these videos raised suspicions?"

"Yeah, but Buddy agreed not to tell Charlie until something more turns up. It wouldn't make much difference anyway, since Charlie already doesn't buy your story for becoming a psychic guide. He thinks you're up to something and wants to catch you in the act."

"Too bad," Frances said. "I thought I had him convinced when I got teary at the end."

"He's insane, Dr. Gourmelon, but he's not stupid."

"I'll be careful," Frances said. "So, Murray, now let's talk about what I need from you."

"Alright."

"I need, as soon as possible, the exact dimensions of the portrait of Ignatius Jones, the length and width of its frame, the width of its frame moulding, and the length, width, and thickness of the wooden stretcher inside the frame."

"What's a stretcher?"

"It's the internal wood frame for the painting which sits inside the painting's visible outer frame. The canvas is tacked to the stretcher."

"Why do you need these measurements?"

"Just accept that I do."

"Because if you're planning to steal the painting, keep in mind that the Portrait Room is monitored 24/7 by video surveillance and a motion detector."

"I will, thank you."

"I've no idea how I'll get your measurements," Murray said. "I'd have to take the painting down."

"Didn't you set up the security system?"

"Yes."

"Then you should be able to figure something out."

"Yeah, well..."

"Also let me know what you see on the back of the painting, like markings on the canvas, and precisely how the canvas is tacked to the four sides of the stretcher, like how many tacks, and where they are."

"I'll do my best, Dr. Gourmelon."

"Now that we're such good friends, Murray, you may call me Sister Frances."

Frances' second stop was at the Loon Lake Inn.

She told Martyn Zimmer, "I'd like to borrow your poster of the portrait of Ignatius Jones."

Martyn hesitated. "Are you asking on behalf of the Ignatius Jones Center?"

"No, I'm asking for me, not for the Center. Why?"

"Last week, just after you checked out of the Inn, a guy called me from the Center, named Murray. He said they wanted to buy it back and would pay me double what I paid for it. I asked why, and he said they had a new policy against selling reproductions of the painting."

"And you told him...?"

"I told him No."

"Good answer, Martyn dear," Frances said, patting his arm. "So, may I borrow it?"

"Yes, of course."

"Thank you."

"I don't suppose you'll tell me why you want it."

"No, Martyn, it's better for you not to know."

"Well, I love a mystery," Martyn said.

"And, please don't tell anyone that I have it, in case you're asked where it is."

"Don't worry. I'll just say that I received a request to return our contented Vermont cows to their place of honor above the fireplace."

It was late afternoon by the time Frances got back to Boston, surrendered her rental car, cabbed to her Institute on Essex Street, and climbed the stairs to her condo. It had been a long day, and she was tired.

There was a note from Tessa on her kitchen table.

"Thank you so much! I hope the rest of your week at the Center went well for you. Please visit me in Anchorage. I'll have lots to show you. Love, Tessa."

Late afternoon in Boston was still mid-day in Anchorage. Frances dialed Tessa's cell number.

"Frances!" Tessa exclaimed when she picked up.

"Hi, Tessa. I've just arrived back at my place and I saw your note. Are you alright?"

"Yes, I am, amazingly. How did the rest of your week go at the Center?"

"Fine, but we missed you."

"Guess what?" Tessa said. "It turns out I don't need a Certificate to impress my clients. I printed and framed one of my photos of the portrait that I emailed to my mom. No one asks to see a Certificate."

"About that," Frances said. "Could you forward to me copies of the photos that you sent your mom?"

"Sure. Hang on." Frances could hear keys clicking. "They're on their way. Should pop into your email any second now."

"I'll look for them as soon as I turn on my PC," Frances said.

"Why do I get the feeling that you're up to something?"

"Because you're an exceptionally sensitive psychic medium, even though you're still very young."

"Will you let me know if I can help?"

"You already have, Tessa dear. I'll fill you in later."

Next, Frances phoned Carter Haas.

"I'm back in Boston and I'm ready to tell you all about the Desmond Wilkins portrait of Ignatius Jones."

"Wonderful!" Carter exclaimed. "I'm still in my office. Come right now. Tell security at the door that you're meeting me. I'll let them know you're coming."

"Not now, Carter," Frances said. "I just drove down from Vermont and need to get settled. How about tomorrow morning, first thing?"

"I'll be waiting for you," Carter said.

Forty Three

FRANCES WAS ONE OF THE FIRST into the MFA when it opened its doors next morning at ten o'clock.

She hustled to the gallery in the MFA's new Art of the Americas Wing which was showing three Desmond Wilkins portraits of prominent New Englanders.

His *William Roberts Longley and his Sister Cecilia Elizabeth* (1882) depicted a couple in riding gear staring down their noses at the artist. His *Meredith Jane Longfellow* (1888) showed a young woman in bohemian dress.

The third Wilkins, *Elijah Price* (1893), portrayed a red-cheeked, middle-aged Boston merchant at his desk examining a book of accounts that was laid open before him.

Contemplating the portly gentleman, Frances thought, *You must have been baffled by your son William's relationship with the notorious psychic, Ignatius Jones, and you were most likely despairing over your daughter Melissa's infatuation with him. I'd guess that you judged William's assassination of his former friend to be justified, even though it led to William's own passing. You probably had little contact with Melissa's daughter Sarah after she was exiled to Vermont. But from all that, you now have a great-great-granddaughter, Lily*

Prestowicz. I believe that you would have liked her, Mr. Price. I'll do my best for her.

Carter was standing in the hallway waiting for Frances when she stepped off the elevator on his floor. He led her into his office.

"Can I get you anything?" he asked. "Tea, coffee, water?"

"No, thanks," Frances said.

"Great," Carter said, dispensing with additional niceties. "So tell me about the portrait of Ignatius Jones."

"It's quite marvelous."

"Does it have the... *powers*... that have been ascribed to it?"

"It does indeed," Frances said.

"I want this painting for our collection. Whom do I call at this place in Vermont?"

"They won't sell it."

"Just to test the waters. Start a conversation."

Frances wrote the Center's phone number on a piece of note paper.

"Ask for the Center's co-manager, Murray Gattis," she said. "Don't mention my name."

"I won't. Thank you, Frances."

"You're very welcome, Carter, and now, in return, *you* can help *me*. I'm looking for an artist who can make a copy of the painting, secretly, without the Center's knowledge."

"How would they not find out? They're likely to see copyist setting up an easel a few feet away from the original."

247

"My copyist will work from a poster reproduction and from photographs taken recently at the Center. Like these, for example."

Frances handed Carter prints of Tessa's photographs.

Carter studied each of them in turn, muttering to himself, "Fantastic!"

Then he passed them back to Frances and said, "I do know a copyist who's very good, and she's particularly into late 19-century American art."

"Perfect. Will you introduce us?"

"That depends on your plans for the copy, Frances. Given your need for secrecy… it raises questions."

"Like what, Carter?"

"Not that you'd do anything illegal, but we have anti-forgery rules, like a copy must be smaller than the original and on the back it has to be stamped as a copy in indelible ink."

Frances gave him a cheery not-to-worry look.

"Actually, I need a copy that only an expert like yourself can tell is not the original. Same size, no stampings on the back. Identical in every possible way."

"Then we have a problem."

"My copy will never be sold to anyone. Once it's served its purpose, I'll destroy it."

"Easy enough to say now."

"You can watch me destroy it, if you like."

"Well…"

"What if you just pointed me in her direction? No introduction. I'll take it from there."

"And my name would never come up?"

"Never. I promise."

PORTRAIT OF IGNATIUS JONES

Carter looked at Frances, thinking about her request, and about her, and how she'd helped him. Then he said, "Her name is Annie Kane. She's working towards her Master of Fine Arts degree at BU. You can find her on Tuesdays and Thursdays in Gallery 232 in the Art of the Americas Wing. Currently she's working on her copy of John Singer Sargent's *Daughters of Edward Darley Boit*. She usually arrives in the early afternoon. Short brown hair, attractive, you can't miss her."

If Murray was surprised to receive a phone call from a curator at the Museum of Fine Arts in Boston, he hid it well.

"How are you doing?" he asked, after Carter introduced himself.

"Fine, thank you," Carter said. "I'm calling about your Desmond Wilkins portrait of Ignatius Jones."

"What about it?"

"May I see it?"

"Sure. I'll schedule a session for you in the Portrait Room with Messenger Charles."

"Who is Messenger Charles?"

"He communicates with the spirit of Ignatius Jones on behalf of visitors to the Center."

"Oh, right."

"There will be a nominal charge of three hundred dollars for your thirty minute session, payable by credit card or via PayPal when the reservation is made."

"That's nominal?"

"It is, for communicating with the spirit of Ignatius Jones."

"My reason for calling is a bit different. If the painting is as wonderful as I've heard, I may want to acquire it for our collection. We are already displaying three Desmond Wilkins portraits at the MFA and yours would make a great addition."

"I'm sure it would," Murray replied.

"I'll have to inspect it first, of course."

"You'd be wasting your time," Murray said.

"Why is that, Mr. Gattis?"

"Our painting is not for sale."

"How about lending it to the MFA, instead of selling it?"

"No can do. Messenger Charles will never allow our painting to leave the Center for any reason."

Carter didn't reply, and Murray asked, "Shall I reserve your session with Messenger Charles?"

"I'll get back to you on that," Carter said.

Forty Four

ANNIE KANE SET UP her easel on a drop cloth about five feet from the John Singer Sargent painting.

She placed her palette knife, paints, and brushes neatly and readily at hand in her compartments drawer. She squeezed paint colors onto her palette to begin her afternoon's work. She mixed a touch of one color with a smidgen of another, and then dabbed the resulting blend to her canvas with quick brush strokes.

Rather than attempting to copy John Singer Sargent's entire monumental *Daughters of Edward Darley Bolt,* Annie was focusing instead on the smallest of the four girls who was sitting on the rug holding her rag doll.

Visitors in the gallery paused to compare Annie's copy to the original painting. "Very well done," one lady said. Annie looked at her and smiled. "Thank you," she said, before returning to her task.

"Excuse me, my dear, are you Annie Kane?"

Annie put down her brush and turned to find out who was asking.

She saw a large woman in a dark green muumuu emblazoned with red and yellow sunbursts. The woman had curly grey hair, kindly grey eyes behind gold-rimmed glasses, and rosy cheeks.

"I guess that's a silly question," Frances said, "now that I see your name shown very clearly on your MFA permit."

Frances gestured towards the museum's copying permit that Annie had left hanging from her easel.

"Not a problem," Annie said.

"My name is Frances Gourmelon."

"Glad to meet you," Annie said, before turning back to her work.

Frances said, "Sorry to bother you, Annie, but I'd very much like to speak with you."

"I'm quite busy now," Annie said. She'd never finish if she chatted with every kibitzer on their way through the gallery. "Perhaps some other time."

Frances persisted, "I understand, you don't know me from Adam. Please let me give you my card."

Annie glanced at the card that Frances handed to her, which read, 'Dr. Frances E. Gourmelon, Ph.D., President, Institute for Psychical and Paranormal Research,' with her address and contact information.

"You're a psychic?" Annie said. "I'm not looking for a séance."

"Of course not, dear," Frances said. "I want to talk with you about the Desmond Wilkins portrait of Ignatius Jones."

For the first time, Annie looked like she might be interested in what Frances was saying.

"Do you know of it?" asked Frances.

"I've only seen it in old photos. But I do love Desmond Wilkins."

Frances said, "I've just returned from a week in Vermont where it's on display."

"I thought it was lost."

"It was, until it turned up in Vermont in a rummage sale."

"I'd love to see it," Annie said.

"Take a look at these," Frances said, handing Annie the envelope with copies of Tessa's photos.

Annie said, examining each of them in turn, "You get the feeling that Ignatius Jones is trying to tell you something."

"That's more true than you realize, Annie," Frances said. "I have a proposal for you. But you should know more about me first. Do your research. Check on the Internet. Ask people you know. And then, if you'd like to hear more, please contact me."

"Can you give me a hint?" Annie asked.

"My proposal involves the Desmond Wilkins portrait of Ignatius Jones."

"I suspected that much."

"I'm in a great hurry, my dear, so if you're willing to hear what I have to say, please do contact me within the next day or so."

Forty Five

To start her investiture as Consort in the Portrait Room, Lily read Chapter Eight of the *Book of Ignatius Jones* as it had just been transcribed by Messenger Charles.

Charles stood beside her, watching her read.

Chapter Eight. Renewing the Cycle of Life.

And I lay with Melissa.

1 Each of us was naked before the other.

2 We touched, her bare skin against my bare skin.

3 She wanted me, even as I wanted her.

4 I entered her, and her body received mine.

5 And I lost myself in her.

6 Her womb demanded my seed, and I gave all that it sought.

7 She was with my child when I passed to spirit.

8 I stayed close to her in spirit when my child was born.

9 And I stayed close to my child in spirit as she became a woman.

10 And she bore a son, and he conceived a daughter.

11 And I stayed close to them in spirit.

12 And my portrait was a portal for my spirit, as I had intended.

13 And the daughter of my daughter's son knew me in my portrait.

14 And she felt my presence.

15 And my Messenger selected her as his Consort.

16 And with his seed, she will bear my children.

17 And through them, I shall return to the physical world.

"I'm not ready to be a mother," Lily said.

Charles reassured her, "Your children won't be a burden to you. They'll be brought up by our Spiritualist Helpers and pilgrim mothers. Children in the Center belong to everyone."

"But..."

"Otherwise, if you weren't ready, why would Ignatius Jones have selected you to bear his children?"

On that, Messenger Charles' logic was irrefutable.

Their ceremony involved just the two of them in front of the portrait of Ignatius Jones.

Charles clicked a button on his remote control device to disable the video camera and checked that its tiny red light had blinked out.

Lily stood in her bare feet next to the tatami mat on the stage in front of the portrait. She wore only a white gown with nothing underneath. Charles, also barefoot, had changed his robe for the occasion, to one made of silk instead of cotton.

She faced the portrait, looking into the eyes of Ignatius Jones, and she felt him surround her, embracing her, nuzzling her hair, and just behind her ear, sending a tingling down her spine.

Her gown, coming undone, dropped to the ground. Hands cupped her breasts. She could feel him behind her, pressing into her, and she arched her back to receive him.

Supported by his arms, she sank slowly to the tatami mat and stretched out on her back with her eyes fastened on those of Ignatius Jones, as he gazed down at her.

Charles said, *Each of us was naked before the other.*

Stepping free of his silk robe, he lowered himself to the floor beside her.

She was lightheaded, inflamed, dizzy.

We touched, her bare skin against my bare skin. She wanted me, even as I wanted her. I entered her, and her body received mine. And I lost myself in her.

He moved inside her slowly at first. She felt every stroke, every shudder, and she could not help herself from crying out as he thrust against her.

Her womb demanded my seed, and I gave all that it sought.

As he surged into her, filling her with liquid warmth, Lily felt a wave of blissful serenity, of singular oneness with her lover, the beautiful man with his wavy brown hair and dark penetrating eyes.

Charles lay beside her for a few minutes, gathering his breath, and then reached for a pillow which he placed beside the tatami mat. He knelt on the pillow, gazing down at Lily, and recited the remaining words to complete their ceremony.

And the daughter of my daughter's son knew me in my portrait. And she felt my presence. And my Messenger selected

her as his Consort. And with his seed, she will bear my children.
And through them, I shall return to the physical world.

"You are now my Consort, Lily," Charles said. "Bless you in the name of Ignatius Jones."

Lily raised herself to sit cross-legged on the tatami mat so she could look directly at him.

"Now that I am your Consort, how shall I refer to you?" she asked.

He was old, and sweaty, and had straggly grey hair on his chest and around his drooping penis and testicles. She wondered whether he was uncomfortable kneeling on his knees that way. Perhaps, being the Messenger, he welcomed such discomfort, like holy men flagellating themselves.

"You may call me Charles when we're alone. In public, though, you'll still call me Messenger Charles."

"Where will I stay?"

She could hardly return to the room that she and Becca were sharing.

"We've prepared a suite for you in the Residence next to my apartment," Charles said. "I'll visit with you there until you are with child."

"No, Charles," Lily said, the first time that she dared to contradict him. "Our visits must be here in the Portrait Room, here with Ignatius Jones."

"I understand," Charles said.

Lily wasn't sure that he did understand, but as long as he agreed, she didn't care.

"What are my duties as Consort?" she asked.

257

"You will help me serve Ignatius Jones. You will bear his children. You will counsel our pilgrim families and give guidance to our Spiritualist Helpers."

"Can I tell them what to do?"

"I prefer to think of it as guidance."

"What about our Protectors, and Buddy, and Murray?"

"No change there, for now," Charles said. "We'll see."

"We'll see what?" Lily insisted.

"How things develop," Charles replied, vaguely. "Meanwhile, the main thing for you, and for both of us, will be our times together here in the Portrait Room. Until you are with child."

Lily stood and reached for her white gown.

She turned towards the portrait and Ignatius Jones, and said, "Whenever you call for me, I will join you here."

And then she phoned her mother.

"Why didn't you tell me that Grandma Prudence was Ignatius Jones' daughter?"

"Who said that she was?" Suzie replied.

"It's in the latest chapter in the *Book of Ignatius Jones*. I'll read it to you, *And the daughter of my daughter's son knew me in my portrait. And she felt my presence. And my Messenger selected her as his Consort.*"

"So?"

"That's me, isn't it?" Lily said. "I'm the daughter of his daughter's son."

"You can't take that stuff seriously, Lily."

"But it's true, isn't it, Mom?"

Suzie didn't answer and Lily said, "Mom?"

"I don't know, honey, it might be."

"So Ignatius Jones is my great-grandfather."

"He would be, yes."

"Why didn't you tell me?"

"Because you're already way too entranced by his damn portrait. Anyway, I only recently found out about it from Frances Gourmelon."

"How did she know?"

"She worked it out after asking Hildy Veysey about Prudence. She wanted to tell you right then but I made her promise to keep it to herself."

"So everyone but me knows my business."

"We meant well, Lily. We're so worried about you. I wish you'd come home. Even if only for a short visit, so we can talk."

"I can't. Not now."

"Why not?"

"I have important duties as Consort to Messenger Charles. For one thing, Ignatius Jones has told Messenger Charles that I will bear his children."

"Oh my God!"

"They will be Ignatius Jones' children, through Charles. Ignatius Jones says that he will return to the physical world through his children."

"Lily!"

Lily could hear her mom gasping and crying on the phone.

"But Messenger Charles told me not to worry since our children will be brought up by the Spiritualist Helpers and pilgrim moms in the Center. They'll belong to all of us."

"That's…"

"So I've stopped taking the pill."

"I can't listen to any more of this," Suzie wailed, and hung up.

"Bye, Mom," Lily said, smiling to herself.

Forty Six

MURRAY WAS RUNNING TESTS in the video room when Buddy entered, followed by Brian Struggles, a newly hired Protector.

"Brian comes highly recommended by Protector Ricky," Buddy said. "They played football together."

"Welcome to the Center," Murray said.

"Thank you, sir," Brian replied.

He was large like Ricky and Jackson, short ginger hair, glasses.

"We got a problem?" asked Buddy, as Murray switched between video feeds.

"Yeah, another video blind spot," Murray said. "Unfortunately, it's in the Portrait Room."

"How so? Didn't our camera catch Pruitt taking her pictures?"

"We'd have missed it if she'd held her cellphone a few inches higher. The painting blocks the camera's view. I'm thinking I'll install another camera a bit over from the first one where it won't be obstructed."

"Do you need help?"

"Lend me Protector Brian. I want backup when I take the painting down so it won't get damaged while I'm working back there. Anyway, I don't want to be alone with it."

As both Murray and Buddy well knew, one of Charles' cardinal rules was never, ever, to leave the painting alone with only one person, Messenger Charles himself being the sole exception.

"Good experience for Brian," Buddy said.

Murray said, "Protector Brian, please turn around while I enter the passcode to disable the motion alarm."

Protector Ricky held the door open to the Portrait Room for Murray, who was carrying a toolbox, and for Brian, who was carrying a ladder.

"Why're you squinting?" Brian asked.

"Fucking smoke," Ricky said.

He waved his hand by his face to clear away the smoke rising from joss sticks in a ceramic brazier on the floor next to him.

"At least you can breathe in there," he said.

Brian spread a silk cloth on the platform in front of the painting. Then, ever so gently, Murray lifted the painting from its hooks on the pillar and laid it face up on the cloth.

Murray said, "I'll take measurements to make sure we put the new camera in the best spot."

He measured the length and width of the frame, and the width of the frame moulding.

He turned the painting over so that it was face down, and measured the distance between the bottom of the frame and the wire attached to the frame that suspended the painting on the pillar.

Without looking up, Murray also measured the length, width, and thickness of the stretcher. He counted the tacks that pinned the canvas on each of the four sides of the stretcher, and measured the spacings between them. He checked the back of the canvas: yellowish color, no visible markings.

Brian stood by quietly and didn't ask any questions as Murray jotted down his observations.

Then Murray got Brian's help propping the ladder against the wall behind the pillar.

Referring to a number that he'd written on his notepad, Murray marked a spot near the top of the wall for the second camera's enclosure. Then, he attached the enclosure to the wall and inserted the camera in its enclosure.

"Is that it?" Brian asked, as Murray came down the ladder.

"Still need an electrician to connect the camera," Murray said. "Meanwhile, let's re-hang the painting…"

The door to the Portrait Room slammed open and a robed cyclone tore down towards them.

"What the bloody hell are you doing?" Charles shouted. "No one touches that painting except for me!"

"We have to install another video camera," Murray said, in a calming voice. "We have a blind spot."

"I don't believe it," Charles said.

"What don't you believe, Charlie?"

"That you would place your hands on the portrait of Ignatius Jones, a portal to the afterlife, like it was nothing."

"I wanted to protect it. We might have bumped into it while we were working."

Protector Brian spoke up to defend Murray. "Also, we needed to measure the painting."

"Why?" Charles asked, looking at Murray.

"To install the new camera," Murray said. "The painting blocked part of the view from the camera that we installed earlier. We had to know the painting's dimensions in order to get a sightline around it."

"We already took those measurements when we designed the Portrait Room and then again when we located the pillar down here on the stage."

Still speaking quietly and calmly, Murray insisted, "I had to check, Charlie."

"From - now - on," Charles said hoarsely, breathing hard, "you - don't - touch - this - painting."

"I got it."

"Leave now! Both of you. I'll re-hang it myself."

Charles sat for a moment to allow the pressure in his chest to subside, and then he lifted the painting back to its rightful place on the pillar.

Protector Ricky cast his eyes down like a guilty schoolboy as Murray and Brian passed him on their way out of the Portrait Room.

Murray paused. "What happened, Ricky? Did you call Messenger Charles to tell him we were in there?"

"No, I didn't. He came by and asked me if everything was alright in the Portrait Room. I had to tell him."

"Don't worry about it," Murray said. "You were just doing your job."

"Yeah, man," Brian said, looking at his friend. "Good job."

Murray called Frances that evening.

"Do you have a pen and paper handy?" he asked.

"I'm ready. Please go ahead."

Murray read off his numbers for the dimensions of the frame, for the width and length of the stretcher, and for the thickness and width of each piece of wood on the four sides of the stretcher.

"Good. Thank you."

"I've got more."

He provided the number and locations of the tacks attaching the canvas to the stretcher, to each of its sides and to its top and bottom pieces."

"Thanks," Frances said, as she wrote down Murray's numbers.

"The back of the canvas is plain and unmarked, but looks yellow from age. The stretcher is secured inside the frame with old nails in each side and top and bottom."

"Right. Good."

"Sister Frances, I must remind you again about the security devices in the Portrait Room."

"Which you can disable."

"I can. That's how I got the measurements. But I had a cover story and even so, Charlie went into a rage when he found out. My point is, both the video surveillance and motion detector systems are clocked continuously. If they're turned off at any time, no matter how briefly, the gap in coverage will be discovered."

"Okay," Frances said.

Forty-Seven

AT TWO O'CLOCK in the morning, a pickup truck coasted slowly with its headlights off down the Center's gravel driveway and came to a stop before it reached the turning circle.

Only the *hoo-hoo-hoo* of an owl nearby broke the almost total quiet.

A sliver of crescent moon did little to penetrate the darkness.

Below where the truck was parked, the turning circle was illuminated in addition, but only dimly, by a single yellow light on the Evelyn M. Billings Residence building.

Two figures stepped out of the truck and unloaded a box from the back. They carried it quickly across the turning circle and deposited it at the Residence entrance.

Then they stood side-by-side facing the residence, unzipped, and urinated against the door.

As they jogged back to their truck, one of them snickered and the other cautioned, "shhh," and the first one replied, "shhh," and now they were both giggling, but quietly, trying to keep a lid on it.

Then they screamed in unison, shattering the silence, "FUCK YOU, ASSHOLES!" and their truck tore up the driveway spewing gravel and exhaust.

Buddy arrived first at the scene, followed by the Center's Protectors, and then by Murray, all in shorts and t-shirts, except for Murray in a cotton bathrobe.

Lights came on in some of the Residence windows but no one else joined the group clustered at the entrance.

"What the hell was that?" asked Murray.

"Some jerks left us a present," Buddy said. "A cardboard box."

"Smells like someone peed," Ricky said.

Murray stepped towards the box.

"Don't touch it!" Buddy warned. "Could be booby trapped."

"I'm just looking," Murray said. "They've written something on one of the flaps."

He leaned closer. "Fuck Portrait Worshipers."

Jackson said, "If it's booby trapped, maybe we should call the police."

"No," Buddy said. "We'll wait until Messenger Charles is here."

"Meanwhile let's move the box away from the Residence, just in case," Murray said.

Buddy told Protector Jackson to get the Center's utility cart from the storage area.

The cart jerked and bumped on the gravel as Jackson brought it around.

Murray said, "It's too unstable on the gravel. Could set off whatever's inside the box."

Buddy said, "Then we'll carry it."

"I'll do it," Ricky said.

"You sure?"

"Yeah, no problem."

The box was about three-feet square but within the grasp of Ricky's long arms.

He lifted it gingerly and began to carry it slowly and carefully towards the back of the Residence. Jackson and Brian stayed with him, one on each side, shining flashlights in front of him to light his path.

He laid the box on the ground behind the Residence, about fifty feet from the building.

"We'll examine it later this morning when we've got daylight," Buddy said. "Meanwhile, Jackson, before you go back to your room, wash the pee off the door, get rid of the smell, and Murray, let's check our video file."

The video showed two figures in hoodies walking towards the Residence, one carrying the box, and the other beside him. Their heads were down so the camera did not pick out their faces.

The video caught them peeing on the Residence door but their heads were still down with their faces shadowed by their hoods.

The light on the turning circle was too dim to make out any details about the figures crossing it towards and then away from the Residence, only that they appeared to be large.

The audio picked up their suppressed laughing and their scream before they drove off.

It was too dark to make out the truck's license plate.

"Any thoughts?" Buddy asked.

Murray said, "The fact they drive a pickup suggests they have blue collar jobs or work on a farm. They were laughing so they think what they did was funny, plus they were probably drinking, and obviously they have a grudge against the Center."

"I don't think what they did was funny," Buddy said.

"We'll find out more when we open the box," Murray said.

After breakfast, Messenger Charles, with Buddy, Murray, and Protectors Jackson and Ricky, marched out to the field to examine the box.

Protector Brian kept the Center's visitors and pilgrims well back for their own safety.

Although the weather was clear, the box was still damp from early morning dew. Otherwise it was exactly as it was left earlier that morning.

"I'll open it," Charles said.

"What if it's rigged to explode?" Murray asked.

"Ignatius Jones would have warned me," Charles said.

He leaned over the box and slit the box sealing tape with a box cutter. He pulled the flaps up, and peered inside.

What he saw made his head throb. There could no longer be any doubt: Their enemies were preparing to strike. The struggle for survival of the Center, and all that it stood for, would soon be upon them.

"What's in there?" asked Buddy.

Charles reached into the box and started to take out pieces of wood.

Murray said, "Broken up picture frame."

Charles nodded grimly, and extracted the rest of the box's contents:

A scruffy pocket size Holy Bible.

Four brass bullet casings in a plastic baggie.

A plain black matchbook with only one match left inside.

A bicycle lock cable with a smashed combo lock.

A GI Joe figure dressed for battle and holding a semi-automatic weapon.

Buddy said, "They probably left finger prints, and the bullet casings can be traced, but we don't need any of that. I know who they are. They're the guys we caught down by the stream."

Protector Ricky said, "They don't care if we know, like they think we can't do anything about it."

Protector Jackson cleared his throat.

"What is it, Jackson?" asked Buddy.

"Maybe they were just blowing off steam after they had too much to drink."

"Looks like a threat to me," Ricky said.

"Then we should let the police know," Jackson said.

"No point in that," Buddy said. "We have to protect ourselves."

Charles turned to Murray, "What do you think?"

"I agree with Jackson," Murray said. "They wouldn't have warned us if they really meant to attack."

Charles said, "Ignatius Jones will guide us."

Forty Eight

THAT AFTERNOON, Charles called Buddy into his office.

"Shut the door," he said.

Buddy pushed the door shut and took a seat in front of Charles' desk.

He dreaded hearing how, once again, he'd let Charles down, this time by allowing two yokels to deliver their hate box to the Residence front door with contents that were threatening and unpleasant but could have much worse.

However, Charles didn't launch into a complaint about Buddy's failures as head of security. Instead, he held up a sheet of paper, and said, "I've transcribed another chapter from Ignatius Jones. It will involve you, so listen carefully."

Charles read the new chapter aloud.

Chapter Nine. Preparing for the Gathering.

A day of judgment will come.
*   1 When my followers are attacked.*
*   2 And my Messenger is disparaged.*
*   3 And my portrait is threatened.*

4 On that terrible day will commence the Gathering to purify the physical world.

5 When those who conspire against me will be called to spirit.

6 As will those who conspire against my Messenger.

7 As will those who disdain my portrait.

8 And those who are close to me will sacrifice to restore the connection between our worlds, to assure life continuous for all who hear and trust my words.

As Charles read these lines to Buddy, he felt good; more than good, *elated*. Ignatius Jones had shown the way. They would resolve their fate on their own terms.

Buddy nodded to acknowledge each line. He didn't understand exactly what Charles was saying, but he was on board, one hundred percent.

Charles said, "We'll keep this chapter to ourselves, for now, Buddy, because others might not understand."

"Sure."

"Do you get what Ignatius Jones is telling us about the Gathering?"

"That our enemies will be defeated?"

"It's about choice, Buddy. We'll each make conscious choices for truth over lies, light over darkness, order over chaos."

Buddy was relieved that Charles confided in him. He would be proud to join Charles, who spoke with such calmness and certitude, in making such important conscious choices.

Charles said, "An attack on the Center will signify that the Gathering has started."

"We will be ready for them, Messenger Charles."

"I'll want Sister Lily at my side while I confirm that the Gathering is underway. You will escort her to join me in the Portrait Room."

"Sure," Buddy said. "We have to protect her."

"Ignatius Jones has called on those closest to him to sacrifice," Charles said. "Sister Lily will volunteer. I will send her to spirit with my own hands."

Checking that he understood Charles correctly, Buddy asked, "By send her to spirit, you mean..."

"I will help her to depart the physical world, Buddy."

"Even though she's your Consort?"

"Our personal sacrifice will have greater meaning precisely *because* she is my Consort."

That Charles would contemplate such a terrible sacrifice caused Buddy to appreciate even more his total commitment to Ignatius Jones and to the Center.

"I'll bring her to you, Messenger Charles."

"And then those who are disloyal to us in the Center must be sent to spirit as well. Use your weapons on Murray and Protector Jackson before they have a chance to resist or flee."

"I will."

"And all witnesses in the Center, whether pilgrims, or visitors, or other staff, they must also be sent to spirit. And also Protector Ricky, after he has finished helping you to send the others to spirit."

That's a lot of bullets, Buddy thought, even as he affirmed to Charles, "Yes, alright."

"And then you must return to the Portrait Room, when you have completed those important tasks, to send me to spirit as well."

"You, Messenger Charles? Why?"

"Once the Gathering gets underway, I cannot stay in the physical world to be captured by non-followers. Do you understand?"

"I do."

"And finally, my old friend, you must join me in passing to spirit, by your own hand."

Whoa, Buddy thought, *that's a passing-to-spirit too far.* Dispatching adversaries and traitors, no problem. Helping others to sacrifice themselves, happy to oblige. But self-sacrifice? When the time came for his conscious choice to cross to the Other Side, he'd choose, *no thanks*. He'd be long gone by the time the police arrived at the Center to count the bodies. Maybe, come to think of it, he'd spare Ricky as well, since the big fellow would be useful to him wherever they ended up.

Charles asked, "Will you do this?"

"I will, Messenger Charles," Buddy replied. "I will. I promise. I will be worthy of your trust."

That same afternoon, Frances received a text from Protector Jackson: "OK to talk now?"

She replied, "Yes. Call me."

She picked up on the first ring.

"I'm at the Aubuchon Hardware with Murray," Jackson said. "He's having an argument with the manager. Apparently they don't want our business any more. I just stepped out for a minute and don't have much time."

"What's going on?" asked Frances.

Jackson described the events that morning with the cardboard box and its contents.

"Messenger Charles was freaked," he said. "Buddy too. It was a message from the local boys that they haven't forgotten what Buddy did to them and to remind us that they'll be back."

"Were you able to reach them?"

"I texted them please to hold off."

"Did you get a response?"

"Yeah, that they're bored with waiting."

"It would wreck everything if they went ahead on their own."

"Next time they won't just leave a cardboard box. And next time they won't get away so easily either. Buddy has promised Messenger Charles that our defenders will be ready for them."

"Please ask them to wait a bit longer."

"How much longer?"

"I don't know yet. I'm still pulling things together."

"Can I give them an estimate?"

"Tell them, we need another month."

"That's a long time."

"Best I can do."

"Okay, I'll try that. Gotta go. Murray's calling me."

Forty Nine

ANNIE KANE RETURNED to her apartment on Beacon Hill, a third-floor studio overlooking an alley, and searched on Google for articles about Dr. Frances Gourmelon.

A profile in the *Boston Globe* described her as Boston's best-known psychic medium. Her clients came from the hub's top political, business, and cultural circles.

A photo in the newspaper's Out & About section showed Frances resplendent in a blue and gold muumuu, posed beside Boston home-boy actor-activist Ben Affleck at a fundraiser for his Eastern Congo Initiative.

An earlier article in the *Boston Herald,* in the mid-1990s, reported the opening of Frances' Institute for Psychical and Paranormal Research on Essex Street. Boston Mayor Tom Menino lauded the Institute as an important addition to the city's spiritual and cultural fabric. The article's headline quoted the Mayor phonetically, "A Treasah for the City of Boston!"

Annie didn't believe in life after death. It had never occurred to her to go to a psychic medium to communicate with her grandparents whom she'd lost to cancer, one only six months after the other.

277

She assumed that psychics who claimed to be in touch with their clients' loved ones must be lying or deluded.

Reason enough to stay clear of the psychic Dr. Frances Gourmelon, however well-known she might be.

On the other hand, Annie couldn't help wondering what Dr. Gourmelon had in mind that involved the Desmond Wilkins portrait of Ignatius Jones.

There was only one way to find out.

Frances said, "First things first," and held out a plate piled high with newly baked chocolate chip cookies.

Annie took one to be polite.

It did taste good, she thought, savoring the cookie's taste-bursts of buttery chocolate. She debated with herself whether to take another. And then decided, why not?

Frances retrieved an easel from the corner of the room. There was artwork on the easel which she turned around so that it was facing out.

"Behold a reproduction of Desmond Wilkins' portrait of Ignatius Jones," she said.

Annie examined the coloring of the subject's face, the silken folds of his cravat, his well-articulated strands of wavy hair, the way his figure stood out against a reddish-brown background and, most of all, the piercing urgency of his coal dark eyes.

Frances asked, "Do you have any doubt that this is a Desmond Wilkins?"

"The brushwork and style are typical Wilkins. But this portrait goes well beyond his other work. It's more powerful. His Ignatius Jones reaches out to you."

Frances said, "That's exactly what happens, Annie. Last week in Vermont, I felt his presence during my sessions with his portrait. I heard his voice from the Other Side."

Reading Annie's expression, Frances said, "Don't be alarmed, dear girl. I'm a psychic medium. I communicate with the Departed."

"Sure you do," Annie said, suddenly regretting her decision to come to Dr. Gourmelon's. "Thank you for showing me your poster, and everything, but..."

Frances interrupted her. "A young woman, her name is Lily, has fallen under the control of the spirit of Ignatius Jones. She's only eighteen. I promised her mother that I would try to break her free and for that, I need your help."

A young woman under the control of a spirit? Break her free?

"I'll go now," Annie said. "Thanks for the cookies."

Frances rested her hand gently on Annie's arm. "Annie, please..."

Annie stayed in her seat, but perched at the edge.

"Because of Lily's strong attachment with Ignatius Jones, she's unable to leave the Ignatius Jones Center which is run by people who are capable of anything. She'll break free only if she concludes that Ignatius Jones no longer resides in his portrait."

Frances paused and leaned towards her visitor. "And that's where you come in, Annie."

Annie said nothing, waiting to hear what came next.

"We need a virtually perfect copy of the Desmond Wilkins portrait of Ignatius Jones."

"Is that it?" Annie asked.

"Yes."

"Well, I don't do art forgery."

"I'm not asking you to, my dear."

"Then, what…?"

"Your copy will not be offered for sale to anyone. We just need it to break Lily free. Once that's done, we'll destroy it."

"I'm sorry for Lily, but why would I agree to do this?"

"Are you asking about money?"

"I'm asking in general."

"Well, to the extent it's about money, I'll cover your expenses and I'll pay for your time. This is the only way I can think of to help Lily. Even now, while she's under Ignatius Jones' spell, she's committing herself to a man who is more than twice her age."

"That's not so horrible," Annie said, recalling her own memorable encounters with charismatic older professors at BU.

Frances said, "The man is serving as a physical vessel for Ignatius Jones, who is her real lover."

"And who is dead."

"Who passed to spirit more than a hundred years ago and who is, among other things, her great-grandfather."

"So the spirit of Ignatius Jones is controlling both Lily and her older man."

"Yes."

"And now the girl is committing incest by proxy with her ancestor who is in the spirit world?"

Annie could help sounding like she was scoffing at Lily's predicament.

"Annie, this is not funny."

"It's just too weird," Annie said. "I don't know Lily. I can't get worked up to save her from her own bad decisions."

"But if you did agree to help, could you do it? I mean, could you make a virtually perfect copy of the portrait based on this reproduction and on the photos?"

Annie looked again at the poster. The reproduction's hues and shades were similar to those that Annie knew were favored by Desmond Wilkins in his other paintings, and it was sharp enough for her to discern his brushwork.

"I could make a very good copy."

"How long would that take you?"

"Maybe a couple of weeks. But that's academic, Dr. Gourmelon, because it still wouldn't be a virtually perfect copy. For that, I'd have to see the original painting."

Which will put an end to this surreal discussion so that I can get out of here.

"I can arrange that," Frances said.

Not the answer that Annie expected.

"You can?"

Frances noticed Annie's surprise and sudden interest. She had finally found Annie's button. She pushed it, hard.

"What I'm offering you, dear Annie, is a once-in-a-lifetime chance to see the legendary Desmond Wilkins painting that's been lost for more than a century. You'll can analyze it in great detail, learn from it, and by copying it, pay homage to it and to Desmond Wilkins."

Now, Annie understood: This wasn't about saving the unfortunate Lily. It was about the painting. No one else in BU's Fine Arts program had ever laid eyes on the Desmond Wilkins portrait of Ignatius Jones, not even her professors. They'd all heard of it, and talked about it at great length, but only she would have actually seen it. By creating a virtually perfect copy of the Desmond Wilkins portrait of Ignatius Jones, she'd make that famous lost masterpiece her own. Where was the harm if her copy were never offered for sale?

"Okay, I'll do it," Annie said.

Fifty

THE EMAIL that Frances received from Murray asked how things were going and shared 'wonderful' news:

Dear Sister Frances,

Messenger Charles asked about your progress recruiting pilgrims for our Center. He also wanted me to share with you our wonderful news that Sister Lily has been formally invested now as Consort to Messenger Charles and is residing at the Center in that capacity. We hope everything is going well for you and look forward to hearing from you.

Yours very truly,

Murray

To which Frances replied:

Dear Murray,

Such wonderful news about Lily! Please congratulate her and Messenger Charles on my behalf. You will hear shortly from a young man who is very interested in the Center. He has been searching for meaning for his life and I believe that he plans to join the Center as a pilgrim. While he is not wealthy, he will be delighted to contribute to the life of the Center in other ways. In particular, since he is an electrical engineer, he could help you maintain the Center's very important systems to ensure everything continues to operate as it should.

Warmest personal regards,

Sister Frances

Frances' nephew Teddie Bulger was not yet aware that he would commit to the life of a pilgrim at the Ignatius Jones Center for Spiritualist Discovery in Tudorsville, Vermont.

However, he was an adventurous young man and Frances knew that he would rise to the occasion, as he had numerous times before when his aunt needed a willing accomplice for her various projects.

Teddie's job as an engineer at Boston's public transit authority, the MBTA, would not pose a problem. He could apply for unpaid leave confident that his Aunt Frances would make him whole financially.

She called him to let him know.

"Teddie, it's your Aunt Frances. I have an important mission for you, dear boy."

"Anything for you, Aunt Frances."

"I want you to go up to Tudorsville, Vermont, near Woodstock. You'll stay at the Ignatius Jones Center for Spiritualist Discovery. They have a painting there that provides a portal to the Other Side."

"The 'Other Side,' meaning spirits?"

Teddie had learned not to argue with his aunt about the afterlife. Her experiences with spirits were real to her. For Teddie, that was all that mattered.

"Exactly," Frances said. "The portrait of Ignatius Jones, one of our greatest psychics, offers a portal to the spirit world. It's on display in a building they call the House of Spirits, in a special room called the Portrait Room. Believe me, Teddie, I've heard the voice of Ignatius Jones in that Portrait Room."

"I do believe you, Aunt."

"Good boy. I'm recruiting you to join the Center as a pilgrim."

"Will I have to pray?"

"No praying, not unless you want to. Your reason for joining is to find more personal meaning for your life from your interactions with the spirit of Ignatius Jones and from supporting the Center's work."

"Cool!" Teddie said.

"Call the Center. Say that you are interested in joining as a pilgrim because of what I told you about the Center but, and this is really important, don't reveal that you are my nephew. Just that you want to set your life on a better course."

"What if they ask how I know you?"

"I'm afraid, dear boy, that you'll have to tell a little white lie. Just say that I've helped you to manage the loss of your father."

"Which is basically true," Teddie said.

"They will ask you to cover your expenses. I'll reimburse you, of course, as well as for your lost income from the MBTA. Also, you'll be expected to volunteer to help maintain the Center."

"Like in a commune."

"Yes, but your talents need not be wasted on washing dishes. When they ask what you can do, be sure to remind them about your skills as an electrical engineer, especially your experience with the MBTA's security systems."

"I can do that."

"There are risks, Teddie. They're expecting trouble from local boys, and you may be drafted to help defend the Center."

"How, Aunt Frances?"

"Buddy Choate, who's in charge of security, has equipped the Center's defenders with firearms."

"I'm not into guns."

"If he hands you a gun and orders you to head out to battle, just leave."

"I will."

"Dear boy!"

Fifty One

TEDDIE TOLD Murray Gattis at the Ignatius Jones Center that he was calling at Dr. Gourmelon's suggestion.

"How do you know Dr. Gourmelon?" Murray asked.

"She helped me when my father passed."

"So you want to come to the Center."

"Yes sir. Dr. Gourmelon told me I could join the Center as a pilgrim so that I could communicate with my father and learn more about the afterlife. She said the Center could use my skills as an electrical engineer."

"I'm sure we could," Murray said. "When do you plan to come to the Center?"

"Tomorrow."

"That's pretty fast."

"I've already taken a leave from my job at the MBTA."

"What do you do at the MBTA?"

"I maintain our security systems that we use for video surveillance and intrusion alarms, both in the stations and inside the tunnels."

"We'll welcome you here, Teddie," Murray said.

It took Murray only a couple of minutes on the Internet to confirm that Theodore (Teddie) Bulger did work for the MBTA, and to find his name in the *Boston Globe* obituary for his father, Steven Bulger, along with his mother's name, Portia Masnaghetti Bulger.

Murray searched on 'Portia Masnaghetti' in Boston. He clicked on a 1970s *Globe* article about a Masnaghetti family bakery in Boston's North End. The whole family worked there including the two children who did so after school, Portia and her older sister, Frances.

So, if Frances Masnaghetti was now Frances Gourmelon, which Murray figured was a safe bet, then Portia's son Teddie Bulger was her nephew.

Gourmelon's plan was afoot. Whatever it was, Murray hoped she'd act quickly.

He'd been getting the evil eye from Charlie since he was caught moving the sacred painting. Now, after the incident with the cardboard box, Charlie had gotten even stranger.

From now on, he told Murray, he was to be addressed by Murray as well as everyone else as *Messenger Charles*, even in private.

Murray thought about leaving the Center, and Vermont, taking with him the cash that was rightfully his, but then he'd always be looking over his shoulder for Buddy's emissaries. He had no doubt that eventually they'd chase him down.

The phone call from Teddie Bulger was a promising sign.

Fifty Two

LILY'S ROOM as Consort to Messenger Charles was luxurious as compared to the space she shared formerly with Becca, and even as compared to the suites occupied by the visiting psychics.

In her bedroom, she had a double bed, a sofa, and a dressing table with a three-panel mirror and upholstered bench; in her bathroom, a Jacuzzi; and in her living area, a working gas fireplace.

Luxurious, like a gilded cage.

Buddy came by to inform Lily about her new living arrangements. "You got a minute?" he asked, grinning amiably as he slid by her to enter her room.

"Sure, okay," Lily said.

They stood facing each other in Lily's living area. Buddy had on his Protector outfit as he did most of the time now, with the wide belt and black leather boots. He hooked his thumbs in his belt and pressed his shoulders back, assuming his military leader stance.

Lily was wearing a white shift, getting ready to join Messenger Charles in the Portrait Room.

"Our enemies did us a favor with the warning they dumped at our door," Buddy said. "Now we gotta prepare, and you're part of that."

"Okay."

Buddy said, still grinning but less amiably, "I need to make sure there's no question about where you are, if you know what I mean."

"Not sure…"

"So from now on we'll keep track of where you go and who you see, starting with a sensor on your door that sends an alert whenever it's opened. Also, the camera in the hallway will monitor your doorway 24/7 so I'll know who's coming or going."

"That's creepy, Buddy, watching the door to my room like that."

"Can't be avoided," Buddy said. "When we're attacked, I need to get you to the Portrait Room first thing, so I have to always know where you are."

"That's fine, but I don't like you watching my door."

"You'll get used to it. Also, from now on, do not communicate in any way with Protector Jackson."

"Why not?"

"His loyalty has been questioned."

"Jackson is a friend. I'll talk with him anytime I want."

"You talk to Jackson, and he's gone. I'll fire his ass."

"You can't… "

"If he tries to talk to you, just tell me, and I'll deal with it."

"I want you to leave my room right now," Lily said angrily.

Buddy made no move to comply.

"Not yet, Sister Lily. I've got more to tell you. I've assigned Protector Ricky to accompany you when you are out of your room, like when you are called to the Portrait Room for your 'special duties,' or when you go to the Café."

"I don't want Ricky near me."

"It would hurt his feelings if he knew that," Buddy said, clearly enjoying himself. "Also from now on, Sister Lily, you won't need to stand in line in the Café. You'll be served at your table and eat by yourself. We wouldn't want our Consort to be forced to share idle gossip with others in the Café, would we?"

"You're trying to make me a prisoner."

"It's for your protection."

"I'll talk to Messenger Charles."

"Sure you will," Buddy said. "Now, give me your cellphone."

"Why?"

"Less temptation to do something you might regret later."

"What if I want to talk with my mom? Or she calls me? She'll be worried if I don't pick up."

"She can leave a message with me. You can talk from our landline phone in our office."

"Get out of my room, Buddy!"

"Not without your phone. Give it to me, or I'll get Ricky in here to take it from you."

Lily handed Buddy her phone.

Lily had no illusions about Buddy. He was a pig, a total pig. But he didn't scare her. Messenger Charles would support her and put Buddy back in his cage, along with his stupid sidekick Ricky. She had been so careful with Jackson. She knew he liked

291

her. She didn't encourage him because Charles wouldn't allow it, and she didn't want to get Jackson into trouble. She counted on Jackson being at the Center. She knew he'd respond if she felt threatened and called for help.

In the Portrait Room, Lily told Messenger Charles all that had transpired.

"Buddy treats me like a prisoner," she complained. "You've got to do something."

Charles' response was not what she expected.

"We are surrounded by enemies. Buddy has instructions from me to prepare for their attack, which includes protecting you, Sister Lily. Everything he's doing is at my request while the Center is under threat."

"I didn't sign up for this."

"Yes, you did, Lily. You are my Consort."

"I'll leave the Center."

"We can't let you go, just yet."

As Charles spoke, he guided Lily to the tatami mat.

Lily looked at the portrait and felt the presence of Ignatius Jones, calming her, and drawing her in.

She'd missed him so terribly after her mom sold the painting. She hated the thought of suffering through all that again, the loneliness, and the longing to hear his voice. She felt incomplete without him.

She'd endured the loathsome touch of Messenger Charles so that she could be with Ignatius Jones. She could put up with her movements being managed by Buddy and Ricky. She could always contact Jackson, or her mom, if she felt threatened.

She would stay, for now.

Fifty Three

ANNIE KANE EXITED the Green Line at a Commonwealth Avenue stop in Boston's Allston neighborhood, one block away from Benny's Art Supplies, her go-to source for her painting projects.

Benny Shavik, a tall, elegant man in his early sixties who still looked as lithe as a dancer, was taking a smoking break on the sidewalk outside his store entrance.

He stubbed out his cigarette in the gutter when he saw Annie approaching. She was more than a loyal customer. She was family. He and Annie's parents had been friends since before she was born. He greeted her with a warm two-handed handshake that turned into a hug.

Annie said, "You look as dashing as always."

"Got to keep up appearances," Benny said.

Annie said, "I'm starting a copy of another Desmond Wilkins painting. I want this one to be just about perfect, even better than my others, so I'm looking for vintage canvas like he used."

"Well, let's see what we can do for you," Benny said, holding the door open for her to go inside.

They descended a stairway to the store, which was located in the basement underneath a street-level outlet for used furniture.

Paint was splashed on the stairway's steps, handrails, walls, and ceiling as if it'd been sloshed on with mops. The same riotous motif of red, yellow, blue, green, white, and purple was carried down into the store on its ceiling and on its support columns.

"I have old rolls of linen canvas out back," Benny said.

While he was off searching for the canvas, Annie pushed a shopping cart to the section of the store where oil paints were shelved.

She found Desmond Wilkins' preferred brand, Schmincke Mussino, and selected the colors that he favored, cadmium yellow, vermilion, Mars red, Mars yellow, Mars brown, burnt umber, rose madder, sienna, ultramarine blue, cobalt blue, viridian green and emerald green. There were only two tubes left of Schmincke Mussino lead white, which Desmond Wilkins always used, and she took both of them. Lead white had become scarce since the EU banned its manufacture and sale in Europe, so Annie stocked up on it whenever she had the chance.

Benny returned after a few minutes holding loosely rolled canvas. "Snagged this at an artist's estate sale," he said. "It's good stuff, and it's old."

"Also I'll need a stretcher made to order," Annie said. "The standard sizes won't work for my painting."

"I've got pinewood pieces," Benny said. "I can make it for you now if you don't mind waiting."

Annie told him what she needed, based on Murray's measurements.

Back in her new studio space in Frances' Institute on Essex Street, Annie cut a piece of Benny's canvas and attached it to the stretcher he made for her, pushing in tacks in the same locations, and with the same spacings between them, as on the original, based on Murray's measurements.

To age the canvas, she brushed onto its front and back a mix of diluted bleach, paint thinner, brown paint, and liquid from cigarette butts soaked in water.

Next day, after the canvas was dry, she added an undercoat of mid-tone cool grey such as Desmond Wilkins used for his paintings in the 1890s, combined with a crackling medium so that fine cracks would appear in her copy similar to those to be expected on a century-old painting.

"Looking good," Frances said.

"I haven't started painting yet."

"Well, I'm impressed by all your preparations."

"Even so, it won't fool an expert," Annie said. "Anyone with a black light can easily tell that the paint isn't old. And even if I could fool the black light, which I can't, carbon dating will expose the age of my paint beyond any doubt."

"Don't worry," Frances said. "Your copy won't be tested with a black light or carbon dating."

"How do you know?"

"I'm a psychic, Annie dear."

Frances rubbed the orange Moonstone on the pinkie of her left hand to enhance her psychic insights on the topic.

"Just make your copy look the same as the original," she said. "That's all that counts."

Annie measured the image on the poster that Frances borrowed from the Loon Lake Inn. It was twenty-one percent smaller than the original painting, both in its length and width, assuming that Murray's numbers were correct.

Not good.

The image that she used as her primary reference had to have exactly the same dimensions as the original.

She brought the poster to the BU print center which made a high-definition full-color copy that was corrected for size.

This excursion cost a half-day, but the delay would have been far worse had she drawn Ignatius Jones as shown in the poster, and then had to start over when the size discrepancy was discovered.

She placed the size-corrected reproduction on an easel next to her work easel, and lined up the photos on a side table where she could refer to them as needed.

Annie started her copy by sketching a rough outline of Ignatius Jones' head, torso, arms, and hands. She positioned them on her canvas to match what she saw in the reproduction.

Then she painted a preliminary background color, burnt umber, also as shown on the reproduction.

Gradually, brushstroke by brushstroke, she added details to Ignatius Jones' features, his hair, forehead, eyebrows, eyes, cheeks, nose, ears, lips, neck, jacket, fingers. She mixed her colors, her medium, and her solvent to mimic the transparency, texture, definition, and gloss of the Desmond Wilkins masterpiece. She experimented, checked, adjusted.

She added a glowing-embers hue to the lower portion of the background.

Then back to Ignatius Jones, refining the details, adjusting colors and composition, applying special Wilkins touches.

After each refinement, she stepped back from her easel a few feet so that she could see her copy as others would see it, and to compare it to the reproduction.

Two weeks after she first applied brush to canvas, Annie's painting looked identical to the poster reproduction of Desmond Wilkins' portrait of Ignatius Jones.

"I can't tell the difference between them," Frances said.

"I've done as much as I can here," Annie said. "What counts is how my copy compares to the original painting."

"So let's go to Vermont," Frances replied.

Fifty Four

THEY DROVE in separate cars to the Ignatius Jones Center consistent with their cover story that Annie was Frances' client, and nothing more than that.

Along their route from Boston into Vermont, leaves on many of the trees on the hills beside the road had turned to yellow, and orange, and brown, and, here and there, to fiery red.

Annie was behind Frances on Route 100A when she saw Frances slow and her turn signal blinking. She followed Frances onto the gravel driveway down to the Center, to the turning circle in front of the Evelyn M. Billings Residence.

Protector Jackson collected their car keys.

"Is everything ready for us in there?" Frances asked.

"Yes, Sister Frances," Jackson replied. "All set for you and Ms. Kane in the House of Spirits."

Frances looked up at the Residence and saw Buddy watching them from his office window. He stepped out of sight when she waved hello.

"So you've come back," Protector Ricky said when they arrived at the door to the Portrait Room.

"Why wouldn't I?" Frances replied.

"I don't know," Ricky said, witty banter not being his strong suit.

Buddy had warned him to watch Gourmelon closely but not to say anything about it since she'd be watching and listening too. It wasn't easy, the way she seemed to look right through him.

"I'm a Psychic Guide," Frances said. "I'll always have a place here at the Center, Ricky."

"Sure," Ricky said. "Anyway, I need to look through your bags."

He took her cellphone, and Annie's, and also their stashes of ballpoint pens that had collected at the bottom of their bags.

"New rule," he said. "Nothing in the Portrait Room that has a sharp point."

Annie realized that she had more work to do as soon as she saw the original Desmond Wilkins portrait of Ignatius Jones.

To begin with, it was more luminous than the poster and Tessa's photos. She'd have to do more to capture that quality.

She set her mind on studying and memorizing notable attributes of the original painting. She would have taken notes had Protector Ricky not confiscated her ballpoint pens. Industrial-strength memorizing would have to do.

Frances said, "Annie, I will attempt now to contact your grandparents. You can join me on our journey to the Other Side by keeping your eyes directly on the portrait."

Annie nodded to acknowledge Frances' suggestion while locking her attention on the painting.

"Ignatius Jones is welcoming us and wishes to help us," Frances said. "He is welcoming you here, Annie. And also your grandmother and grandfather have come to us. What I am sensing here is that they are very proud of you."

"We were very close," Annie said.

The upper background behind Ignatius Jones' head and shoulders was deeper brown than on the poster.

"You told me that their names were Joe and Flora, but that's not what you called them, was it?"

"No."

Ignatius Jones' eyes looked darker than on her copy, almost pure black, but even so they seemed alive, an effect brought out by touches of red and white on their corneas.

"They are letting me know. Did you call them something like GranDad, GranGran…?"

"You're close on that," Annie replied. "GrandPops and Granny."

Frances said, "I'm sensing that they passed to spirit at almost the same time."

"Six months apart."

"I'm so sorry," Frances said. "There was suffering at the end."

"Cancer."

The jewel at the center of Ignatius Jones' gold ring glowed more than Annie recalled seeing on the poster, and its red was closer to purple, like amethyst.

"You carry their pictures with you, don't you Annie?" Frances asked.

"Yes, on my phone."

"They want you to know that they are aware when you look at their pictures and when you are thinking of them. Do you do that often, Annie?"

"Yes."

"They appreciate that, Annie. They know that you did what you could for them. They truly appreciate your love and support at the end. They wish they could have told you that more often than they did."

Despite herself, Annie felt tears coming. "It was the least I could do."

She imagined that she saw both of them standing before her, courtly GranPops with his shock of fine white hair, and Granny full of hustle and bustle as always, just as they looked before they got sick. She could have touched them, if she reached out.

Once back outside, Frances enveloped Annie in a hug.

"Watch what you say because of the surveillance cameras," Frances whispered, "Are you alright?"

"I'm fine," Annie whispered back.

"What I told you about your grandparents is true. I did hear from them."

"Thank you Frances," Annie said, finally pulling out from her hug, but still whispering. "I'll stop at the Loon Lake Inn to write up my notes but then I think I'll drive back to Boston."

"So you won't be at the Inn tonight?"

"I want to get back to Boston before my memory fades of the original painting."

"See you tomorrow, then," Frances said. "Drive safely."

Buddy and Murray watched from their office window. Frances pretended not to see them.

Fifty Five

FRANCES FOUND them staring intently at their monitors when she got to their office. She guessed that they'd scooted back to their desks when she entered the Residence after saying good-bye to Annie.

Buddy looked up innocently from his monitor as if Sister Frances had been the last thing on his mind. "Where's your client?"

Frances replied, "She returned to the Inn for a rest. She felt drained emotionally, hearing from her grandparents. They were very close."

"So it was a good session," Murray said.

"It was indeed. I'll send your share of her fee when I do my accounts at the end of the month. Will that be alright?"

"Sure," Murray said. "Also send us a copy of your credit card statement which shows her payment so that we can keep track."

"You want to check my math?"

"Yes."

Buddy said, "Your pilgrim who you sent to us is working out well."

"Teddie?"

"Yeah, Teddie," Buddy said. "It's good to have a resident electrical engineer."

"He's helping us with our security systems," Murray said.

"I'm so glad," Frances said.

Murray said, "Back to financial matters, we'll owe you a portion of our income from Teddie since you referred him to us."

"Thank you for reminding me," Frances said.

"But, truth is, he's contributing in ways that don't involve actual money so we won't have anything to send you, I'm afraid."

Anticipating Frances' reaction, Buddy grinned when Murray imparted this news.

"Okay," Frances replied. "No problem."

Buddy's grin faded.

"How is Lily doing as Messenger Charles' Consort?" Frances asked.

"She's doing terrific," Buddy said.

Frances stayed for dinner at the Center Café.

The Center's current crop of visiting psychic mediums came in and lined up at the counter, trays in hand, to make their dinner choices.

Frances counted fourteen women and three men. They appeared to range in age from their thirties to their seventies. Two were Asian, and one was black.

She was acquainted with several of them from spiritualist conventions, and some of the others she recognized from seeing their pictures online and in spiritualist journals.

Dusty Hellecker, an acquaintance from Minneapolis, stopped by. "Why Frances, what a surprise! What brings you to the Center?"

"A session with a client in the Portrait Room."

"So you were here before."

"In the first group, just after the Center opened."

"Well, welcome back," Dusty said, and proceeded on her way to join her group at another table.

Other diners entered. Frances figured they must be pilgrims. Two solemn-looking women apparently in their twenties were holding hands. A young man and woman came in with a child, a girl about ten years old.

And then Teddie entered, chatting with another couple whose boy, around thirteen or so, tagged along after them.

Teddie saw Frances and came over to her table.

"Dr. Gourmelon," he said. "It's good to see you."

"How are things working out for you here, Teddie?" Frances asked.

"Great!"

"Are you finding what you were looking for?"

"I am," Teddie said. "Messenger Charles has put me into contact with my father, and he and Ignatius Jones are helping me to learn about the spirit world. And now I'm memorizing my *Book of Ignatius Jones.*"

"Buddy said you've been helpful to the Center."

"Yep. I'm working on updating the security system."

"That certainly is important work," Frances said. "Well, I won't hold you, Teddie. I'll let you enjoy your dinner with your friends."

Lily entered. She came in alone, tall and regal in her white gown. She looked neither left nor right. Unlike everyone else, she didn't stop to grab a tray and stand in line at the counter. Instead, she went straight to a two-seater table at the back of the Café.

She sat with her hands clasped on her table, staring straight ahead. To Frances, she seemed to hold herself remote from everyone around her while also, at the same time, remaining excruciatingly aware of others' watching and judging, totally alone in a room full of people.

A Spiritualist Helper, not Becca, apparently a new hire, took Lily's dinner order and then returned to the kitchen.

Frances picked up her tray to join Lily at her table.

"I'm sorry, Dr. Gourmelon," Lily said. "That seat is reserved for Messenger Charles."

"I promise I'll move when he comes," Frances replied, placing her tray on the table and taking the seat.

"We can't talk here," Lily said.

"Just tell me, Lily dear, are you happy? Because you seem preoccupied."

Lily just looked at Frances, not answering.

"Lily…"

"I have accepted Ignatius Jones into my life and I'm Consort to his Messenger."

"My dear girl!"

The Spiritualist Helper brought Lily's dinner and laid it on the table before her: Roast chicken, rice, and asparagus; green salad on a separate plate; and a basket of bread that smelled freshly made.

"I also asked for ice water," Lily told her.

Her Spiritualist Helper apologized for not bringing it sooner, dashed off, and then returned quickly with a tall glass, a carafe of water, and a bowl filled with ice cubes.

Buddy appeared at the table. "Everything okay here?" he asked, staring at Lily.

"We're fine," Lily said. "Dr. Gourmelon just came by to say hello."

"And now I'm leaving," Frances said. "It was good to see you doing so well."

Buddy grinned at Frances. "Stay in touch."

Frances could feel Buddy's eyes on her as she dropped off her tray, so she didn't take a detour past Teddie's table as she left the Café. She did, however, catch Teddie's eye on her way out and she was fairly sure that he understood what she wanted him to do.

As Protector Jackson handed Frances the keys to her car, he asked, in a low voice, "Any news for the boys?"

"We're making progress," Frances whispered, "Just a few more weeks."

"I'll pass that along."

"Meanwhile, what's going on here? How is Lily doing?"

"I don't know. Buddy won't let me talk to her."

"What do you mean?"

"He says she has special duties as Consort and I've got to keep my distance so as not to distract her. He says it will go badly for both of us if I try to make contact with her."

"But you both work in the Center…"

"I never see her except in the Café, and she always sits alone where Buddy, or Ricky, can keep an eye on her. She never goes anywhere except with Ricky at her side."

"Has she tried to communicate with you?"

"No," Jackson said.

Fifty Six

"WHERE ARE YOU?" Frances asked when Teddie called her later that evening.

Teddie knew why she was asking.

"I'm out of range of the cameras," he said. "I'm sitting on the rock wall at the top of the driveway. I'm using my ear-bud so if anyone is watching, they'll think I'm just out here taking in the fresh air. I'll clear our call from my phone log after we're done."

"Good."

"Strange stuff going on here."

"Like what?"

"Like, every evening after dinner we all have to meet to hear Messenger Charles lecture us about Ignatius Jones and read to us from his *Book*. All of that's fine, but then he does his 'trust' thing. We're all supposed to participate. He asks us, 'Do you trust me?' and we respond, 'We trust you Messenger Charles,' and then he asks, 'Do you trust me completely?' and we chant, 'With all our hearts and minds, we trust you, Messenger Charles.'"

"People in my group wouldn't have responded quite that way," Frances said. Then, thinking of Tammy Bell, she added, "With one exception."

"The pilgrims really get into it," Teddie said. "The staff too, while Buddy is watching them. The visiting psychics, not so much, except for the ones who are signing on as psychic guides. Also, Messenger Charles talks about a 'Gathering' which he says will allow each of us to have our own personal encounters with Ignatius Jones. One of the visitors asked what he meant. He said all will be revealed when the time is right."

"How is Buddy preparing for the attack they're expecting from the local boys?"

"He runs a training camp in the field behind the Residence every morning for his Protectors and two pilgrim men he conscripted. It's like an alarm clock. They start firing their guns at six o'clock, Bam! Bam! Bam! They also practice hand-to-hand combat they're being taught by a Protector who's an Iraq war veteran, Protector William, which seems to involve a lot of shouting. Then when that's done, they stand at attention for Buddy to inspect them before they're dismissed to get breakfast."

"Have you gone out for that?"

"No. And so far, Buddy hasn't pushed me. I think he's still trying to figure me out because you recruited me. The way he acts when your name is mentioned, I don't think he likes you, Aunt Frances."

"I'm not his favorite psychic," Frances said.

Teddie said, "Like I told you in the Café, Messenger Charles channeled my father during our sessions in the Portrait Room."

"So now you accept that we can communicate with spirits?"

"I wouldn't go that far, Aunt Frances, but Charles did seem aware of things about my father. He apologized for what he described as my father's indifference. Even as a spirit, apparently he doesn't want anything to do with me."

"I did warn my sister Portia about your father."

"Well, if she'd listened to you, I wouldn't be here, so I'm glad she didn't."

Frances said, "You also told me in the Café that you're working on the Center's security system."

"Yep. Murray asked me to check on it and to recommend fixes they might need."

"What do they have, Teddie?"

"Well, you know about the video cameras covering public spaces inside the Residence and House of Spirits, and the areas just outside the buildings, plus at Messenger Charles' house in Woodstock. A motion detector system in the Portrait Room sets off an alarm if the painting is moved. They have a door-locking system in the House of Spirits so that all the doors in the building are locked remotely in case of a threat to the painting."

"Can these doors be opened from the inside?"

"No, neither from inside or outside. Once the system is engaged, the doors can be opened only by command from the video monitoring room. It's designed to trap anyone who might try to steal the painting."

"Hmm," Frances said.

"They've installed an electric fence around the perimeter of the property in the back that will shock anyone who touches it. A break in the fence also triggers a loud alarm throughout the Center."

"Can you access these systems, Teddie?"

"I can and do, Aunt Frances. Murray gave me the passwords so I could conduct my tests."

"Teddie, dear boy, if I were to ask you to switch off the security systems inside the Portrait Room for a few minutes, could you do that?"

"Yes, although I'd have to be inside the video monitoring room at the time. And the system would record when and how long the security in the Portrait Room was down. This time gap would be visible to anyone who reviewed the files."

"What if they suffered a power failure?"

"The Center has an electric power generator for backup."

"You know where I'm going with this, don't you, Teddie?"

"Yes, Aunt. You're going to ask me to turn off security in the Portrait Room."

"It could be dangerous for you, dear boy."

"And for you, Aunt, if you're locked in there."

"I know," Frances said. "I'm working on that."

Fifty Seven

THE PORTIONS of Annie's copy that couldn't be fixed by touching up or by painting over, she scraped off her canvas and started fresh.

Now that she'd seen the original, Annie understood better how Desmond Wilkins achieved his effects. She mimicked his use of color accents and his brushstrokes in his rendering of Ignatius Jones' face and in his more loosely brushed representation of his subject's clothing, his jacket, buttons, and cravat.

She spent a whole day reproducing Desmond Wilkins' treatment of Ignatius Jones' eyes.

Starting each morning at eight o'clock, she worked steadily all day taking short breaks only for snacks and to stretch.

Finally, after a week of this, she told Frances, "It's finished."

Once again, Frances compared Annie's copy to the poster and to Tessa's photos, and again, from what she could tell, they looked identical. And, recalling the original painting, Frances thought that Annie's copy matched exactly the original's colors, light, and intensity. Ignatius Jones seemed to reach out from Annie's copy as he did from the original.

As an additional check, Frances examined Annie's copy not as an image of a person but rather as a composition of shapes, colors, and textures. She compared Annie's version to the poster reproduction, segment by segment, starting at the bottom and working up to the top. She found no discernible differences.

"You've done it," Frances said. "You've made a virtually perfect copy of the Desmond Wilkins portrait of Ignatius Jones."

Annie contemplated her creation. She did feel good about it. It could pass as Desmond Wilkin's masterpiece; unless, of course, it were examined by an art expert or scanned with a black light.

"How long until it dries?" Frances asked.

"Figure on a week to become dry to the touch," Annie said. "Two weeks to be safer."

"Then, two weeks from now, I'll pay another visit to the Portrait Room."

"You mean, *we'll* pay another visit. I'm going with you."

"Too dangerous, my dear. I can't ask you to do that. It's enough that you've created this marvelous copy."

"How will you get back into the Portrait Room without a client?"

"I'll bring Martyn Zimmer. You met him at the Loon Lake Inn."

"Dr. Gourmelon," Annie said, "You can ask anyone who knows me, I always finish what I start. Always. I'm not going to bail on you now. You and Martyn Zimmer don't know how to handle paintings, not like I do. You need me there. So if you want to return to the Center with my copy, you have to take me with you."

Just for emphasis, Annie took hold of her painting as if she were about to carry it away.

"Are you very sure that's what you want, Annie dear?" Frances asked.

"I'm positive."

"Alright," Frances said. "I give up. Two weeks from now, *we'll* return to the Center."

She called Murray to schedule a second session in the Portrait Room with her client Annie Kane.

"Two weeks from today, on October 24th," Frances said. "I want the last session in the afternoon."

"Why is that, Sister Frances?" asked Murray.

"I have an appointment in the morning here in Boston that I can't break. We'll be driving up once that's over and you never know about traffic, so I'll need your latest afternoon slot."

"Let me check," Murray said.

He brought the Center's calendar up on his screen and clicked forward to October 24th, the third Friday in October, as Frances requested. He typed 'Sister Frances with client Annie Kane' into the six thirty slot.

"I've got you in the Portrait Room at six thirty," he said. "That's our latest time."

"Precisely at six thirty?" she repeated back to him.

"Yes."

"Good. By the way, separate topic, have you verified that the security system is operating properly? Now that I'm recruiting pilgrims like Teddie Bulger and bringing clients to the Center, I wouldn't want anything to happen to the painting."

"Teddie has checked our security system very thoroughly," Murray said.

"It would make me feel so much more comfortable if he'd check it again."

"No problem."

"In fact, perhaps he could be on duty while we're there on the 24th so that we can be completely sure everything is working."

"Good idea, Sister Frances," Murray said. "I'll take care of it."

"I'm so glad," Frances said. "One can never be too careful."

"I agree."

"What do you know about the Gathering that Messenger Charles has talked about?"

"Charlie told me that it was an event foretold by Ignatius Jones that will bring joy to all of us, like an epiphany. When I asked Buddy, he just grinned at me, the way he does."

"Will you let me know if you find out more?"

"Sure," Murray said, "Meanwhile, we'll look forward to seeing you and your client here on October 24th, at six thirty."

Frances texted Protector Jackson. "Call me."

Jackson called about an hour later.

"Are you outside, away from the cameras?"

"Yes, I'm inspecting the fence."

"Time for you to talk to the boys again."

"What do I tell them?"

"Their time is coming, two weeks from now."

Frances explained.

Jackson said that he would let them know.

"Is there anything else that I can do?" he asked.

"Just behave normally. Do what Buddy says."

Frances texted the same message to Teddie, "Call me."

"What's going on, Aunt Frances?" he asked, when he called her ten minutes later.

She told him.

Fifty Eight

PSYCHIC TAMMY BELL couldn't believe the awful news she heard when she turned on her radio at breakfast.

The story was confirmed in sickening detail on the front page of her *Philadelphia Inquirer*: Shawn Berwick was found alive in a house in Bala Cynwyd just outside Philadelphia.

Shawn had been missing for four years. He disappeared when he was six years old, last seen by neighbors out riding his bicycle.

Now, out of the blue, he turns up *alive*.

On the radio, and in the morning paper, the story was repeated *ad nauseam*, covering every possible angle. Neighbors reported seeing a school-age boy at home during school hours. A social worker called on the house. The man and woman who came to the door looked scraggly, and unkempt, and seemed evasive. They claimed initially that Shawn was their son and was staying home because he was sick. Then they said they were taking care of him for relatives, then that he was adopted. The social worker became suspicious. She asked to be let into the house to talk with Shawn. The couple refused. Then she called the police.

Police identified Shawn based on photographs that were taken just before he disappeared and age-progressed to show how he would look at ten years of age. His identity was confirmed by unique marks on his lower back, and a DNA test removed any remaining doubt.

Shawn's parents, Mark and Jean Berwick, were staying with Shawn in Hahnemann University Hospital where he was being evaluated for physical and mental trauma. First reports from the hospital indicated that Shawn was in generally good health.

Good news for almost everyone involved, but not so much for psychic Tammy Bell who, after Shawn went missing, had informed Mark and Jean that their son was dead.

She'd also shared with the Philadelphia police her insight, based on what she received from Shawn's spirit, that his body was buried in a park not far from a playground. Police squads and their cadaver dogs searched parks all over the city, all the while trailed by media crews. Understandably, in retrospect, they failed to locate the young boy's remains, although they did discover several adult bodies so their efforts were not entirely fruitless.

Tammy's dreadful revelations generated headlines such as "Psychic Tammy Bell To Shawn's Mom and Dad: Your Boy is Dead," and "Psychic Tells Cops: Tip From Shawn, Search Near Playgrounds for My Body."

Now, reporters would be calling, asking snarky questions.

In fact, she *had* sensed a presence. The voice she heard sounded like a boy's voice. There was a lot of noise, as always, but she could make out words, like 'Shawn,' for example. So she hadn't totally invented her messages from the lost boy, as some might claim, even though she did fill in the gaps.

She rehearsed what she would tell the reporters, "I'm delighted for Shawn and for his parents." And, "Psychics are people and like anyone else, we can make mistakes."

They would accuse her of tormenting Shawn's parents when they were most vulnerable. Never mind that at the time, Shawn's mother claimed that she still believed Shawn was alive, so it wasn't like Tammy caused the mother to give up hope, but still.

And the taunts would follow.

"Do you have any more leads on where the body is buried?"

"What else did Shawn's spirit tell you?"

If that weren't enough, her relationship with the Ignatius Jones Center for Spiritualist Discovery had taken a bad turn ever since Messenger Charles made Lily Prestowicz his Consort.

He had no more time for Sister Tammy, his first Psychic Guide. When she phoned to report on her progress recruiting more pilgrims, he expressed only perfunctory gratitude and he never asked how she was doing otherwise.

Obviously, Messenger Charles didn't care about her now that he was entertained by his blonde teenager slut.

Mostly her phone calls got through only to Murray or Buddy, and messages that she left for Messenger Charles were frequently not delivered, or so Charles claimed.

She had recruited more pilgrims than anyone else, nine in all, including two children in pilgrim families who represented the future of the Center, and she had not yet received a single payment. She knew for a fact that her pilgrims had donated significant sums to the Center. She was due a share of that money. Murray kept assuring her that her compensation was being processed and would be sent momentarily, but it never arrived.

They'd discover that Tammy Bell would not play their fool.

They owed her respect, money, and gratitude, and they would give her what they owed.

Otherwise, she'd expose to the world their plan to murder Tessa Pruitt, a plan that she wormed out of Protector Ricky with no difficulty at all since his very large body was operated by a very small brain.

Tammy had no issue with their plan to murder Tessa. The girl deserved to be punished for swearing falsely on the *Book of Ignatius Jones*. However, the authorities would undoubtedly take a different view.

Tammy decided to get out of Philadelphia until the Shawn Berwick fiasco quieted down.

Murray picked up when she called.

"Sister Tammy, what a pleasure," he said.

"Is Messenger Charles available?" asked Tammy.

"He's out at the moment. Shall I take a message?"

"No point, since it seems he doesn't get my messages."

"Well, I'll make sure he gets this one," Murray said.

"Never mind. Just let him know that I'll see him in person tomorrow evening."

"You will? Will you be visiting us tomorrow?"

"Yes, Murray. Can you arrange to have my room at the Residence ready for me?"

"Of course, Sister Tammy," Murray said. "We all look forward to seeing you."

"I'm sure you do," Tammy said.

PORTRAIT OF IGNATIUS JONES

Murray noted in the Center's online calendar for Friday, October 24th, "Sister Tammy arriving. Prepare room in Residence."

Fifty Nine

FRANCES LOCKED THE DOOR to Martyn Zimmer's office, which she and Annie were borrowing for a delicate procedure.

"Being plump has its benefits," Frances said.

She lifted off her purple muumuu and dropped it over the chair beside her.

She was dressed now only in her slip and bra. She'd sewn plastic clips onto each of her bra straps in front, just below her shoulders. The clips, shaped like clothespins, were tiny but they had strong springs and serrated jaws.

She spread parchment paper on Martyn's desk.

Annie removed her copy of the Desmond Wilkins portrait of Ignatius Jones from its flat box where it was stored during their car ride from Boston, laid it face down on the parchment paper, and then pulled out the tacks that she had used to fasten the canvas to its stretcher.

She clipped the canvas to Frances' bra-straps, with the painted side facing out so that Frances' body heat wouldn't come directly into contact with the paint.

Then she used the same bra-strap clips to hold a sheet of white silk in front of the painting, to protect it from rubbing against Frances' muumuu when she moved or was sitting.

322

PORTRAIT OF IGNATIUS JONES

A nylon band around Frances' thigh was held in place by Velcro and by a suspender connected to a belt around Frances' waist. Two cotton pockets were sewn onto the band and hung from it on the inside of her thigh. In one of the pockets, Frances placed a wooden-handled tool designed to pull the tacks that attach a painting to its stretcher. In the second pocket, Frances placed a claw hammer with a rubber handle and hard plastic head. She secured both tools in their respective pockets with Velcro strips on the tops and bottoms of the pockets.

Then Frances raised her arms and Annie fitted her muumuu back on, over her arms, so that it covered her body and her attachments.

They left their bare wood stretcher, tacks, and carrying box in Martyn's office, with a note. "We'll pick these up on our way back to Boston."

Frances also left in Martyn's office his poster of the portrait of Ignatius Jones, with a second note, "Thanks! I owe you, Frances."

On October 24th, the sun sank behind the hill west of Route 100A and the Ignatius Jones Center for Spiritualist Discovery at five forty in the afternoon.

Twilight was giving way to dusk at the Center when Frances and Annie arrived there forty minutes later, at twenty minutes after six.

Protector Brian took their car and they walked directly and in Frances' case, very stiffly, to the Portrait Room.

Ricky met them at the entrance, blocking the door.

"Let me have your phones, anything that can be used as a camera, sharp objects, and any liquids."

He collected their cellphones, pens, and pencils.

"Any liquids?"

"No," Frances said.

"How about you?" Ricky asked Annie.

"No for me, as well," she replied.

"I have to examine your purses."

He rummaged through them, opening plastic containers of aspirin and Tylenol that Frances was carrying, opening glasses cases, feeling the purse material for hidden compartments.

"Now raise your arms," Ricky said. "I've got to wand you."

"Is that totally necessary?" Frances asked. "Our session in the Portrait Room is scheduled to start in two minutes."

"Guess you should have arrived sooner."

He waved his handheld device over Annie's body, up one side and down the other, and along each of her arms. It squawked when he passed it near her chest.

"That's my bra," Annie said. "Do you need to take a look at it?"

"No, no, that's okay," Ricky said. Then, leering, "Unless you want me to."

"Hurry it up," Frances said. "We've driven a long way for this session and I'll make sure Messenger Charles hears about it if you waste our precious time for your nonsense."

"Just doing my job."

"Be that as it may, let me remind you that I'm a Psychic Guide in the Ignatius Jones Center for Spiritualist Discovery, where you work on the staff, which means you work for me, and I will not take it kindly if you run that infernal thing around my body."

PORTRAIT OF IGNATIUS JONES

Although Frances' curly grey hair reached only as high as Ricky's chest, she leaned her square frame towards him and glared up at him like Winston Churchill defying the Nazi horde, daring him to raise the wand towards her.

Ricky wilted.

"You may go in," he said, standing aside and opening the door to the Portrait Room.

At six thirty two, Frances and Annie descended the stairs in the Portrait Room down towards the stage.

They each took a chair facing the portrait.

Frances said, "Annie, I'm going now to ask Ignatius Jones for his help in bringing us back into contact with your GranPop and Granny."

"Thank you, Dr. Gourmelon."

"Ignatius Jones knows that you love them and that you miss them."

"I do."

"I'm receiving something now from GranPop. He's so proud of your work, Annie. And Granny is too."

"I know they were."

"They are, Annie. They are still. But I'm sensing a question from Granny."

After a pause, as if she was overhearing a conversation, Frances said, "What I'm sensing, I think, it's very personal, Annie, it's about your plans to have a family. She wants to know when..."

It had gotten dark out on the field and woods behind the Residence when, at six forty, alarms connected to the fence began honking, blurting, and beeping.

"The fence is cut!" Buddy shouted, running out of his office, and down towards the area where Protectors and pilgrim volunteers were trained to muster in emergencies.

On his way, he stopped at the tool room and unlocked the Center's new gun cabinet. He grabbed pistols and rifles and ammo and stuffed them in an athletic bag.

The floodlights behind the Residence illuminated the portion of the field that was close to the buildings but they did not reach farther down towards the stream where now there were brilliant flashes, followed by bangs, and then the pop-pop-pop of gunfire.

Buddy handed out firearms to Protectors Brian, William, and Jackson, and to pilgrim Henry, a heavy-set man in his early forties.

"Where the bloody hell is Ricky?" Buddy shouted.

"At his post at the Portrait Room," Protector Brian said.

"Get him now. We need everyone here."

Teddie was busy working on a software problem in the video monitoring room. When he heard the alarms, he followed protocol by setting the remote locking system for the House of Spirits. Then he deviated somewhat from protocol by disabling the video and motion detector systems inside the Portrait Room.

The lights in the Portrait Room blinked. Frances' watch gave the time as six forty plus thirty seconds. She glanced up at the two video cameras. The red lights on both of them had gone dark.

In what could only be described as complete panic, Teddie flipped the Center's other video cameras off, and on, and off again.

He announced over the PA system, "This is Pilgrim Teddie Bulger. We are under attack. All defenders are requested to join Buddy in the mustering area immediately. All others at the Center are instructed to stay in their rooms with their doors bolted until further notice."

When the alarms sounded, Protector Ricky realized the Center's peril. After all his practice on the firing range behind the Center, now at last he could shoot at real live targets.

First, however, he had to secure the Portrait Room. Sister Frances and her client would have to be pulled out even if they did have time remaining on their session. He lunged to open the door but it was locked, and his card-key didn't work. He was about to call Buddy, or Murray, when he heard banging at the entrance to the House of Spirits.

Protector Brian was outside, hammering on the door. He yelled, "Buddy sent me to get you, man!"

"Gourmelon and her client are still in there," Protector Ricky said. "I can't leave until they're out."

"This door is locked." Brian said. "Can you open it from the inside?"

Protector Ricky remembered: The remote locking system.

"Shit! I can't. The House of Spirits is locked down in emergencies. I'll have to wait here."

"I'll tell Buddy," Brian shouted. "At least with you in there and all the doors locked, the painting is safe."

Messenger Charles was back at his house in Woodstock, resting during his quiet away-time while visitors met with Ignatius Jones. As usual, he'd left orders not to be disturbed except for the direst emergency.

His cellphone rang.

"What is it?" he demanded.

Buddy said, "We're being attacked. They've come across the fence. There's gunfire, and explosions."

Indeed, Charles could hear loud banging from Buddy's end of the call.

"Where is everyone?" Charles asked.

"Our defenders are with me, our Protectors and defender pilgrims, except for Protector Ricky, who's trapped in the House of Spirits because of lock down. Everyone else has been instructed to stay in their rooms."

"Including Sister Lily?"

"Yes."

"What about Murray?"

"I assume he's still in our office," Buddy said. "He said he'd wait there for me."

"Don't let him leave the Center," Charles said. "I'm on my way. Push the attackers back. Keep them away from our buildings. They may try to burn us down."

"Don't worry," Buddy said. "We're better armed this time."

"If you see them coming, shoot them, Buddy."

"We will," Buddy said.

"Good. And be ready in case this means the Gathering has started."

"I am ready, Messenger Charles."

Charles slipped into his pocket the switchblade knife that he purchased so that he would be equipped for the sacrifices to be carried out in the Portrait Room.

"I'm leaving now," Charles said. "I'll be there in twenty minutes or less."

Sixty

"SHOWTIME!" FRANCES SAID.

She lifted the original Desmond Wilkins portrait of Ignatius Jones off of its hooks on its pillar, and laid it face down on the hardwood floor.

She raised her arms and Annie pulled her muumuu over her head, and draped it on a chair.

She unclipped Annie's copy of the painting from her bra straps and laid it on the floor, next to the original.

She took the claw hammer from its cloth pocket on her thigh and handed it to Annie, like she was handing a scalpel to a surgeon. Annie used it to pull the nails that were securing the original painting and its stretcher inside its frame. She stored the nails in one of her shoes.

Frances handed Annie the tack-pulling tool. Annie removed each of the tacks that fastened the canvas of the original painting to its stretcher, and dropped the tacks inside her other shoe.

Annie laid the original Desmond Wilkins canvas on the floor several feet away from where they were working.

Then, Annie centered her own canvas on the original painting's stretcher. After folding the canvas edges over the stretcher, she pressed in the tacks through the existing holes in the canvas and into the existing holes in the stretcher underneath the canvas.

She positioned her copy, now attached to the stretcher, inside the frame. She tapped in the old nails to hold it in place.

She hung her copy of the portrait of Ignatius Jones on the pillar.

Frances slid the hammer and tack puller tool into their respective pockets on her thigh strap, and locked them in with Velcro.

With Annie's help, she clipped the original Desmond Wilkins canvas and its silk protector to her bra straps.

Annie lifted Frances' muumuu over her head, letting it down carefully to cover her slip, the painting, and the tools.

Forty eight minutes after six. The switch took just over seven minutes, a minute faster than their best practice run.

At six fifty, the red lights on the video cameras in the Portrait Room came back on.

Frances was saying, "Granny knew you would make good decisions, Annie. She supported you, whatever you did."

"That's true," Annie said. "It meant…"

The door to the Portrait Room was thrown open. Protector Ricky called down, "You've got to leave now, Sister Frances. We're evacuating the House of Spirits"

"Why?" Frances asked. "Has something happened?"

"You heard nothing?" Ricky asked, incredulous. "I was banging on the door."

"Not a thing. We're soundproofed in here. We were communicating with Annie's grandparents. What happened?"

"The Center was under attack. They cut the fence, and they were shooting."

"What do you mean?" Frances asked. "Shooting guns?"

"Guns?" Annie asked. "Did you say *guns*?"

Ricky said, "Don't worry. We scared them off."

"I have to leave now," Annie said. "I won't stay where people are shooting guns."

"We'll leave as soon as I settle accounts with Murray," Frances said.

"No, no, no, right now!" Annie demanded, her voice rising in panic. "Call him later!"

"Okay, dear, we'll leave now," Frances said. "Protector Ricky, can you give us back our stuff and then get my car for us?"

"I have to stay at my post here, Sister Frances," Ricky said. "Sorry."

Annie screamed, "I've got to leave NOW!"

Frances told Ricky, "I'm afraid Annie is in a very fragile state. She can't manage this kind of stress. Perhaps you can call Protector Jackson to get our car."

"I'll need a go-ahead from Buddy."

Frances said, with a gritty edge to her voice that was startling, coming from her, "Last chance, Ricky, before I make some calls on my own."

Frances had stared down many tough guys in her time, beginning with neighborhood thugs when she was growing up in Boston's North End. Ricky was large and not too bright, but he got the message.

"I'll get ahold of Protector Jackson," he said.

"Good decision," Frances said. "Please hurry."

Buddy split his defenders into two groups.

He assigned Protector Jackson and the two pilgrim volunteers to remain close to the Center in case a second attack targeted the buildings.

Then, carrying large flashlights, and with their guns at the ready, he and Protectors William and Brian went to check the electric fence where it had been cut, and then to patrol the property down by the stream where they'd heard gunfire and seen muzzle flashes.

The acrid smell of gunpowder from explosives and gunfire hung in the air but they saw no one as they raked their flashlight beams back and forth across the property. No signs of the intruders. All was quiet. Nothing down near the stream except for birds, croaking frogs, and their own footsteps and heavy breathing.

"They could be hiding in the woods, watching us," Protector William said. "We're sitting ducks out here."

Buddy considered firing into the woods to put a scare into whoever was there. But then, recalling Sergeant Lawrence's warning, he decided against it. They'd have a problem if they shot someone who was technically not trespassing on their property. Also, the defenders back at the Center might mistake their gunfire for another attack and start shooting at *them*.

"Let's get back to the buildings," Buddy said. "Good work, men. We taught our enemies a lesson tonight."

Sixty One

CHARLES FOUND nothing out of place in the Portrait Room.

Everything looked normal. His portrait of Ignatius Jones still hung where it was supposed to. The two chairs down on the stage had presumably been left there after the last session with the portrait.

"No one came in or out of here?" he asked Protector Ricky.

"No one, except for Sister Frances and her client," Ricky replied.

"Frances Gourmelon was inside the Portrait Room during the attack?"

"Yes, Messenger Charles, but all of our doors were locked. She was in here until it was over."

"Where is she now?"

"She left. Her client was screaming about the gunfire."

"So she's gone."

"Yes."

"Let's look around again," he told Murray and Buddy.

Again, they didn't see anything unusual. Everything in the Portrait Room seemed to be in order.

Buddy said, "Let's check the videos."

Pilgrim Teddie Bulger was still in the video monitoring room when Messenger Charles, Murray, and Buddy crowded in.

"Rack up the videos from the Portrait Room from six thirty on," Messenger Charles said.

They saw Sister Frances and her client enter the Portrait Room at six thirty two and descend towards the stage. Sister Frances set up their chairs facing the portrait, where the chairs still remained when Messenger Charles inspected the room.

They heard her say that she was in touch with Ignatius Jones who would help her to communicate with 'GranPop' and 'Granny.' Then she was telling her client that 'Granny' was proud of her but also concerned about her plans for a family when, at six forty, the video stopped.

"It just went off," Charles said. "What happened?"

"We were having problems in the whole security system," Teddie said. "All of our cameras were cycling between off and on. I don't know why. Maybe as a result of the electric fence being cut. Maybe there was a surge."

"That's just great!" Charles said. He whirled towards Murray. "You're our security genius. Did you know about this?"

"I'm finding out now for the first time," Murray said. "Just like you."

Wheeling back to Teddie, Charles asked, "Who are you, again?"

"I'm pilgrim Teddie Bulger, Messenger Charles. I was with you in the Portrait Room when you were in contact with my father."

"Why are you here in the video monitoring room?"

"I'm an electrical engineer. I was asked to help out with the security system."

"Who asked you?"

"I did," Murray interjected. "I thought it would be a good idea to get someone in here who knows what he's doing."

Charles said, "So, Teddie Bulger, how did you become one of our pilgrims?"

"I was searching for more meaning for my life and Dr. Gourmelon said I should consider the Center."

"You've got to be shitting me!"

"No, why?"

"Gourmelon recruits you into the Center as a pilgrim, and she just happens to be in the Portrait Room when the Center is attacked and we lose video, at the same time that you just happen to be at the controls in the video monitoring room?"

"I don't understand," Teddie said. "Dr. Gourmelon told me wonderful things about the Center. I thought she was well regarded here."

"Of course she is," Murray said. "Why don't we watch the video where it comes on again?"

At six fifty, the video system was restored and showed Frances and her client still in their seats, facing the portrait. Frances was reporting that 'Granny' would support her client's decisions when the door to the Portrait Room opened and Protector Ricky yelled down that they had to leave.

"What about the motion detector?" Charles asked.

"That got turned off as well," Teddie said. "There was a lot of confusion."

Back in the office, Charles told Murray, "From now on, keep Teddie Bulger away from our security system."

"It wasn't his fault," Murray said.

"Maybe it wasn't, maybe it was. I don't know."

"Alright," Murray said.

"Why didn't I know earlier about Gourmelon and Bulger, that she recruited him?"

"You were copied on all the documents, Charlie. Seems you've been too busy lately to read them."

"Have you forgotten, Murray? I'm *Messenger Charles* to you, not *Charlie*."

"Right. *Messenger Charles*."

"Send Gourmelon a message for me. She's done here. No more Psychic Guide. No more visits to the Portrait Room. No more visits to the Center, period. I don't want to see her again. Ever. She's not welcome."

"Fine."

Charles stared hard at Murray.

"You let Bulger get his hands on our security system."

"I told you why. He's an electrical engineer. He knows how these systems work."

"Yeah, well..."

"What?" Murray asked.

"You, too. You stay out of our security system. Leave it to Buddy."

"Wait..."

"No. No more waiting."

Turning to Buddy, he said, "Buddy, keep Murray out of the video monitoring room. Let our Protectors know. He's not allowed in. You got that?"

337

"Got it, Messenger Charles," Buddy said.

Turning back to Murray, Charles said, "And also stay the fuck out of the Portrait Room until further notice."

"If that's what you want," Murray said.

"Yeah, and if you think it's because I don't trust you, you're reading me correctly. And Murray…"

"Yes?"

"Don't wander off. You know we'll find you."

Teddie Bulger asked Protector Jackson to fetch his car.

"Are you leaving us?" Jackson asked.

"I'm afraid so. Things haven't worked out here for me as well as I hoped."

He left a note addressed to Messenger Charles on the bed in his Residence dorm room.

"Dear Messenger Charles, I am not well suited for the life of a pilgrim here at the Center so I am leaving to explore other paths. I'll always be grateful to you and to the spirit of Ignatius Jones for the insights you have shared with me. With love and my complete trust, Pilgrim Teddie."

Sixty Two

AD THE GATHERING STARTED?

The Center was attacked. The attackers were armed. They had explosives. Casings from high-explosive fireworks were found on the property down near the stream.

But why then were there no bullet shells, nor footprints or other disturbances on the property?

"Looks like they stayed outside the fence even after they cut it," Buddy said. "They must have been scared off when they saw us coming after them."

But that makes no sense, Charles thought. The attackers had to expect the Center would be defended. Why didn't they exploit their initial advantage of surprise?

Was it a coincidence that the video cameras and motion detector failed in the Portrait Room at the very moments when they were most needed? And that when these events occurred, Pilgrim Teddie, who was sponsored by Frances Gourmelon, was left in charge of the security system?

Gourmelon! From the first moment he laid eyes on her in her multicolored muumuu, Charles knew she would be trouble. She doubted him as Messenger. She helped blasphemer Tessa Pruitt escape. But the Portrait Room looked the same after

339

Gourmelon's session there with her client. The portrait of Ignatius Jones remained in its place on the pillar, as it was before.

Charles couldn't identify any specific effects of the night's events, but something had changed, he was sure of it.

He needed to consult with Ignatius Jones.

Nothing! Charles stared fixedly into the dark eyes of Ignatius Jones and received nothing. Silence. Dead air.

He checked that he had disarmed the video cameras. Their red lights were dark. He asked, speaking aloud, "Where are you? Have you deserted your Messenger?"

The only presence in the Portrait Room at that moment, either in the physical world or in spirit, was Charles himself.

His neck hurt more than usual. He pulled his shoulders and elbows back to stretch his muscles. Maybe he was too distracted to receive messages from the Other Side.

He had to decide soon about the Gathering.

Perhaps Ignatius Jones' silence was a test of his readiness to make a conscious choice for sacrifice.

Sister Tammy ventured out of her room after the all-clear.

She was still tired after her long drive. It didn't help her mood that she was awakened from her nap by banging noises, and explosions, and people yelling, and then the PA system ordering everyone to stay in their rooms with their doors bolted.

She saw Buddy in the hallway. He seemed to be in a hurry. He looked down a stairwell, then opened the door to a supply room, peered inside, and slammed it closed. She noticed that he had a handgun holstered on his belt.

He was striding past her when she stopped him. He looked annoyed to be waylaid, which she didn't care in the slightest about. She asked, "What was all that commotion?"

"The Center was attacked," Buddy said. "We drove them off."

"So it's safe now?"

"Yes, Sister Tammy, all safe now."

When Buddy started to move on, down the hall, Tammy said, "Hold on, Buddy, I'm not finished."

"What is it?"

"I need to talk with Messenger Charles."

"He's not available at the moment."

Here we go again, thought Tammy.

"Buddy, just take me to him, now."

"As I said, he is unavailable."

Tammy's smile became as rigid as an uplifted middle finger.

"You'd better make him available or I'll let the world know about your plans to kill Tessa Pruitt."

Buddy said, "I don't know..."

"Yes, you do know, Buddy. The bridge at Quechee Gorge. The whole thing. Messenger Charles *will* talk with me. The Center will pay what I am owed. I will be treated with respect. You, Buddy Choate, will do as I say, or so help me..."

No way was Buddy going to dump this fresh steaming pile of psychic turdstew in front of Messenger Charles who had enough to contend with right now. There was no time or space to deal with Sister Tammy's complaints. How had she found out about Quechee Gorge? And now she was trying to push him around like Gourmelon did, and like the nuns did before her?

341

"Let's discuss this in your room, Sister Tammy," said Buddy. He willed his tone to sound calm and sympathetic. He reached out to guide her back to her room. She snatched her arm away.

"Don't touch me," she said. "We'll discuss it right here."

Thinking fast, Buddy said, "I'll take you to Messenger Charles. He's at his house in Woodstock. You can drive us there in your car."

"Fine."

"Protector Ricky will bring your car around to the front of the Residence. Can you meet us there in ten minutes?"

"I'll be there," Tammy said. "Don't keep me waiting."

Buddy called Ricky.

"Different psychic, same plan," he said.

"Looking forward to it," Ricky said.

Sixty Three

NEXT MORNING, Charles posted a note on the bulletin board in the Center Café.

Fellow believers: The Center is operating normally after the disturbances of last night. I can personally assure you that the Center is well-protected by our defenders, and there is no cause for alarm concerning our safety here. Fortunately, the spirit of Ignatius Jones remains with us as always in the Portrait Room. Yours sincerely, in his name, Messenger Charles.

Nevertheless, the visiting psychics' sessions that day in the Portrait Room did not go well.

Five minutes in, Kevin Sugino, a psychic based in San Diego, pushed up from his chair, declaring, "Waste of time."

Judy Belle Obermeyer, from Memphis, stayed on the stage for her full fifteen minutes. She sighed heavily, shifted her weight from one large buttock to the other, leaned forward with her head in her hands, and moaned imprecations. When she stood and turned to leave, her face was red and slicked with perspiration. "I don't know what happened," she said. "We communicated before."

Cristina Morales from New Mexico allowed a little over two minutes before giving up, shaking her head as she left the Portrait Room.

Prue Wilson, from Concord, New Hampshire, tried for five minutes. Salli Levy from Chicago, five minutes. Bruce Chatwin, from Newark, two minutes. The others decided not to bother. They followed Bruce Chatwin out of the Portrait Room.

Later that afternoon, Protector Ricky accompanied Lily to the Portrait Room.

He checked her purse and then, smirking, held the door open for her and bowed her through.

"Have fun," he said, giving her a broad wink.

She ignored him.

Down on the stage, Charles fingered the switchblade knife in one of the pockets of his robe.

If the Gathering had started, it was not happening in the way that he expected. He needed guidance from Ignatius Jones.

Lily's sacrifice will bring Ignatius Jones back to us.

He watched Lily descend the stairs to the stage. She stopped there, facing the portrait.

Standing close behind her, Charles reached around her to grasp her breasts, and pressed himself against her.

Lily jumped like she'd been shocked. She shook him off. "What are you doing? Who said you could touch me like that?"

She saw him now as he really was, not as Ignatius Jones, but as Charles Philip Tucker, a gross old man with jowls, puffy eyes, and a reptilian smile.

"You are my Consort," Charles said.

"No," Lily said. "You're repulsive."

She pushed past him to leave the Portrait Room.

"Wait!" Charles said.

Lily turned to face him.

Charles held the switchblade knife hidden in his hand. It would take but a second to flick out the blade. Even if she didn't give herself willingly to the sacrifice, he could still easily reach her with the knife to send her to spirit.

She scowled. "What?"

Charles took a step towards her.

She didn't back up. She wasn't afraid of him; he was just an old man.

Charles was about to open his knife when he realized, looking at Lily, that she meant nothing to him. The girl standing in front of him was only a teenager with a bad attitude, a virtual stranger. Sacrificing her would be pointless. He slipped his knife back into his pocket.

"Never mind."

"Fine," she said. "Pervert."

She stalked up the stairs.

Charles wasn't sorry to see her go.

They had nothing in common apart from Ignatius Jones and it occurred to Charles, as he stood alone with the portrait, that he no longer found the great psychic to be as compelling as he once did.

Later that evening, Sergeant Zach Lawrence and a patrol officer arrived at the Evelyn M. Billings Residence.

Protector Jackson came out to the turning circle to meet them. They told him to get Buddy Choate.

"Hello, officers, what's going on?" Buddy asked them.

"Do you know Tammy Bell?"

"Of course. She's one of our Psychic Guides. We are very fond of Sister Tammy here at the Center."

"When did you see her last?"

"Yesterday evening. She asked for her car, after she got settled in her room. She had driven up from Philadelphia."

"How did she seem to you?"

"She seemed tired. I think things were not going well for her back home."

"Did she say anything to you?"

"Just to get her car. Also she said to tell everyone good-bye, which sounded strange to me. But as I said, she was very tired."

"Then why did you let her drive if she was so tired?"

"It wasn't up to me. She makes her own decisions. A very formidable woman."

"And you weren't concerned that she didn't return?"

"I never thought about it. I wasn't aware she hadn't."

"You just said you haven't seen her today."

"We've had a lot going on here recently so I didn't register the fact that I haven't seen her. If I had, I would have assumed she was sleeping in, and anyway I'm not in the habit of checking her room. What's this about, officers?"

"Tammy Bell's body was found in Quechee Gorge under the bridge. Her car was parked nearby. Apparently she jumped."

"Oh Jesus, Mary, and Joseph!" Buddy exclaimed. "That's terrible! I had no idea. She was such a good friend to all of us."

Sixty Four

FRANCES' PHONE RANG. She checked Caller ID, and picked up. "Hi Suzie, are you calling about Lily?"

"How did you know?"

"Ah, well…"

"She called me," Suzie said. "She's coming home! She told me she made a mistake. That the Center is falling apart."

"What about the portrait of Ignatius Jones?"

"I asked her that. She didn't want to talk about it."

"What about Charles?"

"She didn't want to talk about him either."

"Well, I'm glad Lily has come to her senses."

"She said she heard you were at the Center last night when they had a big disturbance. Is that true?"

"Yes, Suzie, I was there."

"Well, I don't know what you did, Frances. Whatever it was, thank you. Thank you for returning my child to me."

Frances called Carter Haas.

"Do you have more news about the painting?" he asked.

"Yes, Carter. I believe the Ignatius Jones Center will be more receptive now to a reasonable offer."

"Why? What's happened there?"

"It's a long story. But if they do agree to sell, Carter, you will of course need to validate the painting."

"Of course."

"Before you deliver it to your experts, can you do me a tiny favor?"

"Certainly, what is it?"

"Bring it here first, to my Institute. Leave it with me for an hour."

"So that you can communicate in private with the spirit of Ignatius Jones?"

"Yes, Carter, for one last time. It's a personal thing."

Sixty Five

CHARLES ASKED Buddy and Murray to join him at his house in Woodstock to discuss their upcoming visit from the MFA's Carter Haas.

"Are you sure that you want to include me?" Murray asked. "In view of the trust thing."

"Don't be an idiot, Murray. I need your big brain to help us work out our options."

When Charles opened his front door, he was wearing an open-necked cotton shirt, linen slacks, and soft leather loafers.

"You look different," Buddy said. "Your robe…"

"Time to move on," Charles replied.

"Amen to that," Murray said, thinking to himself, *Charlie is back.*

"So, Murray, tell us what you know about Carter Haas," Charles said, after they'd made themselves comfortable at the same kitchen table where in times past they'd hatched and plotted out their schemes.

"He's a curator at the Boston MFA. He first called me about five, six weeks ago. Said he heard we had the Desmond Wilkins

349

portrait of Ignatius Jones. He said the MFA already is showing several Wilkins paintings and he wondered if we'd consider an offer from the MFA to purchase ours."

"And you told him?"

"That we wouldn't sell it. Nor would we lend it to him. But I said that he was welcome to come see it if he scheduled a session with you, Messenger Charles."

Charles ignored Murray's dig.

"And he didn't call you back until yesterday?"

"Nope."

"Did he say why he called you yesterday and not earlier?"

"He said he'd been thinking some more about our painting and decided that he wanted to see it."

"What about our session with Ignatius Jones?"

"I told him that would no longer be necessary."

"So it's a coincidence that he called you after we lost contact with Ignatius Jones and everyone left the Center?"

"I don't know."

"Maybe he heard from Gourmelon," Charles said. "She's in Boston."

"Maybe so," Murray said.

"What are our options?" Charles asked.

"We should get what we can for the painting," Buddy said.

"I agree," Murray said. "Now that it's no longer providing a portal to the spirit world."

Was that another dig? Again Charles ignored it. Murray had a point, after all. How could anyone believe that an oil painting was a portal to communicate with spirits?

"Okay, I'll show Haas the painting. See what he has in mind."

Charles segued to the rumor passed along to him by Rosana Pereira, the woman who came to clean his house each week. Rosana was vague about her source, and she didn't know the details, but apparently there was a suicide recently that seemed suspicious and was under investigation by police. The suicide victim's name was Tammy Bell.

"What's this I hear about Sister Tammy? That she committed suicide?"

"What?" Murray exclaimed. "When?"

"Yeah, she did." Buddy said. "Three nights ago. The night the Center was attacked. Tudorsville cops came by the next day. They were asking when we saw her last. I told them I saw her that night after the all-clear, when she asked for her car. She said she wanted to go out. I didn't expect she'd be gone for all eternity."

"I didn't know she was at the Center," Charles said.

"She came up from Philadelphia specifically to see you, Charlie," Murray said.

"No one told me."

"I guess I forgot."

"Me too," Buddy said.

Murray said, "I thought she was just going to fuss that we hadn't paid her."

"Do we owe her money?"

"Yeah, well, she thought so, but we never got around to putting our Psychic Guide agreement in writing, so she had nothing on us legally. Anyway, I figured her visit would not be a top priority for you and then it slipped my mind with all the excitement that night."

"So you saw her," Charles said to Buddy. "Did she strike you as being depressed?"

"Yeah, she did. I think she had some problems at home."

"Wonder why this wasn't reported anywhere," Charles said.

"We may see something about it in this Thursday's *Vermont Standard*," Murray said.

Charles asked, "How did she do it?"

Buddy said, "She jumped off the bridge at Quechee Gorge."

"Jesus H. Christ!" Murray said.

Charles stared at Buddy, not saying anything, definitely not wanting to know more.

Carter Haas parked in front of the entrance of the Evelyn M. Billings Residence.

The place seemed deserted. He saw no other cars, nor anyone outside on the grounds or visible in any of the windows. He heard a breeze rustling through bushes that had lost their leaves. Birds were chirping, cars rumbled by on Route 100A, and his shoes crunched on the gravel. But no human voices.

The entrance door to the Residence was locked. Inside, the lights were off and it looked dark and empty.

Carter rapped it with his knuckles and called out, "Hello? Anyone there?"

Finally a man appeared at the door and opened it.

"You must be Carter Haas," he said.

"Yes, and…?"

"I'm Buddy Choate, co-manager here."

Buddy offered an friendly grin as they shook hands.

"No need to move your car. Not much traffic today."

"Where is everyone?"

"We're between visitor groups," Buddy replied. "Our staff and pilgrims are enjoying some time off before the next group arrives."

"When will that be?"

"Very soon," Buddy said. He gestured towards the House of Spirits. "Messenger Charles is waiting for you in the Portrait Room."

Buddy opened the door to the Portrait Room and pointed down towards Charles, who was seated on the stage, facing the portrait.

"Head on down," Buddy said. "You'll be in good hands with Messenger Charles."

Charles's expensive clothes and soft cheeks gave him the appearance of an investment banker, similar to others of that ilk whom Carter had met and entertained among the MFA's many wealthy benefactors.

"There it is," Charles said, looking at the portrait. "What do you think?"

Carter noted the distinctive Desmond Wilkins flourishes in the brushwork and use of color, and the way that Ignatius Jones seemed to reach out from his portrait to confront and engage his visitor.

He also knew instantly that the portrait of Ignatius Jones that was hanging in front of him did not belong in the pantheon of Desmond Wilkins' masterpieces. He could tell that its paint had dried recently, possibly even within the last few months. No doubt the paint would glow under the ultraviolet black light that he always brought with him to examine works of art. He didn't

353

need his black light for this painting. He already knew what the test would show.

It was an *excellent* copy. It *could* have been a Desmond Wilkins. To an untutored eye, it would be accepted as one. Carter assumed this was Annie Kane's handiwork, and that Frances was involved. Evidently, Charles had no idea.

"It's a wonderful work of art," Carter said. "You get a real feeling for Ignatius Jones."

"Yes," Charles agreed. "We're very proud of this painting."

"Desmond Wilkins was a great artist. One of our most popular at the MFA."

"How does this compare to his other paintings?" Charles asked.

"There are many similarities, in terms of technique and style, but your painting is unique, Charles. Quite unique."

"That's what we think too," Charles said.

Pushing a bit, Carter said, "I heard that you and others in the Center believe you can communicate with Ignatius Jones through this portrait."

"That's been our experience," Charles replied.

"And that you've published a book with the collected words that you've received from Ignatius Jones."

"You're well informed."

"Just based on what I've read on your website."

Changing the subject, Charles said, "You told Murray Gattis that the MFA would like to add this to your collection."

"Yes, I did say that."

"Are you still interested?"

"Mr. Gattis said you would never part with it. So I suppose my interest would be pointless."

"That depends," Charles said.

"I'm afraid that my acquisition budget is quite depleted," Carter said. "I couldn't offer you what this painting is worth."

"What would that be, in your opinion?"

"That's irrelevant, isn't it, since I can't offer that amount. But if I may, I could suggest another way for your fine work of art to be added to the MFA collection."

"I'm not going to donate it," Charles said.

"No, I have in mind a permanent loan."

"Which means what?"

"You would retain ownership while the painting is on display at the MFA."

"How long is 'permanent?'"

"We'd agree on a time, like fifty years."

"And how do I benefit from that, exactly?"

"A plaque in our gallery will state that this fine Desmond Wilkins portrait is on permanent loan from the collection of Charles Tucker."

"Charles Philip Tucker."

"Whatever you want."

"Also you'd need to mention the Ignatius Jones Center for Spiritualist Discovery."

"We could do that," Carter said. "On permanent loan from the collection of Charles Philip Tucker and the Ignatius Jones Center for Spiritualist Discovery. Also the MFA would take responsibility for protecting and insuring the painting, and your ownership of this work of art would be sheltered from future litigation."

According to Murray, the pilgrims were muttering about suing. They wanted compensation for what they gave up when they left home for the Center, with a kicker for mental distress. If they won, they might be awarded a punitive settlement beyond what he could pay from ready cash, in which case they'd go after his assets, including his painting. He'd prefer for it to go on display at the Boston Museum of Fine Arts rather than fall into the hands of embittered former pilgrims.

"So whoever came after me in court couldn't get the painting?"

"Not without a struggle. The MFA has substantial legal resources."

"I'll think about it," Charles said.

"One thing I need to mention," Carter said. "Before we display this painting at the MFA, we'll have to verify that it's truly the Desmond Wilkins portrait of Ignatius Jones that it appears to be."

"Feel free," Charles said. "I already had an expert check it out."

"Glad to hear it, because there are a lot of fakes out there."

"Of this portrait of Ignatius Jones?"

"Possibly. I don't know for sure. Unfortunately, some people try to take advantage. That's why we can't take anything at face value."

"Nor should you," Charles said. "It's a shame how some people are like that."

"No money?" Buddy said. "Fuck!"

"Let's auction it," Murray said. "An original Desmond Wilkins painting; his long-lost portrait of psychic Ignatius Jones. We could raise a pile."

Charles said, "I like that idea except for one thing."

"What's that?"

"The MFA guy hinted about fakes."

"So what? You told us you had it vetted by an expert."

"I did. But I wouldn't call him a museum-level expert. I'm not sure he'd catch a good forgery."

Buddy asked, "If the portrait is a fake, how were you and the others able to communicate with the spirit of Ignatius Jones?"

"I'm not saying that it is. I'm saying I'm not sure."

"So we sell it, the buyer has it tested, and if it's a fake, we say we're sorry and give his money back," Murray said. "Where's the risk?"

"Hard to prove we didn't know what we were selling," Charles said. "Who would believe us, given our earlier, uh, business ventures? We could get sent away."

Buddy said, "On the other hand, if the painting is real, and you give it to the MFA for nothing, we'll leave a lot of money on the table."

"Why a permanent loan?" Murray asked. "Why not just donate it if you're afraid to put it on sale?"

"It's the principal of the thing," Charles replied. "I don't like giving it away. 'Permanent loan' means I still own it even if it's hanging in the museum."

Murray said, "It's your painting, Charlie, but Buddy and I put a lot into the Center."

Buddy said, "How about all three of us get credit for lending it to the MFA?"

"I guess that's better than nothing," Murray said.

"Sure," Charles said. "If that makes you both feel better."

He winced and shifted his shoulders, trying to relieve the ache in his neck.

"Are you alright?" Murray asked.

"Yeah, sure, I must have pulled something," Charles said.

"Maybe you should see a doc."

"It's just a strain," Charles said. "It'll go away eventually."

He asked Murray to make the necessary arrangements with Carter Haas.

Sixty Six

MURRAY WATCHED the two men in blue overalls pack the painting in a flat rectangular wooden box, and then load the box into a white unmarked van.

Then he called Charles, who was waiting back at his home in Woodstock to hear from him.

"They've got it," said Murray.

"Okay," Charles replied, and put down the phone.

Three hours later, the white van arrived at the Institute for Psychical and Paranormal Research on Essex Street in Boston. It stopped, with its flashers on, in front of the 'No Stopping Anytime' sign.

Frances met the two men in blue overalls at her door, and led them to her room in the back.

They deposited their box on a table.

Frances asked them to return in an hour to pick it up to complete its journey to the MFA.

She and Annie took more time, this time, to return the original canvas to its original stretcher and frame, reversing the switch they made at the Center.

When that was done, Frances placed the original Desmond Wilkins painting on the easel. They sat, in silence, gazing at Ignatius Jones.

He was in the room.

Frances felt the tiny hands of her babies, and she heard them chatting and laughing, her darling girls, MingMei, Jeannie, Minal and Pamela, and her dearest boys, Warren and Malcolm.

Annie sensed that her Granny and GrandPops had joined them. She felt warmed by their company, as she always did.

She realized then that she had an opportunity to feel their presence whenever she wanted, whenever she was close to the portrait. She and Frances could keep the original portrait of Ignatius Jones. Frances could send the copy on to the MFA. It would soon be revealed as a fake, but that would not be their problem.

"I know what you're thinking," Frances said. "It won't work. We must stick to the plan."

The two delivery guys left with the original Desmond Wilkins portrait of Ignatius Jones and Frances returned to the back room.

She said to Annie, "Now we need to dispose of your copy."

Annie had set her copy on the easel, where it awaited its fate.

"Yes, I know," she said.

"How would you like to do it?"

"I put a lot into that painting."

"My dear girl, it is a great achievement," Frances said. "But isn't that the problem, the risk that your virtually perfect copy will fall into the wrong hands?"

"I'll stamp it on the back as a copy. I'll use indelible ink. That way, no one can pass it off as the original."

"Your choice, my dear," Frances said. "But keep it under wraps, just for yourself to enjoy."

"Its existence will remain our secret forever," Annie said.

Sixty Seven

FRANCES READ in the *Spiritualist Testifier* about Tammy Bell's passing.

The article was accompanied by a headshot of Tammy resting her chin on her hand. She was smiling confidently, perhaps with a touch of superiority as one might expect of someone who spoke with the Departed on a regular basis.

Passing of Noted Spiritualist Tammy Bell at 53 in Vermont.

Spiritualist Tammy Bell passed to spirit recently in Vermont. She had gone out for a drive while visiting the Ignatius Jones Center for Spiritualist Discovery, where she served with great distinction as a Psychic Guide and was known to others at the Center as Sister Tammy.

Her body was found in Quechee Gorge, a picturesque tourist site in Vermont.

Police are investigating, although the cause of her passing is believed preliminarily to be suicide.

Bell frequently appeared on TV and spoke on radio programs.

It was during such media appearances that she claimed to have communicated with the spirit of Shawn Berwick, a boy who went missing several years ago. However, Shawn Berwick was since discovered alive and well, an embarrassment for Bell that may have contributed to her possible depression.

While being interviewed on a Philadelphia radio station, Bell predicted that she would live until she reached her 90th birthday. While many of her predictions were amazingly accurate, that was not one of them, as we now know to our deep sorrow.

Fellow spiritualists can take comfort that they will most likely hear again from Tammy Bell when she speaks to them from the Other Side.

Frances called Murray on his cell, and he picked up.

"Sister Frances," he said.

"I just read about Tammy Bell."

"Yes, it was quite a shock to all of us here."

"To all of you? That she committed suicide at Quechee Gorge?"

"Frances, please believe me, I knew nothing about it until I heard about it later."

"What about Charles?"

"He had no idea either. I'm sure of it."

"And Buddy?"

"He told us what he told the police, that she asked for her car and then drove off. He said he thought she seemed depressed."

"Murray, I wasn't fond of Tammy Bell, but…"

"I understand, Frances," Murray said. "If you feel you must share your suspicions with the police, then go ahead. On my end, I have nothing to offer except speculation, so I won't get involved."

After thinking about it, Frances concluded that she knew no more than Murray about what happened to Tammy. She also wasn't inclined to have the police take an interest in her role in the events of October 24th, the day of Tammy's passing. So she let it go.

Sergeant Zach Lawrence returned to the Center, accompanied this time in a second car by Major John Pierce of the Vermont State Police Criminal Investigations Unit.

Pierce did all the talking after Sergeant Lawrence introduced him to Buddy Choate.

"Tell us again about the last time you saw Ms. Bell," Pierce said.

"It was around seven thirty, or a bit later, I'm not sure of the exact time, but it was already dark out," Buddy said. "She stopped me in the hallway of our Residence, just outside her room, and asked for her car to be brought around out front."

"Why did she need to do that, and not just get it herself?"

"Our policy is that only staff can drive the visitors' cars on our property, for safety reasons."

"Then you had her car brought to the front of the Residence."

"Yes."

"Who was driving it?"

"Ricky Fotis. He's on our staff."

364

"Then what?"

"Ms. Bell took her car keys and drove off. I thought she would be back soon. She looked real tired, since she'd driven up earlier that day from Philadelphia."

"Did she say where she was going?"

"No. Not my business."

"We need to talk with Ricky Fotis."

"No problem. I'll call him whenever you're ready."

Ricky told the same story, just as he and Buddy had rehearsed. He kept it short and simple.

"I drove her car from the lot in the back to the front of the Residence. She was waiting there for her car. I gave her the keys. She didn't say anything, got in the car, and drove away."

"She didn't say thank you?"

"No. Nothing. Just took the keys."

Among the fingerprints in the car were matches for Ricky's prints. This was explained by the fact that he'd driven the car on the Center's property.

No one who was at the Center that evening recalled seeing Tammy Bell receive her car keys from Ricky Fotis. Some thought they saw headlights of several cars, and maybe some people near the cars, but they couldn't tell for sure in the dim light of the turning circle.

The Vermont State Police appealed to the public for help, asking anyone who was in the vicinity of Quechee Gorge on the night in question to contact the VSP if they saw Ms. Bell or her car. Pictures of her and her car were published in newspapers and shown on TV.

A truck driver who drove across the bridge over Quechee Gorge at about the time the medical examiner estimated that she died said he might have seen a woman and two men, and that one of the men was very large, and that the men seemed to be supporting the woman as if she was intoxicated, but he couldn't be sure, given the dark and also because he was watching the road especially carefully, not being comfortable with heights and therefore nervous on bridges. He wouldn't be able to identify anyone because he didn't see their faces.

The medical examiner concluded that Tammy Bell's death was caused by injuries sustained in her fall. He identified an injury to her head that might have occurred earlier but he lacked enough information to issue a definitive statement about it.

Major Pierce brought Ricky Fotis in to the VSP's Royalton Barracks for additional questioning.

Ricky stuck to his story.

Sixty Eight

CHARLES SAT in his kitchen looking at the remains of his dinner, a pork chop and rice. They were still on his table, unfinished. He wasn't hungry.

Outside it was dark. Days had gotten short now that November had arrived in Vermont.

His house was quiet except for rattling and hissing from his radiators.

He had always felt comfortable in his own company. It had never bothered him to be alone at night.

But now, he was aware that he had his large house to himself. He could feel the jab of loneliness, not just the lack of someone to talk to, but existential aloneness, the sense that he confronted a world and universe and eternity in which his existence made no difference whatsoever.

Charles suspected that allowing Ignatius Jones to touch his mind had made him susceptible to such thoughts.

He was distracted by the nagging, persistent ache in his neck. He couldn't shake it. And also now a squeezing in his chest, not for the first time, but worse now. Probably from the pork chop. He shouldn't have eaten any of it.

He missed Evelyn Billings. She was 102 when he met her, and frail, but he couldn't stop thinking about her fragile hands and sky-blue eyes and tough sense of humor. To come right down to it, she was the only woman he ever loved.

He felt guilty for taking her money to build the Center, not a familiar or welcome emotion. But now he couldn't help thinking that he took advantage of Evelyn and he was ashamed.

He welcomed the pain in his chest. He deserved it.

He felt lightheaded when he stood to leave his kitchen, almost losing his balance. Sweat beaded on his face and neck and under his arms. Maybe it was due to the heat being thrown off by the radiators, although he didn't feel especially warm.

Gripping the banister on his stairs because of the dizziness that threatened his balance, he made his way carefully to his basement room where he first showed his portrait of Ignatius Jones to Buddy and Murray.

The easel was still there, empty.

He was short of breath. He couldn't breathe because of the pain in his chest.

Maybe he should call someone, but his phone was upstairs in his kitchen.

He lay down on the floor on his side, and pulled his knees up to his chest to make the pain go away.

"Oh wow!" he said.

Buddy put his phone down and told Murray, "I keep getting Charles' voicemail. He should have answered by now."

"Maybe he turned off his phone."

"I've been calling him since yesterday morning."

"Did you try texting him, or email?"

Buddy nodded. "I'm not a complete idiot. Something's wrong."

"Let's go to his house," Murray said. "I'll bring his emergency house key from his office."

Murray pressed Charles' doorbell. No response. He knocked on the door, and Buddy called out, "Charles!" No response.

Murray used the emergency house key to open the door, and entered the security code on the pad that was on the wall just inside.

Buddy called Charles' name again. Silence in the house. No response.

They checked his kitchen, where food on his kitchen table and the pan on his stove were giving off a rank smell.

They looked upstairs. His bedroom was neat and tidy and unused.

They found his body in his basement room, on the floor near the easel.

Charles' eyes were open and his mouth was stretched in a grimace. His skin had an ashen grey-blue pallor.

"Oh shit!" Buddy said.

Murray checked the body for a pulse because he thought he should, not because he expected there might be one.

Two Years Later

Sixty Nine

THE DESMOND WILKINS portrait of Ignatius Jones hung in the Andrea and Carl J. Samuelson Gallery on the second level of the MFA's Art of the Americas wing, on the wall opposite the Wilkins' portrait of Elijah Price, father of the man who shot the great psychic.

The painting was a hit for the MFA, as reported in the *Boston Globe*.

Curator Carter Haas claims that he is overwhelmed by the public's response to the MFA's portrait by Desmond Wilkins of famed psychic Ignatius Jones. Indeed, this reviewer noted that the portrait does exert a powerful effect, particularly on women visitors. "It's speaking to me," Denise Lescalillo of Bedford said. "I can't explain it." The painting was acquired on permanent loan from the collection of Charles Philip Tucker, Murray Gattis and Buddy Choate. Earlier it was on display in Tudorsville, Vermont, at the Ignatius Jones Center for Spiritualist Discovery.

Congestion in the gallery was exacerbated by visitors who stopped, transfixed, in front the portrait.

The MFA imposed a limit of three minutes' viewing time per visitor. Visitors who overstayed were requested by gallery attendants to move along in order to enjoy the MFA's many other wonderful works of art.

On weekends, one of the gallery attendants on duty was a tall young woman with long blonde hair. She wore the MFA attendants' uniform, a white shirt with a small blue bow tie, blue blazer, and blue trousers.

According to her MFA badge, her name was Lily.

She told visitors to the gallery that she was working part-time as an MFA intern while studying fine arts at Boston University. She commiserated with their desire to stay longer. She told them that she too felt a powerful attachment to the portrait and to its subject.

One day while Lily was on duty, a woman entered the gallery pushing a baby stroller. The toddler in the stroller had blonde hair and dark eyes. She gazed around the gallery at all the people and returned their smiles, a good-humored, well-behaved child.

Suzie Prestowicz, interim mommy for little Melissa while her real mom attended BU, waited to the side while Lily conversed with other gallery visitors. Finally, the others moved on, and Suzie gave Lily a hug.

Lily picked up baby Melissa from the stroller.

"How's my baby girl?" she cooed. "Is Granma Suzie treating you alright?"

"Yes," murmured Melissa.

"You do as she says, okay?" Lily said.

"I will," replied Melissa softly.

"She's such a good girl," Suzie said, and Melissa pressed her head against Lily's shoulder, pleased, and embarrassed.

Then, looking over Lily's shoulder, Melissa caught sight of the portrait of Ignatius Jones.

She stared at it, fascinated.

She stretched her arm towards it.

"Closer!" Melissa demanded.

"Shhh," Lily said.

Melissa squirmed in Lily's arms, straining to reach the portrait.

"Hold still," Lily said, gripping her more tightly.

Melissa screamed, "I want closer!"

BOOKS BY **PETER DAVID SHAPIRO**

Ghosts on the Red Line

Commuters see their Departed on Boston's Red Line trains. Consultant Harry West is hired by the Massachusetts Bay Transportation Authority to investigate. His project turns personal when his ex-wife Alexandra Ben-Tov meets their beloved daughter on the Red Line, who looks like the teenager she might have become if she had lived.

Are the visitors on the Red Line ghosts or hallucinations? Either way, when Harry's team discovers the source of the visitations, the MBTA declares it will bring them to an end.

Alexandra has a brilliant idea: Build Visitation Rooms that replicate the features of Red Line train cars so that people can continue to meet their loved ones.

But not everyone approves. The Archbishop of Boston seeks to get Visitation Rooms banned in Massachusetts. And a gangster who frets that his victims might return from the dead warns Harry and Alexandra: Cancel Opening Day for the first Visitation Room, *or else!*

"An intriguing and comfy psychical (and psychological) mystery" (Amazon)

"Fascinating, multi-level novel" (Amazon)

"Altogether wonderful!" (Amazon)

Available in Paperback, eBook, Audiobook
www.ghostsontheredline.com

The Trail of Money

Consultant Harry West is hired by the government in Hong Kong to evaluate a business deal promoted by the son of one of the richest men in Asia. But after Harry arrives in Hong Kong, he discovers the assignment is not what he expects. His client wants him to find evidence of money laundering and corruption, evidence that will kill the deal.

Harry has no experience investigating criminal schemes. He harbors doubts about his courage, being all too aware that the people he might expose will stop at nothing to protect themselves. However, he needs the work. He takes on the assignment.

Soon it requires him to draw on resources that he never knew he had.

Along the way, Harry's journey is shaped by two women in Hong Kong, an American journalist who is investigating the same deal and a long-lost love who comes back into his life.

A suspenseful story about intrigue, revenge, and the bonds of love and memory, *The Trail of Money* keeps the reader guessing until the end.

"Jealousy, doubt, a nice dose or two of sex, and a lot of twists of the tale" (Goodreads)

"Marvelously twisty thriller" (Amazon)

"Fascinating plot-driven story" (Amazon)

"Fast-paced suspense novel that will keep readers on their toes!" (Amazon)

Available in Paperback, eBook, Audiobook
www.thetrailofmoney.com